SMOKE IN THE VALLEY

Steve Frazee

Chivers Press • G.K. Hall & Co.
Bath, England   Thorndike, Maine USA

This Large Print edition is published by Chivers Press, England, and by G.K. Hall & Co., USA.

Published in 1997 in the U.K. by arrangement with Golden West Literary Agency

Published in 1997 in the U.S. by arrangement with Golden West Literary Agency

U.K. Hardcover ISBN 0–7451–8859–1 (Chivers Large Print)
U.K. Softcover   ISBN 0–7451–8884–2 (Camden Large Print)
U.S. Softcover   ISBN 0–7838–2046–1 (Nightingale Collection Edition)

The text of this Large Print edition is unabridged.
Other aspects of the book may vary from the original edition.

Set in 16 pt. New Times Roman.

Printed in Great Britain on acid-free paper.

British Library Cataloguing in Publication Data available

Library of Congress Cataloging-in-Publication Data

Frazee, Steve, 1909–
    Smoke in the valley: an original gold medal novel / by Steve Frazee.
        p. cm.
    ISBN 0–7838–2046–1 (lg. print : sc)
    1. Large type books.   I. Title.
(PS3556.R358S46   1997]
813′.54—dc21   96–48191

CHAPTER ONE

Like a crippled bug struggling from a deep rut the Whitlock wagon came at last from the canyon of the Arkansas River in the summer of 1866. Ahead was a valley running far and wild to snow-patched mountains that jumped suddenly across the sky. Major, the oldest Whitlock boy, was driving. He saw how Ma stiffened after one quick look at what lay ahead.

'Are we going beyond them angry things?' she asked.

'I reckon we got to.' Major let the oxen rest. He guessed the other wagons would be waiting in the valley; they were always waiting for the Whitlocks, and in that was a shame which was hard for Major to bear. He was almost nineteen, a square-faced, solemn looking youth. Sometimes his sister and his brothers accused him of acting like an old man. During the war he'd stayed home, trying to do for the family and hold things together while Pa was away at the fighting.

Ma said, 'Dorcas, look here at what's ahead.'

Dorcas was somewhere back in the wagon, and mad because Ma wouldn't let her walk along with Jude. Dorcas didn't answer, so Ma just let her be.

The oxen, Fawn and Steuben, set themselves against their yokes slowly when Major urged them on. They were sore-footed and their backbones were gauntly ridged. It would be a blessing if they could rest a week or two.

Not that Pa was worried one mite about the oxen, or anything else.

Pa was down there by the river with the second oldest boy, Lafait, the two of them having a free and easy time as they hunted for game. Now and then Major caught a glimpse of them in the cottonwoods. Pa was carrying the buffalo gun, slouching along careless in the old hat he'd worn when he marched with General Grant. Right beside him with the long rifle was Lafait, his wild thatch of black hair riffling in the hot wind.

That's the way they went all day long, worrying about nothing but the chance of getting a bead on game. Oh, they knew where the wagon was, sure enough, and if it got stuck in loose gravel or hung up high and dry in the rocks, they would drift in to help, staying just long enough to get it moving again before they went scooting back to their happy partnership of hunting. You might hear their rifles down by the river anytime, or maybe high on the piñon hills. Then along about dusk they would show up after camp was made. Maybe they would have a bunch of young rabbits or a hog-snouted beaver that Ma declared was nothing but a pig with fur, and wickedly unnatural

2

meat for human bellies. Quite often Pa and Lafait would come in with big-eared deer.

Major was sure he could not remember every place where the wagon had been stuck, but he was sure that Pa and Lafait could recall every place where they'd shot game. It was a fair country for game, Pa said, as if he was a judge of such things. Back on the hill farm in eastern Kentucky he'd never been known as much of a hunter before the war. After he came back from three years of marching and fighting under General Grant, Pa seemed to have lost all interest in the farm that Major and Lafait, and even young Jude, had worked so hard to keep going during the war.

Major had been real proud of what they had done with land that wasn't much to begin with, but when Pa came back he looked at the farm with eyes that were seeing something else, and he said sort of absent-like that they had done real well while he was away; and then the whole thing just blew out of his mind.

He got himself a buffalo gun by trading off one of the mules that Major had hidden a dozen times from Unions and Confederates alike, and then he took to roaming the hills like he was looking for something.

Pa said the fighting had him all loosened up and stirred around, and that it would take a little time for him to get hold of himself.

Some folks said the big sergeant's marks on Pa's uniform had plumb dazzled him, but Ma

3

wouldn't have anything to do with that kind of talk. Oh, she could get bitey enough with him when she wanted to, but generally she never did. During the war she'd worried herself thin about him. When he came back so bad unsettled and he didn't want to do any work, maybe she didn't like it, but still she didn't get mean about it.

Then Uncle Lafe popped up from somewhere—he was one of Pa's uncles on the Whitlock side. Uncle Lafe was busting with stories about a wonderful country just over the Rocky Mountains. Why, a man could have land as far as he could see with no more trouble than just declaring it was his.

'Uh-huh,' Ma said. 'What grows on this land—Indians?'

'Now, Delia!' Uncle Lafe laughed. 'Oh, there's an Indian or so out there, sure enough, but that ain't what I'm talking about.' He talked about many things, bright mornings that made a man feel young, grass waving in the wind, game swarming in the hills, fish slopping in the rivers like a bunch of wallowing hogs, and distances that made a man feel like the world was just a beginning thing. He could make you see places where you'd never been, Uncle Lafe could, but he never did get around to telling what the land would grow.

Ma said, 'Zeb Whitlock has got more land right here than he knows what to do with.'

'Worn out, rocky,' Pa said.

4

'You always made a living on it,' Ma argued, but you could see she figured she was losing from the start.

Lafait was eager to start any old time. The idea of Going West had a big fine sound. Major and Ma, they weren't so set on throwing away something you had for sure on the chance of having a whole lot more—if everything turned out all right. Jude, over there on the hill hunting arrowheads, was all for the change. Him and Dorcas were twins and they had a way of sticking together, so when Lafait convinced Dorcas that a trip across the buffalo prairies was a wonderful thing, Jude was pretty well won over too.

The Whitlocks knew there was no doubt about their going when Pa gave Sheba away. Sheba had been the best hound dog for miles around but she was too old for a long wagon trip.

Uncle Lafe told Pa all about a shortcut through the mountains out West. It would take a mite of digging here and there and maybe some double teaming now and then, but wagons could get through, Uncle Lafe declared. He should have been along during the last two weeks in that canyon. Oh, he was aiming to come, sure enough, but when he went down on the Ohio to say goodbye to a woman he knew, he got in a scrape with some steam-boaters and got shot flat out dead.

Ma said that in every generation of

Whitlocks there was one fiddle-footed male who was bounden to get himself killed for trifling reasons.

Now that they were getting where Pa wanted to be, Major hoped that Pa would take a stronger hold on things, but he wasn't doing so. Pa didn't feel bad about being last, nor about being off hunting when the train was sweating and digging its way past bad places. Pa said he figured he'd contributed quite a bit by passing on the news of where the Promised Land was and by knowing right where the shortcut through the mountains was.

About the last twenty miles was when the Whitlocks had been behind the worst. Oh, somebody would always ride back every day to see how they were coming along, and whoever it was always managed to get in a few words about how hard the others had worked that day to make a little progress. That didn't bother Pa none but Major felt that the Whitlocks were getting by on the sweat of others.

Ma was staring hard at the mountains, like they were mortal enemies. They seemed to soar straight up from the great valley, a long marching line of them with blue pyramids along the bottom where the trees grew thickest, and then the trees went up and straggled off to nothing, and above that was a grayness of rocks standing solid in the sullen sky.

What bothered Major the most was the

thought of getting over those rocks with the wagon.

On the easy going of the plains they had gone clean past Pike's Peak, which was supposed to be the great mountain of them all, and so it had appeared at the time. Maybe that was what was making Ma stare so. She must have thought the worst was over when they got around Pike's Peak, and now she was seeing a whole land full of grim mountains standing solidly across the way.

Major heard a shot somewhere down by the river. It was a light charge so he knew that Lafait must have shot a rabbit with the old Pennsylvania rifle that was almost as tall as Lafait.

'They're so terrible looking,' Ma said. 'So bare and awful looking.' She couldn't take her eyes from the mountains.

'There's trees down below.'

'And nothing but terrible cold rocks up above.'

Major knew how she felt. There was sadness in the memory of the wooded mountains of Kentucky, lost so far behind them, and an anger against Pa for bringing the whole family a thousand miles from home.

'I'll be glad to get away from them,' Ma said.

Major wondered if the wagon and the oxen would hold together to get the Whitlocks on to the land Uncle Lafe had talked about so glowingly.

7

Wind with a sticky heat in it was blowing down here in the valley, but above the mountains the sky was dead and quiet, the color of long-ago Shawnee bullets Major had dug from trees on the Whitlock farm. It might have rained up there but the valley was dust dry.

Dorcas decided she had sulked long enough over being made to ride in the wagon. She scrambled up on Grandma Ripley's chest and stuck her head out. 'Can I walk now, Ma?'

'I'll tell you when,' Ma said.

Dorcas' expression twisted into argument. Her face was fair, delicate, oval, golden from the sun. Right now it was dusty too. Her hair was golden colored. She was slim-legged and graceful and could run like a sprite. 'I'll look out for snakes,' she said.

Ma was making her ride because a rattlesnake had almost bit her two days before. Ever since they'd left Kentucky, Major had noticed how Ma had been awful worried about something happening to her younguns, the younguns, as he saw it, being everybody but him. He saw Dorcas looking to him for help.

'Maybe if she stays away from the rocks, Ma—'

'No use to jaw about it,' Ma said.

'At home I went barefoot, with copper snakes laying in the dust any old place, and nobody said never mind about it,' Dorcas complained. 'Look at Jude over there prancing

8

around as big as you please.'

Ma didn't say anything. Arguing was no way to get around her, Major knew. He shook his head at Dorcas. It was best to keep still for a while, and then he'd see what he could do to help Dorcas. That snake had scared the daylights out of her; she'd be real careful from now on, Major figured.

'I'm wearing shoes,' Dorcas said. 'And I think—'

'I'll thank you to get those shoes off Grandma Ripley's chest this instant.' Ma never did get a mean look, but when she had been bothered too much, her mouth thinned out and her eyes began to snap. At such times even Pa was careful about his tongue.

Dorcas slid back across the chest and settled down somewhere on the bedding in the jolting depths of the wagon.

Sometime later Major let the oxen rest while he strained to see if he could make out any sign of the wagons ahead. He couldn't see them. Hills running out on both sides of the river prevented a full view of the valley, so he guessed the train would be on beyond those hills. He drove on slowly, noticing how the wagons had spread out side by side to keep out of each other's dust. He pointed that fact out to Ma. She nodded without interest.

Major didn't rush because he could tell Ma was still a little bitey. She kept looking at the mountains. Major went on quite a spell before

9

he spoke again.

'With all the wheels grinding and all the riding and tramping around, the game must have got scared away from right here.'

'That's likely,' Ma said.

'Snakes too, I guess,' Major said, keeping his face straight ahead.

'I swear there's something in the water out here that makes younguns disrespect their parents,' Ma said. 'Trying to team against me that way.'

Major kept a solemn look on the dusty backs of Fawn and Steuben. From the corner of his eye he watched Ma.

After a long time he caught a faint smile on her face. She said, 'You can walk a spell now, Dorcas.'

Dorcas was already on the chest. She went around Major's back, hit the seat lightly, and went over the wheel like a flying squirrel. She was running toward Jude when she struck the ground.

'Jeem's cousin!' Ma said. 'Just suppose she'd slipped and run her legs atween the spokes!' She watched Dorcas race away and then she looked hard at Major.

'I would've stopped real quick,' Major said.

'Indeed!' Ma sounded real mad but Major knew she really was not. Lately she hadn't been getting honest mad at him at all, not like she had at the other children.

You could see now that it was raining hard

10

on the mountains. The tops of some of them were cut clean off by the storm. Major saw Ma shake her head slowly. 'It's a-pouring water up there,' she said, 'cold, shivery water spouting down on those cruel rocks.'

She sounded like she was talking to herself. Her quietness gave Major an uneasy feeling as he watched the furious storm working on the great peaks. The hot wind was making the sections of the canvas top between the bows rise and fall like the flanks of a hard-worked horse. Dust drifted up from the feet of the oxen.

They heard the boom of Pa's big buffalo gun, and then the sharp and spiteful crack of Lafait's rifle. Shortly afterward Lafait appeared on the high gravel bank and waved for Major to bring the wagon to him. He waited only until he knew his signal had been seen, and then he dropped from sight again.

Jude and Dorcas ran from the piñons when they saw that Major had veered far off the trail. They reached a rocky point above the river at the same time as the wagon. On slabby, dark rocks that ran like a slide into the water, Lafait and Pa were skinning out two young does. In the sunlight the blood was bright against the stones and the roily water.

Jude's face was smudged with dust and his ragged shock of fair hair was lifting to the wind as he stood on a rock and jeered down at Lafait. 'Did you kill another fawn, Lafait?'

11

Pa's white grin flashed in his crinkly beard as he made quick, sure strokes with his knife. Lafait tried to be like him and pay Jude no mind, but the boy in Lafait came out after a moment, and he shouted up at Jude, 'You shut your mouth!'

It was a sore point that always stuck to Lafait's hide like burrs. During the first year Pa was gone to the war, Lafait had sneaked away with the long rifle and killed his first deer, a tiny spotted fawn that he carried home and dumped proudly on the chopping block. Jude turned white and sick with anger when he saw the fawn. He called Lafait names and tried to fight him.

Ma tried to explain to Jude that they needed the meat, and that Lafait had done a fine thing, but Jude got all cold and silent about it and wouldn't talk to anyone. When Ma put the first of the meat on the table, Jude sat with his hands in his lap and stared at the rest of them as if they were about to eat Sheba, or worse yet, one of their own brothers.

It tainted the meat for all of them, so Ma fed it to Sheba.

Looking down at the water, Major said, 'I think the river's coming up.' It had been roily in early afternoon, but now the color was darkening. Twigs and small limbs were floating in it.

Ma barely got their names out in protest before Jude and Dorcas went leaping down the

12

bank to see for themselves how the river was rising. They ran along the water's edge, shouting, throwing stones out toward the deep current. Pa turned his head once to look at them and then he went on with his skinning.

All at once Major had the feeling that he and Ma, looking down from the wagon, were sort of like the mountains, apart from what was going on below. It was as if the two of them were one division of the Whitlocks and the others a group to themselves. It was not a pleasant feeling.

Then Major looked up the valley, worrying ahead, wondering where the other wagons were. They'd wait, of course, but it wasn't fair to hold them up so much. Major wished Pa would worry more about such things.

Lafait and Pa rough-butchered the deer and slung the meat in the green hides when they brought it to the wagon. He was a big man, Pa Whitlock, with a crinkly black beard that he trimmed to look like General Grant's. His eyes were puckered from squinting and from laughing. To hear his tales about the war, you'd think there was only a funny side to it. Not even when Lafait urged him would Pa tell about the mean side of fighting and dying, although the Whitlocks knew well enough from Cousin Ahab, who had come home weak and crippled from Spotsylvania Courthouse, that Pa had been in the thick of things.

He slung the meat in the back of the wagon

and came around to look at the oxen, but he only glanced absently at Steuben and Fawn, as if he expected them to be in good shape without any caring from him. He might have washed the blood off his hands and wrists when he was down at the river, Major thought.

It was easy for Major to think of a lot of things that Pa might do better than he did, but Major didn't get too free with his ideas because Pa could be a mighty sudden man when he was riled up.

Major said, 'Looks like we're farther behind than ever.'

Pa squinted ahead. 'You got dust in your eyes, boy. Anybody can see the wagons just beyond that point up there.'

Major couldn't see no wagons. For the life of him he couldn't see anything but empty land and a storm rolling out from the mountains.

Pa pointed. 'You see 'em, Lafait?'

Lafait was short and wide like most of Pa's folks, with the swarthy Whitlock coloring. His brows were dark and heavy. His eyes were black and quiet as rifle holes as he peered upstream where Pa was pointing. 'I see 'em. You're right, Pa, Major's got dust in his eyes.'

Pa and Lafait hefted their rifles and walked on. Major twisted around to locate Jude and Dorcas before he sent the wagon on slowly toward the storm swept mountains.

Ma said, 'I'll never settle where those cruel rocks are looking down on me day and night.'

14

CHAPTER TWO

Before Major reached the wagons the hot valley turned chill under a hard wind that billowed the wagon top. Ma called for Dorcas and Jude to come back to the wagon and Dorcas' voice came plaintively between gusts of wind, 'Wh—a—at, wh—a—at, Ma?'

They held out as long as they dared, Jude and Dorcas, knowing well enough what Ma wanted, even if her words had not been clear to them. Then they came racing out of the piñons with dead branches held to their heads, pretending they were buck deer.

Major watched them with a fond but envious wonder; it seemed so long ago that he had romped like that all free from worry.

Pa and Lafait were just a little ahead of the wagon when it reached the train encamped on a flat above the river. The men and older boys were having one of their eternal pow-wows at Rawl Judson's wagon. From the looks of the camp Major guessed the wagons had been waiting here at least two days.

Judson shouted so everyone could hear him, 'Here comes the cow's tail.'

Pa grinned a little, not at all put out. 'We generally show up.' He and Lafait joined the group of men, Lafait standing solemn and square as he grounded his tall rifle.

'We figured to cross this morning, but we didn't,' Judson said, 'and now we misdoubt we can make it.' He was the elected leader of the train. He spoke with some chinchiness, like he was trying to put the blame for the delay on the Whitlocks.

Pa squinted at the river. He rubbed his whiskers on his shoulders and said, 'Why didn't you cross?'

'Argument,' Judson answered sourly. 'They made me leader of this train, and then, by God, all they do is argue about what I say.'

Major studied the river beyond the little meadow where oxen were grazing. The water was up a startling heap since he'd last seen it down there where Pa and Lafait killed the deer. It was darker, with lacy slaps of foam jumping from the waves, and it was now carrying fair-sized branches and some small trees.

On the far side of the river was a square looking cabin of twisty cottonwood logs, with a canvas top peaked in the middle from a center pole. Smoke was drifting out of an unfinished fireplace. Back in the trees Major saw five or six horses.

The Malone children went noisily out to gather firewood to store under the wagon, while Mrs Malone and the oldest girl, Malinda, began to rig up a canvas out from the high box of the wagon to protect their cooking place.

Major watched Malinda for a while, and then he drove the wagon over to a camping

16

place and unhitched the oxen. He walked behind them when they went rumbling toward the river, not because any harm could come to them here, but because he wanted a closer look at the cabin across the Arkansas.

It wasn't much, except for size. Above the growling of the river he heard laughter and talk. Though it was a very crudely built place over there, it spoke of a settled kind of warmth that did not come from campfires that would be left behind forever when morning came. He doubted that Lafait and the other younguns would understand his feelings.

A tall man in buckskins ducked through the low doorway and came down to the river with a leather bucket that had white U.S. letters on it. He nodded at Major before he bent down to scoop up water. He looked about as old as Pa but his face was cleanly shaved.

The man dipped water and threw it away. He tried another bucketful and after picking out some twigs and dead leaves decided it was the best he could do.

'You going to cross tonight?' he shouted.

Major glanced up the hill at the conference, where the arm waving and gestures indicated that affairs were far from settled. 'Don't know,' he yelled.

The buckskin man shook his head at the river. He indicated with the edge of his hand against his stomach how deep the water was, about four feet; and then he motioned toward

17

the oncoming rain and measured a foot higher on his body. 'Better stay over there!' He went back to the cabin.

Major wished he could have talked more to the man. He was a friendly acting fellow who reminded Major of Colonel Gadsen, back home. So absorbed was Major in watching the stream that he didn't hear Malinda Malone until she came up close behind him.

'What you thinking about there, Major?'

'Nothing. Just a-looking at the river.'

For a while they stood together in silence, watching the onrushing flood. Malinda had lost her hair because of a bad fever the spring before. It was not yet grown out enough to bear exposure and so she was still wearing an old woman's gray bonnet. Under the stiff, weather-stained brim her face was strongly alive and eager.

'Are we going to walk tonight?' she asked.

It was never much, a stroll to a rocky point, a few minutes together at dusk in a grove, a short walk on a plain in clear view of the camp, but the moments served to isolate them briefly from the grind and bustle and worry of the camp, to make them feel that they were alone and responsible only to each other.

'I guess,' Major said, 'if we don't cross the river.'

Malinda started away. 'I got to go back now and help Ma.'

Major watched a tree go past in the swift

current. It rolled sluggishly and its silt covered leaves made a seething sound in the dirty water. Always before the Arkansas had been a cool and friendly stream, swift and rocky, but easily forded if you used a little judgment picking the right place. Now it was running so fast you could see that the heavy current in the middle was inches higher than the water at the banks. Although the other bank was only a hundred feet away, Major guessed this was the worst water crossing he had ever seen.

He started toward the loud council at Judson's wagon. The women had taken their cue from Mrs Malone and had their cooking fires going under canvas. Oppressed by the oncoming rain, most of the younger children were hanging close to the wagons, but Jude and Dorcas were still going full tilt, playing duck-on-a-rock with some of the Pilchers.

An odd desire to join in the game came over Major, but he knew that such things lay far behind him, lost all at once when Pa went away to the fighting. Major went on to the council.

'What are we going to do?' Judson was saying. 'We voted once to cross and now nobody wants to abide by the vote.'

'It wasn't strong enough on the one side,' Marv Wright said.

'Well, by God, why did we bother to vote at all, if that's the way we're going to act?' Judson asked.

'I ain't taking my wagon into the river to lose

19

it, not after coming this far,' Matt Jessup said.

Joe Marion stomped around and looked at the storm. 'We should've crossed when it was low. From the look of things, the longer we wait, the higher it'll be.'

'The river will go down again,' Malone said.

'It could do anything.' Judson looked around at the camp. 'The question is, do we stay here the best part of the summer waiting and trying to make up our minds?'

The men looked at the river. They looked at the storm. You could see they were in no rush to make their decision.

Major was of a mind to speak a piece about what the buckskin man had said about waiting, but he could see that his words would be lost, so he said nothing.

In desperation Judson turned to Pa for advice. Pa was leaning on his gun, with his eyes a-twinkle as if he were getting fun out of the argument. 'What do you say, Whitlock?'

'Yeah,' Wright demanded. 'How would General Grant handle this?'

Pa eyed Wright an instant to make sure he was not trying to make fun of General Grant. You could make fun of Pa, but if you tried to say anything light about General Grant, Pa got bristly pretty fast. He eyed Wright and decided it wasn't anything serious. 'Well,' Pa said in his deep, slow voice, 'I'll tell you—if there was something to fight over there, General Grant would've been across two days ago. Now it looks like there ain't no hurry.'

'Not with you, there never ain't,' Joe Marion said. And then, with a blast of wind that scattered ashes and rattled canvas, the rain came driving in icy cold. The council broke up in a hurry.

Out in the meadow the oxen grumbled as they turned their rumps to the storm. Children scrambled into wagons or dived under them. The Marions, who travelled in high style with a tent, were running into it when it blew down and left them threshing in a tangle of canvas and ropes. The men who ran over to help weight the tent down with rocks to keep it from blowing away didn't laugh and joke like they had one time before when the same thing had happened; but that had been long ago, way back on the plains.

Water ran from Pa's whiskers as he sat under the wagon with his sons and Dorcas. He kept the breech of the buffalo gun under his coat. 'Minds me of the time when we was foraging down in Mississippi...'

Major didn't listen to the story. He kept looking through the rain toward the cabin across the river. They were snug and warm over there and tomorrow they didn't have to get up at dawn and start on toward unknown mountains with a wagon that was ready to fall apart.

The rain slanted in under the canvas above Ma's fire. It disappeared silently into the back

21

of the Union great-coat she was wearing. Major wondered how many times he had seen her like that since they left Kentucky.

'How far is it now to the place Uncle Lafe told us about?' Major asked suddenly.

'A fair piece of travelling.' Pa's eyes squinted down like he was laughing inside. 'You ain't afraid we'll be left behind, are you, boy? With me knowing the only sure way we can get wagons through them mountains, you think Marion and Judson are going to run off and leave us?'

Pa's words gave Major a dishonest feeling that he had to swallow before he said, 'No, I guess they won't.'

Pa laughed. 'You bet they ain't.' He leaned back against a wheel and called to Ma, 'Ain't that meat about ready, Delia?'

For fifteen minutes the valley danced with rain. There were surges of it so blinding that at times Major could not see the river. Then suddenly the storm was gone. People emerged from shelter and tramped around on sweet, new-smelling earth. Blue sky was breaking above the mountains that had spawned the downpour. Still a half hour high, the evening sun appeared and sent a great fan of light streaking down through the dissipating sullenness.

Ma stared at the golden rays shafting through the dark clouds. 'It looks like stairsteps to heaven up there, I do declare,' she said.

'Council!' Judson bawled.

Now there was fresh material for argument. Marion contended that the rainy season had set in and that they had better act quick before the river got worse. Somebody suggested that there must be better crossings either up or down the river.

'There ain't none better down, I'll tell you that for sure,' Pa said. 'Leastwise, not the way she's booming now.'

Judson pointed out the fact that they had to cross here because the hills pinched off wagon passage less than a quarter mile ahead on this side of the river, and there were no crossings in between.

Pa said he was willing to swim across the river and talk to the people at the cabin to see if they had anything to offer. 'I never heard nothing about a rainy season out here but maybe—'

'Won't do no good to ask questions of that bunch over there,' Ross Pilcher said. 'They got no wagons, no families, no nothing. They wouldn't be reliable. They might tell us anything that came to mind.'

If having a family made a man reliable, Pilcher should have been a humdinger for steadiness. He was responsible for fourteen children, six by his first wife, four who belonged to his second wife, and four more as a result of the second marriage.

'What are we going to do?' Judson demanded. 'We voted once to cross. If we're afraid to try it now, what are we going to do when it gets higher? We could spend the rest of the summer right here, arguing and waiting.'

'It might go down,' Wright said. 'And again....' He shrugged and gave the Arkansas a worried look.

'I say let's get across there tonight,' Marion said. 'We got plenty of time to do it if we don't stand here jawing.'

Major had seen it happen before, bitter argument that appeared too strong to be smoothed away, and then all at once agreement. That was the turn affairs took now.

'Hitch 'em up!' Judson shouted.

Older boys went running to the meadow to get the oxen. Husbands went to their wives to explain the necessity of the sudden move. Major heard Mrs Pilcher shouting angrily at Pilcher. Mrs Malone threatened to hit her husband with the cooking pot. With weary patience Ma passed out meat, not quite fully cooked, to her family and began to pack her utensils in the wagon.

Pa came up to Major while he was hitching up the tired oxen. 'Don't be in no great hurry, Major,' Pa said. 'Let's see what happens first.'

Five men came out of the cabin and ranged themselves on the bank when they saw that the train was getting ready to attempt a crossing. The buckskin man shook his head but he didn't

24

give any advice.

Marion was to make the first try. He drove his wagon down to the edge of the river, with all his family in it, and there he stopped while the men gathered for a last conference.

At the edge of the councilling group, Jude came up to Major and nudged him. Jude pointed to a stick stuck in the sand at the edge of the water. 'It came up that far while we were breaking camp.' Jude indicated three or four inches with his fingers.

'You put the stick there?'

'Sure, I did.'

Jude was always measuring things, or figuring how heavy work could be done, or planning the building of something. On the ferry coming across the Mississippi he had spent the trip in the engine room, while Ma was looking frantically all over the boat for him.

Marion said he thought he could float the wagon across by angling downstream to where the oxen could get their feet on the bottom of a gravelly place about a hundred yards below the cabin. He kept looking at the river and you could tell that he had lost some of his enthusiasm for the crossing. Then he made his wife and children get out of the wagon and that was a sure sign that he was plenty scared.

'I'll go on across,' he said, 'and then we can use the cable to help the rest of you.'

The cable was a big rope that the men of the train had bought from the owner of a burned-

25

out steamboat. They took turns carrying it because it took up so much room in a wagon. Marion had it with him now, to be strung across the river once he reached the far bank.

'Going downstream ain't the right way,' Jude told Major. 'They ought to swim some oxen over first and then use the cable to hold the wagons upstream so they could swing across like a ferry works.'

'How do you know how a ferry works?' Major asked.

'Uncle Lafe told me.'

Marion's oxen sniffed the dirty water and began to bawl when he tried to force them into the stream. It took men on both sides of the team to get the animals started into the river. They waded out slowly. When they were belly deep the water was breaking hard against them, surging up their sides. They tried to swing back toward the bank. Marion whipped them on straight ahead and shouted at them.

Suddenly they were in swift water and the current swept them downstream. For an instant Major thought the tongue was going to snap as it swung around, but the river was thrusting hard against the wagon too. The wheels ground on the rocky bottom as the weight of the oxen and the drive of the water slewed the wagon to a quartering course.

It floated, its big top rocking, the swimming oxen churning into the high current. For a count or two Marion was headed directly where he had planned to go. The picture changed in an instant. The off ox struck a submerged rock. Its head and shoulders lifted above the flood. The heavy tongue swept it under as the back of the wagon swung with the current, and then the other ox was fouled and helpless, drowning.

The back of the wagon swung on downstream. Dragging the struggling animals with it, the wagon drifted on past the place where Marion had thought to land. It struck rocks and almost turned on its side. The water smashed it on. Those on the bank heard the crashing of tough oak spokes when the wagon went against great rocks that stuck above the current.

There in the churning water the wagon held, hard slanted to one side, with the top trembling. One of the oxen heaved itself about the surface for an instant and then it sank again. Marion was clinging to the high side of the seat.

'He can't swim! He can't swim!' Mrs Marion moaned.

Major ran with the rest of the wagon men. Across the river the others were running downstream too. Major was a fair swimmer and he thought maybe when the wagon tipped and dumped Marion out, he might be able to get out far enough to grab him. And then, even with the wagon, Major had a close look at the savage, saw-edged rapids below the wagon.

The water made a churning hell's broth against black rocks and Major knew that no swimmer could ever help another man out of there.

The wagon was shuddering, grinding lower into the water as the river tried to break it up. Stricken motionless, Marion held to the seat with both hands, looking helplessly at his friends and his family on the bank only fifty feet away.

Matt Jessup yelled, 'A rope! Get a rope!'

Several men scrambled away at once. Across the river the buckskin man had already thought of the idea. He had a rope and he whirled one end of it with a rock tied on it. It fell fifteen feet short of the wagon and the water whipped it downstream. He began to draw it in again. His companions were shouting at Marion and hooking their arms at him, telling him to jump.

Marion leaned out and moved one leg like he was going to climb down from the seat, and then he got all still again. The buckskin man was wading out to make his rope reach, while his companions held to him with a chain of hands. He got out about ten feet and the water knocked him over and it was all his friends could do to haul him back.

The wagon slewed around. It tilted with a sudden jar and looked like it was going clean over and then it caught again on the rocks, but you could see it wasn't going to last much longer.

Major didn't even see the swimmer until Lafait yelled, 'Get out of the way!' Lafait was scrambling along the bank with a rope that made a deep bow downstream on its way out to a man who was being swept toward the wagon. It was Pa!

He came against the wagon and went under. An instant later he hauled his head and shoulders above the water, with one hand holding to the side of the wagon. He held up the end of the rope and shouted at Marion, but Marion shook his head. He didn't want to slide down the tilted seat to reach the rope. You could hear Pa cussing something awful. Everyone on the bank yelled at Marion to grab the rope.

Pa pulled himself up a little higher. His legs were kicking downstream and it didn't look like he could hold on much longer. 'Grab it, goddamn you!' he bellered.

At last Marion inched down the seat and reached out. The water slapped at his arm and he jerked back, and then he knew he had to do it. He reached far out and got the rope.

'Tie it around you!' Judson shouted.

There wasn't time for that. The wagon started to go, and still Marion wanted to stay with it. By then the men on the bank had crowded Lafait clean away from his end of the rope, with so many of them grabbing it. They pulled Marion off the wagon while it was tipping over. Major saw the wagon roll on its side and then it went slamming and bumping down the rapids and he couldn't see Pa any more.

'He got caught!' someone shouted.

Major ran along the bank. He came against a willow thicket that cut off his view of the river. He lost time crashing through it and when he came again to the bank, there was no sign of Pa. The wagon was below him, close to the other side of the river. It was grinding along on its side, with the top ripped away. On below it the Marions' household goods were floating away.

The buckskin man and his companions ran out of the trees. They shouted at Major and waved him back when he began to wade from the bank. He was already swimming before he caught on to what they were trying to tell him: Pa was on his side of the river. Major turned back then.

Pa was against the bank, clinging to some willows. His face was pale and he was gasping as Major splashed over to him. Men were pounding through the willows, shouting.

'Pa, are you hurt?' Major yelled.

Hanging there with one arm hooked around some willows on the bank, Pa looked tuckered out and half drowned. The corner of his mouth was cut and blood was running down his beard into the muddy water. 'I'm fine,' he said, and then he gathered his strength and rolled up on the bank and lay there gasping. 'Gawd, there's

30

a power to that water, I'll tell you.'

Lafait came busting through the willows with a whole bunch behind him. Pa got up then. He wiped at the blood with the back of his hand. 'No river got a Whitlock yet.' He felt his head. 'Lost my hat, by Ned! I wore that hat—' He turned toward the river, as if he expected to see it floating in.

'Naw,' Lafait said. 'You throwed it on the ground before you swum out.'

'Marion's all right,' Judson said. 'We hauled him in with no trouble.'

Ma shoved through the men with Pa's hat in her hands. It was twisted up like she'd been trying to wring water out of it. All at once she grabbed hold of Pa and hung on tight.

'Here now, Delia,' Pa said, 'don't you carry on.' He patted her on the back with a big wet hand, looking sheepish at the folks watching him. Then he took the hat from Ma and began to straighten it out.

'That was a big thing you done, Whitlock, a real big thing,' Marv Wright said real loud, like there was folks around that didn't know what had happened. He went on talking without giving Lafait no credit for helping Pa by getting two ropes and tying them together while everybody else was running down the bank yelling.

Lafait, he didn't mind none about being overlooked. He was so proud of Pa he was ready to bust his buttons.

31

On the other side of the river the men had followed the wagon to where it was caught once more in the rocks, this time upside down but out of the bad current. The buckskin man plunged in suddenly and swam out far enough to grab something floating away from the wagon. When he worked back in toward the shore the others waded out and helped him tug, and then the wagon people could see what it was that the buckskin man had saved.

It was the big cable.

'That's something at least!' Judson said.

All the Whitlocks were proud of Pa as they walked back to camp with him.

CHAPTER THREE

Major and Matthew Pilcher swam over with the first six oxen in the morning. The Arkansas was another foot higher then on Jude's measuring stick and it was carrying trees big enough to smash a wagon to flinders. There was nothing to do but plunge in when it seemed that the way was clear.

Out in the heavy current the force of the water scared Major. A gritty wave top slapped him in the face when he had his mouth open to breathe. For an instant he thought he was strangling but he coughed it out and tried to shout encouragement to the oxen. When he saw the ox ahead of him heave its shoulders out of the water, he knew they had made it, but it was not just the coldness that made him shake when he let his feet down and struck a sandy bottom. He stood up and looked back. They had been swept downstream a hundred yards.

Matthew Pilcher acted like it was nothing. 'That warn't bad a-tall,' he said.

'Easiest swim I ever had.' Major wasn't going to give Matt anything. They were the same age. They hadn't liked each other from the minute the Pilchers had joined the train back in Kansas. Some of it was on account of Malinda Malone, and some of it started when they got into a wicked fight because one of the young Pilchers tried to cheat Jude in a jackknife trade.

Matt was red-headed like most of the Pilcher boys, heavy framed and tall. He already had a lot of hard muscle on him, and before long he was going to be a powerful man. He was the oldest Pilcher boy. Their real ma had started in with the names Matthew, Mark, Luke—but when it came time for John, Pilcher said she had been mad at the preacher over something, so she named the fourth boy Noble.

The buckskin man and his friends were waiting on the bank when Major and Matt drove the oxen ashore. Right off the buckskin man introduced himself as Jim Goodwin. He said it was a nervy thing for two young men to swim the oxen across the river, considering how it had come up.

'It was nothing like my pa did when he saved Mr Marion off that wagon last night,' Major said.

'Oh! So that was your pa, huh? That was a real brave thing he did and no mistake.'

Major guessed he sort of had Matt shoved in the corner for a while.

Goodwin's friends were a ragged, wild looking bunch. All of them were carrying pistols and knives. They were young men but they were heavily bearded. Some of them wore parts of Confederate uniforms and others had parts of Federal blue clothing. Back home they would have been taken for bushwhackers at a glance. They acted decent enough but they weren't friendly like Goodwin. From the way they grinned and looked at each other as they watched the wagons getting ready to come down to the river, Major sensed the great difference between them and the people of the train.

When Goodwin asked him, one of the ragged bunch did come over to help lay out the cable. His name was Bill, and he was a dark, slender man with quick eyes. He wore an old Union blouse. You could see where the corporal's marks had been removed.

'How far are you going?' he asked Major.

'A long ways yet.' Major looked at the mountains. 'Beyond them—someplace. What kind of place you fellows going to have here?'

34

Bill was puzzled for an instant and then he grinned. 'Goodwin's, you mean? Oh, he's starting a city. Be as big as Nashville one of these days, I reckon.' It was hard to tell whether he was serious or not.

They strung the cable out and hitched the six oxen to it. On the other side of the Arkansas Judson tied a rock onto a rope and heaved it over, and then by means of the rope the cable was hauled across to where the wagons were. The first one was already in position, hub deep in the water, angled upstream into the river. The men over there unhitched the oxen and led them away and tied the cable to the tongue.

They had the crossing figured out just as Jude had said, although it was not because of anything that he had said. Major and Matt put the oxen into a slow pull from upstream above the cabin. They drew the wagon out until it floated. A dozen men on the other side yelled, 'Easy, take it easy!'

Matt grumbled, 'What do they think we're trying to do—jerk the tongue out?'

The wagon floated. Water crested high against the square front of it when it swung into the current. It rocked from side to side and the oxen had all they could do to hold the weight against the driving river, and then the angle of the pull swung the wagon quickly across the current. After that all Major and Matt had to do was keep the team in a slow, steady pull to draw the wagon in without turning it over or breaking wheels on submerged rocks.

They breathed easier when it was across. No one had taken the chance of riding the first one over. Major and Matt had to unhitch and take the oxen down to haul the wagon out of the way before they could bring the next one across. All the Pilchers came over in the second wagon and after that there was plenty of help.

Major stayed with his job until men arrived to take it over, and then he walked down to satisfy his curiosity about the cabin. It wasn't much of a place. You could see daylight between the logs. The window holes were so small the room was gloomy inside in spite of flames in the unfinished fireplace.

Across one end of the room was a roughhewn counter. Stacked against the wall behind the counter Major saw sacks of flour and other goods. His estimation of Goodwin fell a little. The man hadn't looked like a storekeeper but that must be his business.

Sitting against the wall or just slouching around the room were all of Goodwin's friends. They had lost interest in the crossing and were now passing a jug around. In the dim light they were a shadowy looking bunch. They didn't say anything to Major as he stood awkwardly in the middle of the room. When his eyes opened up a little he made out Bill sitting on a crooked stool near the fire.

'Is this the place that's going to be as big as

Nashville?' Major asked.

'Sure is,' Bill said agreeably.

'When is it they figure on finishing the distillery?' one of the men asked.

'Next week,' another answered.

'I don't think they'll get the railroad through in two months, like they figure. It'll be winter sometime before we hear a whistle. I'll bet on that.'

'What railroad?' Major asked.

'The one that's built halfway through the hills already. You must have come up the river, or you'd have seen it.'

'Two thousand settlers they plan on before Christmas.'

'That'll work all right. I hear the sawmills up the river got enough lumber drying now to build five hundred houses, but what I want to know is where they going to graze those five thousand cattle Robbery is bringing in this month?'

'What are you grinning about, boy?'

Major looked around him. They were all serious, and they made him feel like he'd insulted them. He got an uneasy feeling that maybe he was wrong thinking they were just funning.

'I think this boy wants to call us liars. Us, the people that have sweat and bled to get this place started, and he thinks we're lying. What are we going to do about that, boys?'

Major backed out of the room. It was hard

37

to believe what they had been saying, but still, they had been so serious about it ... And then he heard them laughing inside, hard enough to split themselves.

'Talk about a wet-eared hillbilly!' a man said.

Major felt sheepish enough and mad enough to go back and fight, but he walked away quickly from the laughter.

All the wagons weren't across the river yet, but there was already a council going, and, as usual, an argument. Judson was for pushing on at once. Others were for camping and sending men ahead to scout the next crossing. It was the women who finally settled the argument. Everything in the wagons had been soaked by the crossing. A delegation headed by Mrs Malone declared that the women were not going a foot farther until they had dried out their possessions.

*   *   *

It was a bright, clear day. Unless you looked at the surging river, it was hard to believe there had been a pouring rain such a short time before. Pa and Lafait went hunting. Major helped Ma get the stuff out of the wagon. When he lifted down Grandma Ripley's teakwood chest, Ma frowned and rubbed her hand across the new scars on the top. She set great store by the chest, for it, along with a few things inside it—a teapot and some china dishes and some small painted pictures of her ancestors—were about all she had left of her family.

She stared at the chest for a while and then she looked at the mountains. When she began to take the sodden bundles from the inside of the chest, she told Major, 'I won't need any more help.'

Just in case it did rain again, Major fixed the canvas over the cooking place. He went down the river with Marion and some of the others to see what could be saved from the wrecked wagon. It was lodged in the rocks a mile down from where they had last seen it, out in rough water, with part of the bed and one broken wheel showing. Marion shook his head and they all went back to camp.

Judson and some of the other men were having a loud discussion with Goodwin about the valley as a place to settle. 'Sure, you'd like to see us light down here,' Judson said. 'What with you having a store and all, it wouldn't hurt you a bit, would it?'

'Why, no, it wouldn't,' Goodwin said.

'What will this land grow?' Pilcher asked.

'Where there's good bottoms, you'll find wild hay belly deep.' Goodwin shook his head. 'I wouldn't guarantee anything else.'

'We've got to have wheat and corn ground,' Malone said.

Goodwin nodded. 'Maybe you'll find it over

39

there where you're headed. I can't say because I've never been there.'

In spite of his buckskins and the hard, brown look of him, Goodwin was not the adventuresome man Major had first thought. He was a little disappointed in Goodwin, although the man did have a steady, solid look about his eyes and mouth.

Judson indicated the cabin, from which sounds of laughter and talk were coming. 'Where do they live?'

Goodwin shook his head. 'They're not the settling kind.'

'Yeah.' Judson looked at the wagon men and they all seemed to know what he was thinking.

Along about suppertime Major was walking with Malinda beside a little green-edged run when he saw Pa and Lafait coming back from hunting. Malinda saw them too and seemed to be displeased. All of a sudden she said, 'Are you going to have a place of your own when we get over the mountains?'

'In time, I figure to. First, I'll have to help Pa get started, but after that—'

'Seems to me you're helping a little more than you should. How long is this "after" you're talking about?'

'What do you mean by that?'

Malinda kept looking out to where Pa was striding along with a deer on his shoulders. 'It ain't like you didn't have folks to raise Jude

40

and Dorcas. That's what I mean, Major. You're a grown man, and your family is all in one piece, not like some that got busted up by the war. You don't have to try to be the father.'

'I ain't trying to be.'

Malinda gave him a straight look. Her voice was sharper than he'd ever known it when she said, 'Saving a man from the river is a right fine thing. Nobody denies your pa is a great swimmer. Why didn't he swim the first oxen across this morning, instead of you and Matt Pilcher?'

'I don't know what you're talking about,' Major said hotly. 'Why didn't Matt's pa swim the oxen over, since you're trying to make a big argument over nothing.'

'Matt's pa can't swim. That's one good reason.'

'I ain't going to argue with you, Malinda. You don't make sense.'

'Neither do you, doing everything for your family that your pa ought to be doing. You'll go right on doing it too, just as long as you want to make a fool of yourself!' Malinda swung around and went back toward camp.

'You just wait a minute!'

'You just go to hell, Major Whitlock!'

She had a bad temper, that Irish girl, and this wasn't the first time she'd tried to get mean about Pa. Let her go. By tomorrow she'd be sorry and ready to make up.

Major waited until Pa and Lafait came up to

him. Pa swung the deer to the ground. 'You should see the fish in that little run over west.' Pa measured in the air with his hands. 'Dangdest red color on them fish I ever seen.' Pa walked on toward camp. 'You boys take care of that deer so's your ma can pass it around to folks.'

Lafait gave Major a sly look. 'Big fight with Malinda, huh?'

'None of your business.'

'Her and Matt will be walking together now, with you sulking around like a hound dog with a mouthful of bad meat. Girls just ain't worth fooling with, Major.'

'How do *you* know?' Major started to pick up the hind legs of the deer. He moved on around and took the front legs. 'Get a hold of it.'

'Yeah,' Lafait grumbled. 'Give me the heavy end, huh?'

'I been carrying the heavy end of a lot of things for a long time. Shut up and let's go.'

As they carried the deer on into camp Major considered the fact that Malinda was about right. Pa did have a way of dropping burdens just as handy as he'd shed this deer for someone else to take care of. Shooting game was the easy part of it; the work and mess began right after you pulled the trigger.

Tonight would be a good time to have a little talk with Pa about what was going to happen once they got across the mountains to that

42

place Uncle Lafe had talked about.

Ma glanced at the deer and said, 'Whack it up and pass it around. I swear it keeps a body busy giving away the game Pa and Lafait bring in.' She caught a look in Major's eye as if he was thinking she was making mean of Pa's hunting more than was necessary. That was just what Major was thinking, too. 'Be thankful your Pa is a good hunter, young man,' Ma added.

Whenever she called one of the boys 'young man' it meant she was ready to get bitey. Major said, 'I'm awful thankful.' He got away before Ma could get after him in earnest.

CHAPTER FOUR

The big fire was throwing brightness on the faces of the wagon people as they danced on a flat place where the leaves and sticks had been cleared away among the trees. Major watched glumly as Matt Pilcher paired off again with Malinda. That Matt, he acted like he was quite a man, grinning and bobbing his red head and prancing around like a prairie chicken.

And Luke Pilcher there, with his ears as red as the top of his head, hopping around with Dorcas. When they'd had the first dance while waiting for the ferry on the Mississippi, they'd tried to get Luke to join and he'd gone twisting

43

away like a swamp rabbit. Ma oughtn't to let a lout like him even go near Dorcas.

Pa was having himself a time. He always did when it came to dancing. He'd danced with dang near every woman in the train, whooping and kicking his legs out and making the women smile. Oh, he was a great one for dancing, and a lot of other things that didn't amount to much. For an hour Major had tried to get a chance to talk to him but Pa was too busy. At first he'd said the talk could wait until tomorrow and then when Major said it could not, Pa had promised to come over in the shadows where Major was waiting and see what he had on his mind.

Major leaned against a tree and tapped his foot in time with Marv Wright's fiddle. The whole bunch from Goodwin's store had come up to watch the dance at first, and then all of them but Bill had gone back. Bill was dancing with Essie Broome, Mrs Pilcher's oldest girl by her first husband. With his pistols off, Bill didn't look much different from any other of the young men, except for his wild beard.

When Wright stopped for a rest, Pa still didn't come over to talk and Major knew he'd forgotten all about it, so he went out to the group of men where Pa was talking and waited until he could get Pa's attention. They walked back into the shadowy grove.

'What's the matter, Major?'

'I been wondering about when we get settled.

44

I want to have a place of my own soon as possible—'

'Sure you do, boy, sure you do,' Pa said. 'You're older now than I was when I married your ma. I mind the time—'

'I want to know how long you figure on me helping you get settled and all.'

Pa said, 'Hmn,' down deep in his chest. 'Well, now, that's hard to say. That depends on things.'

'Say, I help you get a cabin built for Ma and the others, and the planting done next spring.'

'Yes,' Pa said, real slow. 'That would be a start, sure enough.'

'The way I see it, it would be quite a start.'

'Now don't you try to get mean with me, boy. I might need you for a spell longer than we figure. It depends on things.'

'What things?' Major asked.

'I said not to try to get mean.'

'What are the things—you mean me keeping on doing work that you can do better, and ought to be doing?'

Major's head struck the tree. He saw white flashes and there was a ringing in his ears and he knew that Pa had cuffed him a good one. Major tried to fight but Pa shouldered in hard and held him against the tree. He was like a bear. It was always a discouraging thing to try to fight Pa because if you did get in a good lick, he'd haul off and knock you about fifteen feet.

Major wanted to get things settled right, so

45

he quit struggling and said, 'Let me go. You and me got to get something straightened out.'

'Well, now that's better.' Pa stepped back. 'Ain't nothing much to straighten out. After we get fixed up good where we're going, we'll see about you having a place of your own. I'll do a little thinking on it in the meantime.'

'I been thinking it over. I'm going to do what I want to do, whether you like it or—'

Major landed on his back in a tangle of old branches. He could see the stars above the trees, but his head was full of roaring noises and his body was numb. He knew Pa had whacked him a real heavy one this time.

Pa said, 'You make a man lose his patience, Major.' Pa went back to the fire. By the time Major got up and hauled his strength into one piece, Pa was laughing and joking at the fire and telling a big story to some of the men. The sad part of the whole thing was, he hadn't taken Major seriously enough to be mad at him.

I'd leave him right now if there was any chance for me, Major thought; but there was no chance, unless he figured on being like a wandering animal. Almost everything he owned was on his back. He was in a far, strange country. And there was Ma and the young ones to think about.

Major stayed in the shadows, watching the dance. If Malinda missed him, she sure did a good job of pretending she didn't even know he

46

was within a thousand miles. He could change that all right when the time came, but there was going to be more trouble with Pa, once they got over the mountains. That would just have to be.

After a while Malone and Jessup and some of the others got tired of dancing. Malone said, 'Let's go over to Goodwin's trading post and have a couple of drinks of his bad whiskey.' Pa and some others were all for that.

Goodwin grinned and said, 'I doubt there's any of that bad whiskey left by now, the way the boys were going when I left.'

'Let's find out,' Pa said.

'You fellows are used to good whiskey where you come from.' Goodwin was pleasant about it but you could tell he was trying to keep them away from the store. 'I'm honest when I say I don't think there'll be any left.'

'Damn'dest storekeeper I ever seen,' Malone said. 'Trying to discourage business.'

'He ain't.' Jessup laughed. 'He's being sly. Come on, boys.'

A half dozen men went trooping out of the firelight and away toward the store, with Pa's deep voice a-booming away right in the middle of things. Goodwin hurried away after them. When the dance picked up again, only the young folks were much interested. Major observed that Bill had got Dorcas away from Luke Pilcher, and Luke didn't like it a bit. He was standing with some of his brothers and you could see he was trying to work up a storm. When you had trouble with one of the Pilchers, you had trouble with several of them.

Major sized up Bill again and decided it might take quite a few Pilchers to have any luck with him, even if he wasn't as big as an ox.

Sure enough, Luke got something started right after the dance ended, when Bill took Dorcas back to where Ma and some of the other women were sitting on boxes at the edge of the tromped space. Luke pushed Bill lightly in the chest and said flat out he guessed Bill better not dance with any more girls from this bunch of wagons. Other Pilchers, brothers and half brothers, were standing behind Luke.

They didn't scare Bill. He said, 'I asked Mrs Whitlock if it'd be all right, and then I asked Dorcas, so I guess you clodhoppers ain't got no say.'

'Yup, we have,' Luke said, and took a big swing at Bill, and the other Pilchers tried to crowd in to help. Right then was when all the tomcats got loose. Bill knocked Luke heels-up with one wallop. Then he ducked and went through the mass of other Pilchers like cavalry splitting through infantry. As he passed he slugged one of them in the belly and you could hear the grunt fifty feet away.

When the others got untangled and turned around, Bill was into them again. Men were bellowing and women were screeching angrily. Major saw another Pilcher reel back like he'd been hit with the end of a pole. Bill was doing real well, and the wagon men, for all their yelling, weren't trying to stop the fight.

One thing about the Pilchers—you could hurt 'em but they didn't quit easy. One of them tripped Bill and another one kicked him in the side of the head as he was getting up and after that they were getting the best of things, even before Matt came charging in. Major's dislike of Pilchers was heavier than the common sense law that wagon folks always stuck together, and he was feeling like an old hound with a sore paw anyway, so he kicked out a fair club from the brush where Pa had piled him up. He went Pilcher hunting.

Matt was his first target. Major rapped him once on the head from behind. Matt turned around from trying to murder Bill and gave Major a startled look. Pilcher heads were known for hardness, and Major shouldn't have forgotten. The next time he did better and Matt dropped like a dead coon falling from a tree.

Well pleased, Major looked for another handy red-topped skull, but someone grabbed his arm and someone else took him from behind and he went sprawling on his face close to Mrs Malone's feet. 'Get up! Get up!' she shouted at him.

He was getting up when Rawl Judson grabbed him, and by then some of the other men had quit yelling for the fight to stop and were doing something about it. They pushed

Pilchers back and dragged Bill off Luke close to the edge of the fire. Matt was still stretched out like Grandpa Betters sleeping in the sun on his cabin porch back home. He looked real good, Matt did.

Judson shouted, 'That's plenty for the time being!'

There was a silence while the women shook their heads as if to say it was the awfullest thing they'd ever seen, and while the Pilchers glared at Bill and Major. Bill was pretty wobbly but he was glaring right back. Matt grunted and twitched his feet a little, like he was trying to come to life.

It was then the two shots came from the direction of the store, sort of muffled and real quick on each other. Some of the women jumped. The men looked uneasily at each other.

'What was that?' Mrs Wright asked. Her husband was one of the men who had gone to the store.

Judson let go of Major. 'I'll go see,' Judson said. 'Like as not it was just one of those wild men shooting through that canvas roof.'

'It's awful quiet though,' Marion said. He nodded at Judson and they started away.

The sound of gunfire never failed to snare Lafait's interest. He trotted away after the men going down to the store.

Luke said, 'If you think this is all, Major, you just got another think coming. We—'

'Hush,' Mrs Marion said.

The women were all quiet, with their heads turned toward the silence in the direction of the store. Matt struggled around and sat up, but even his brothers didn't give him much attention. They stared at Bill when he walked off. It was then that Major, too, went down to the store.

The blanket over the doorway was pushed part way to the side. He could see men moving around slowly inside and someone was saying something in a low voice. All at once Lafait ran out through the doorway. He bumped hard against Major and Major tried to stop him. 'Hey, what's the matter?'

Lafait didn't answer. He went pounding away into the darkness. Major went inside. Men were standing so close together he couldn't see what was going on.

'What's the difference if he had a gun or not, Goodwin? A man tries to kill me, I got a right to see he don't.' That was one of the ragged bunch, a tall man who, like Bill, wore a faded Union blouse.

'You could have got out of it different, Grove,' Goodwin said angrily.

Major pushed his way between men until he came against a table with two candles on it. He saw then what the trouble was. Pa was lying on his back on the dirt floor near the counter, with his eyes wide open, with one arm stretched oddly from his body. Light from the fireplace

51

shone on his crinkly beard and high cheek bones, and deep in his whiskers his mouth was open as if he was just going to say something. The middle of his shirt was darkly stained.

Pa was dead. He was laying there dead on the floor while the men shifted around uneasy-like, paying no mind to Major, who had his hands set like claws on the table as he stared, with his mind all numb.

'You want to go tell his wife, Grove?' Goodwin asked bitterly.

'I didn't start it,' Grove said. His beard was sandy, his eyes blue. They held a mean, tough look, as if he wasn't going to take any more from Goodwin or anyone else in the room. All his friends, except Bill, were lined up with him. If they had been a little drunk before, they were steady enough now.

Goodwin was the only one in the open space between the two groups. He kept looking from one bunch to the other.

Malone said, 'What are we going to do about it, Judson?'

'Yeah,' Grove said, 'let's hear what you've got in mind.'

After a little, Judson said, 'An argument over General Grant ain't no reason for shooting an unarmed man. We'll have to have some kind of trial and—'

'Unarmed, hell! He was killing me with his hands,' Grove said. 'You ain't going to have no trial over me.'

Major looked around slowly. He saw Bill standing at one end of the counter. His face was bloody and dirty from the fight with the Pilchers. He was wearing his pistols again and the knife was in his belt. Oh, he was one of them all right. The whole bunch ought to be hanged, or lined up and shot, like they did in the army.

Major watched the wagon men. They were quietly angry, and there were more of them than Grove had behind him. Nobody could say they weren't tough. Major had seen them push wagons through sand with their teeth clenched and their neck cords standing like ropes. They had rolled rocks that would have strained a team of mules. They were hardened men who stood by each other in all kinds of trouble.

But they just stood there. At last Judson said, 'Go tell Mrs Whitlock, Jessup.' He walked past the table and went over to Pa then and said, 'Let's carry him out of here.'

It came then to Major that no one was going to do anything about Pa's death. Anger so cold that it sickened him ran through Major. If he had a rifle he'd lift it quickly and kill Grove.

The wagon men gathered around Pa to lift him. More men from the train came into the room, asking questions, and then Major saw Lafait working his way stiffly and without hurry along the right-hand wall. Someone dragged the table aside so the wagon men could swing toward the door, and when they turned, carrying Pa like a heavy log, there was

53

once more a clear space.

Lafait was at one end of it against the wall. Suddenly Pa's buffalo gun jumped up from his side and levelled at Grove. A minute before, Major would have killed Grove himself, but now he shouted, 'No, Lafait, no!'

Goodwin grabbed the barrel and drove the muzzle down just as Lafait pulled the trigger. The gun made a fearful loud explosion in the room. The men dropped Pa and some of them stumbled over him as they tried to jump outside. Grove's friends drew their pistols and swung them around the room as Goodwin wrestled the buffalo gun away from Lafait, who scarcely struggled to hold onto it, so that when Goodwin got the gun, he fell against the counter with it.

Light from the big fireplace fell across Lafait's face. His swarthy skin was pale. He looked square at Grove, who had a pistol in his hand. 'Give me time to reload and I'll get you,' Lafait said.

Grove stared at him quietly for a long time. 'You his kid?' he asked.

'Give me a fair chance and I'll get you.' Lafait reached toward Goodwin, as if he thought Goodwin would hand the rifle back.

You could see Grove didn't like it. He was puzzled, maybe even scared a little like he was seeing something he couldn't understand.

One of his friends said, 'Let's get out of here.'

'No,' Grove said. 'We'll stay as long as we please.' He shook his head at Lafait. 'I got no quarrel with you.'

White, with his dark eyes burning, Lafait turned away and walked out of the room.

'He's going for another gun, Cy,' one of the ragged bunch said to Grove.

Grove raised his voice, 'You wagon people better see that he don't come back here with it! You hear me?'

Major straightened up from leaning on the table. Except for turning his head, he had been so rigid that he now felt aches in his back and arms. They were taking Pa through the doorway, and it was so narrow that only two men could hold onto him. Judson was behind. Pa's body bumped the ground as they got him through the doorway.

Major started out and then he remembered Pa's buffalo gun. He went over to Goodwin. After looking at Major for a long moment, Goodwin gave him the rifle.

Grove said, 'Don't come back here with it, youngster.' He was threatening and at the same time begging a little.

Major looked at him and said, 'You dirty sonofabitch,' and then he walked away.

CHAPTER FIVE

Before noon the train was six miles away from Pa's grave near the crossing, and for the first time in many weeks the Whitlock wagon was not at the tail end. Major had thought to start in the usual place but Judson told him to go behind Wright's wagon, which was in the lead.

Major overheard the Pilchers arguing some about it, saying that the whole train would be held up on account of having the Whitlocks so far forward, but Judson got mad and shut them up. The Whitlocks were holding close together now. Jude and Dorcas were in the wagon, sometimes talking in low voices to each other, but most of the time silent back there. Ma was with Major on the seat as usual, with Lafait walking off to the left of the oxen.

That fellow in the store the night before had been sure enough right when he said Lafait was going after another gun. Lafait had got the Pennsylvania rifle, but the wagon men caught him and made him behave, and that meant taking the gun away from him and having guards watch careful all night to see he didn't get another gun and go back to Goodwin's to kill Grove.

Major guessed that Lafait was calmed down now, although Lafait hadn't said ten words all morning. He just walked along outside the

56

dust, carrying the long rifle and thinking his own thoughts.

Ma was awful quiet too. She sat straight-backed, looking at the mountains. Mrs Malone had made more wailing over Pa's death than Ma had. Ma hadn't cried hardly a-tall, but even now when Major said something to her she was a long time answering and you could see that something was froze and still deep inside her.

This was the best traveling the wagons had seen in a long time. There were no hills to speak of and the ground was fairly smooth. Bunchy looking grass grew everywhere. Looking far ahead, you might think the ground was richly covered with grass, but it took only a glance down from the wagon to show the big dead spaces between the clumps of grass. On the gently sloping hills the wheels ground against gravel. There wasn't much soil on the high spots of the valley, that was certain.

By now everyone could see that the mountains right in front were not the ones they had to cross, for the valley turned to the north and appeared to run forever. Maybe, like Uncle Lafe had said, there was an easy way to get over the snow-patched peaks somewhere up ahead. But Major doubted that.

The way his mind was running Major felt that maybe he wasn't grieving properly for Pa. Oh, he was thinking of Pa a good deal, but a lot of the time he was worrying about himself and the rest of the family and the way the right front wheel was acting. After the rain and the soaking the wagon had got in the river, the wheels had been some better, but they had dried out quickly enough. Now the spokes were squeaking as they worked in the hubs and some of the wedges between the tires and the fellys were coming loose.

It would take a pile of doing to hold the wagon together and get it over the mountains. The worst of it was that most of the doing would have to come from others in the train who had extra oxen and extra wheels.

At the nooning Major was examining the oxen's sore feet when Marv Wright came over to him.

'How do they look, Major?'

'Fawn's ain't so bad but Steuben—his are getting worse.'

Wright glanced at the mountains. 'Don't you worry no more than necessary. You're going to get there. I got spare oxen and the Lord knows Marion has got a-plenty of them now, what with no wagon to pull, and since he's attached to me now, I reckon I got the right to suggest a thing or two about how he uses his oxen, wouldn't you say?'

'I reckon,' Major said. Wright and Marion were first cousins. They ought to stick together and help each other, but the Whitlocks were no kin of any of them. Major rolled the meaning of 'attached' around in his head. He didn't

58

think he'd like to have the word applied to him. It meant you didn't have the things you ought to have and couldn't do the things you ought to do.

'You and Malinda Malone are a-figuring, ain't you?' Wright asked.

'We was, yes.'

Wright nodded. 'It'll work out. Lafait's old enough to be taking hold now. I expect your ma will marry up again someday, too—'

'My God, Mr Wright! Pa ain't hardly—'

'Oh, not right away of course. But that's the way things go, Major. My own pa was killed a-feuding when I was just a scaper. Few months later my ma married up with a distant cousin from North Carolina, and I can't say but what she got a better man.

'But that ain't what I came to talk about. I want to help you get where we're going, same's I'd help my own kin. My boys are little. It'll be seven, eight years before they can help me much. Getting settled is a chore, Major. I figured maybe you'd work for me a while. I can pay you enough to—'

'I want a place of my own, soon's I can get Ma and the children fixed up.'

'Sure you do. You can have it. You can take up your ground, you and Malinda. Meantime, I can use some help and pay enough to keep you going. You think it over, Major, and see how it strikes you.'

Major watched Wright walk away. Folks

said Wright had made himself some money running cotton up the Mississippi during the war. He was willing to help the Whitlocks get over the mountains and then Major would feel bounden to work for him. That wasn't Major's idea of things. You could work for someone else back home, if that's all you wanted.

Major went to see what Malinda thought about Wright's offer. She was helping her mother cook and as usual there were a half dozen young Malones eyeing Major and making jibes. In a country so big you couldn't see the end of it you still had no more privacy than a fat hog at an auction.

'Go ahead,' Mrs Malone told her oldest daughter, and then she took a swipe at three or four children who were making impudent remarks. 'Will you leave the lad in peace, him with his father just laid away!'

Fifty feet away from the wagon Major told Malinda about Wright's offer.

'It *would* be a chance for us to get started,' Malinda said.

Major felt as if he had swallowed something big and cold; that wasn't the answer he'd wanted from Malinda. She saw he didn't like it and said, 'Maybe it would be only for a little while.'

'I can't help him and Ma get settled at the same time, and us too.'

'Lafait can do what you've been doing.'

'I'm not sure he's old enough.'

'He's old enough to try to kill a man.'

'That doesn't count,' Major said. Last night when Lafait was facing Grove his terrible stubbornness made him seem grown up, but he wasn't like that in all things. Major couldn't explain it to Malinda. For one thing, she didn't like Lafait in the first place.

'There you go,' Malinda said, 'you'll be afraid to leave your mother when you're an old man.'

'It's not just Ma, it's Jude and Dorcas mostly.'

Malinda was getting sharper by the second. 'The way Dorcas was carrying on with that Bill last night, you won't have her on your hands very long.'

'All they were doing was dancing. I don't know what's got into you, Malinda. You jump at me every time I open my mouth.'

'Are you going to work for Wright or not?'

'I don't know.'

'What's so bad about it? Somebody has got to help you Whitlocks over the mountains. If Wright wants to do it, it seems like the least you could do is help him a little too in exchange.'

'That's just it,' Major said miserably. 'I don't want to be bounden to him for anything.'

'You're too proud for your own good.' Malinda started away. 'I got to help Ma.' She looked back over her shoulder. 'And you ain't got nothing to be proud about, if you stopped to think a minute.'

61

Maybe she was right. He didn't think he was a prideful man; but it was just that it was hard to forget that Pa had been slack in a few things.

Major went back to the wagon to eat. Lafait had already wolfed his food. He kept looking to where cottonwoods marked a small stream coming down from the mountains. 'I better hunt this afternoon.'

Ma gave him a long look. She didn't speak.

'I reckon I'll take the buffalo gun.'

'Leave it be,' Ma said. 'Leave it be for a while.'

Lafait never had been one to do much arguing with words. He watched Ma for a second and you could see that she had won. Lafait picked up his long rifle. He didn't leave because just then Judson said in a loud voice, 'Man coming this way.'

The rider was moving at a slow trot. It wasn't until he was close to camp that Major knew it was Bill. The wagon men sort of bunched against him at once, and some of them dragged rifles and shotguns out of their wagons. Bill came straight up to the Whitlocks. He didn't get down, and after one swift look at the wagon men, he pretended they weren't there.

Bill looked directly at Ma. 'I'm right sorry about your man, Mrs Whitlock.'

Ma took him in real careful, the old Union blouse, the pistols, the young eyes looking straight out from the beardy face. She nodded slow and said, 'Thank you, young man.'

That looked like about all Bill had come to say, for he started to turn his horse. He did glance at Dorcas as he was swinging around but he didn't make anything big of it; and then he stopped when he saw how the Pilchers had worked in behind him, standing there with their rifles.

'We going to let him go?' Matt Pilcher said. 'He's thicker 'n oak roots with that bunch that killed Whitlock.'

'Yeah, you're going to let him go,' Lafait said. 'Nobody wanted to do nothing last night about Pa, so you ain't bunching up now on one man that wasn't there when Pa got shot.'

You could tell that Lafait didn't give a damn for all the Pilchers. He was as deep mean and strange as he had been the night before when he tried to shoot Grove.

'That's right,' Judson said, kind of ashamed because Lafait had spoken first. 'Maybe this man keeps bad company, but we all know he was dancing at the fire when Whitlock got shot.' Judson walked over to the Pilchers. 'Let him go.'

'Suppose I don't?' Matt asked.

Judson started to explain that Matt didn't have anything against Bill, except a knuckle fight, and that nobody in the train had a lawful right to arrest Bill, but Lafait, always impatient with words, cocked his long rifle and said, 'Get out'n his way, you Pilchers, or I'll shoot Matt

63

in the mouth.'

The Pilchers got out of the way and Bill rode off.

'That was the right thing to do, Lafait,' Ma said, 'But you're getting too almighty depending on a rifle gun. If you're so all-fired set on Bill, why didn't you leap in last night when him and the Pilchers was a-struggling?'

'Fighting with fists is for kids and fools,' Lafait said. He walked off toward the mountains.

The way Ma watched him, with a tired, thoughty look making her face sad, you'd'a thought Lafait was going away for good.

'Hitch up!' Judson yelled.

Major had the Whitlock wagon ready to pull out as soon as any of the rest, but this time when Judson told him to fall in behind Wright, Major shook his head. He took his regular place at the end of the train. Fawn and Steuben had done well enough during the morning but they would be falling behind again as soon as their sore feet got a little worse.

Ma made Jude ride on the seat beside her. 'You've got to quit pestering Lafait,' she told him. 'Don't fun him about killing fawns and the like.'

'I only do it to make him mad. He knows I don't mean it.'

'I know,' Ma said. She looked out where Lafait was disappearing into the trees beside the little stream. 'Don't do it no more.'

As they went on Ma started to put her arm around Jude. She wasn't looking at him, she was staring at the mountains, but she made to hug Jude without thinking, which was something she hadn't done since he was real little, or unless he was hurt and bawling his head off. Jude didn't like it and he tried to wiggle away. Major saw Ma nod to herself as she took her arm off him.

'Can't these younguns walk a while?' Major asked.

'Who you calling younguns?' Jude protested, and Dorcas stuck her head out and joined in the protest.

'They can walk for a spell,' Ma said. 'But stop the wagon first.'

When Jude and Dorcas leaped down and ran off to join some of the Broome younguns, Major told Ma about Wright's offer. 'Is that what you were a-telling Malinda about, when you come back to eat looking so sad?'

'I told her. She thought I ought to do it.'

Ma held on to the jolting seat and looked ahead. The space between the Whitlocks and the next wagon was widening. 'What do you say you ought to do, Major?'

'I don't know. We got to get over the mountains.'

'Yes. To that golden place your Uncle Lafe talked about. I never did get him to say what was over there, except ducks in the marshes, and deer and elk tromping the hillsides.' Ma

65

smiled like she was poking fun at Uncle Lafe and forgiving him at the same time.

'How long ought I to work for Wright?'

'I didn't say you ought to work for him a-tall. We'll all do what we got to do, but let's see first what that is.'

Major felt some better. Ma had a way of giving you strength when you had something twisty bothering you that looked like it couldn't be beat no way. If Pa had been like that ... But it was best to try to forget Pa and keep on doing the things that had to be done. Right in the midst of his forgetting, Major felt tears running down his cheeks.

Fawn and Steuben plodded on, getting more sore-footed at every step. Before long some of the young Pilchers, jeering and happy, drove the spare oxen right on past the Whitlock wagon, and then it was for sure behind everything. Judson rode back on his bay horse. 'Wright says he can lend—'

'Never mind what Mr Wright says. We can get along for a while,' Ma said. 'Thank him just the same.'

Judson tried to act like he wasn't worried, even if he had said last night that the train ought to hurry as much as possible while the going was good. He went trotting away with a wave of his hand, as if to say everything would be fine.

'Might be we could trade the buffalo rifle gun for a team,' Ma said.

66

'Best we could do would get one ox for it. Lafait's got his heart set on that gun. By rights, he ought to have it.'

'That gun cost a real good mule.' Ma's voice trailed off like she was thinking a long ways back, clean back to home.

By late afternoon the train was two miles ahead, crawling along in a lazy cloud of dust, wriggling its way through brown hills. Major lost sight of it for a while and then he saw it again when he was just coming out of the hills. The train was then dusting along on a smooth looking slope that ran clean back to the wide blue skirts of the mountains. All at once the wagons dropped from sight as if the earth had gulped them down and Major knew there was a heavy break of some kind in the ground ahead.

It was a wide, flat valley, a bottom covered with tall grass. The train was already across it and far beyond when the Whitlocks came to the gravelly hill that led down into the valley. Jude and Dorcas were waiting at the bottom of the hill with a team of oxen.

'Wright done that,' Major said, but he knew he should be thankful, for the hill across the valley appeared as steep as the one he was about to descend, and in the meadows themselves the wheel tracks were black and deep in torn-up ground and he saw pry poles sticking out there in the mud.

The road down the hill was full of rocks ground out by the wheels of the wagons that had gone before. Although it was an angling descent, Fawn and Steuben had a hard time holding. The wagon kept crabbing downhill as it jounced over rocks that Major would have missed if he could. They gave the shaky wheels cruel treatment and once Major thought the right front one was going to crash into flinders, but the wagon held together and he brought it to a stop beside a grove of cottonwoods at the edge of the valley.

Jude and Dorcas led the team over. They were Marion's oxen, Major saw, but he knew who had sent them.

'It's a bad place out there,' Jude said. 'You sink in deep.'

'I can see that,' Major said, looking ahead at the churned black earth. Not all of the wagons had tried the same ruts but all of them had sunk in.

'Mr Judson said the camp would be about two miles ahead.' Jude backed the extra team toward Fawn and Steuben.

For a moment Major was of a mind to try it without the help of Marion's oxen, but he knew that would be foolish. 'Hook the chain,' he told Jude.

'Where it looks the worst seemed to be the best.' Jude pointed. 'After you get past that last pry pole out there, the best way is to the right. Jessup and Malone got through there without no trouble.'

Jude drove the lead team. He had a way with

animals, Jude did. They seemed to know just what he wanted as they went into the mud with steady, even power. Major watched the black ooze, threaded with long grass, pushing up around the legs of the wheel team. Cooling, healing mud was what old Fawn and Steuben needed for feet.

The wagon never reached the first pry pole slanting upright in the mud. Major heard the right front wheel going and yelled for Jude to stop. The mud was up to Major's knees when he got down to look at the wheel. Two of the spoke ends he could see had popped out of the felly. The wheel was a twisty looking thing that would get worse with every turn in the heavy mud.

He glanced up at Ma quickly and she read his thoughts. Jude and Dorcas came around to look at the wheel. Jude said, 'My God, that one's a goner.'

'Watch your language, young man!' Ma warned.

'We'll haul it out backwards and fix the wheel over there by the trees. Hitch your chain on back, Jude,' Major said.

Marion's strong oxen hauled the wagon out almost by themselves. All Major did with his team was hold the tongue straight. With a cottonwood stick Major scraped mud until he could see how bad off the wheel was. It was a wonder it had held together long enough to get out of the mud after those first two spokes popped loose. One section of the felly was split and the tire was hanging over. The tire itself was worn thin. Likely it would come apart before they got across the mountains.

Major looked at Ma. 'Looks like I'll be working for old Wright.' He tried to grin.

'Get the cooking things out of the wagon, Dorcas,' Ma said. 'Jude, you help Major with the oxen. How long will it take to fix the wheel, Major?'

Fixing the wheel wasn't what Major was thinking of. He kept looking at it and said doubtfully, 'Maybe I can patch it out somehow, but the others ain't much good either—'

'Fix one at a time,' Ma said.

The way she said it, as much as the words, was to stick in Major's mind all his life.

Supper was about ready when Lafait returned, coming up the valley from the direction of the river, instead of from the mountains where they had last seen him headed. He was carrying a buck that almost bowed him down. You could see that he was so tired he was ready to drop.

'Why, that's bigger than any Pa got!' Jude exclaimed.

Lafait was pleased. Praise from Jude was the most welcome of all; he got so little of it.

'It's as fine a buck as I ever saw, I declare,' Ma said.

Lafait loosened up some. 'I seen quite a few

70

big-ears along the river.'

He could have killed a smaller one, Major thought. With that Pennsylvania rifle Lafait could pick a bird out of the air that some grown men back home couldn't hit with a shotgun. Next time he probably would bring back a smaller deer, but on this first hunt, with Pa gone, Lafait had felt bounden to kill the biggest buck he could find.

Ma had turned back to her cooking real quick and was dabbing at her eyes like smoke had got in them. Major was blinking a little himself when he said, 'A grown man would have worn out trying to carry that buck.' Lafait was wide and stocky but he was still a boy; he must have near killed himself carrying the deer.

'Is the river still roaring, Lafait?' Jude asked.

Lafait shook his head. 'Down to nothing again.'

Ma straightened up from the fire. 'The chances are we can get some wheel parts from Marion's wagon then.'

'That's what I was thinking,' Jude said.

Even with Pa gone and wagon trouble on their hands, the Whitlocks had to laugh a little. Looking back afterward, Major knew that they were that first night in the grove about as strongly bound together as a family could be.

Marion and Judson rode into their camp at dusk. Major told them about the wheel and about their plans to go get some spokes and

71

other parts from the wrecked wagon.

'That's fourteen miles back,' Marion said. 'It's simpler to borrow a wheel from Wright or Malone.'

'It ain't so simple to pay it back,' Major said. 'You folks go ahead. We'll catch up all right when you hit the mountains again.'

'There ain't that much rush,' Judson said. 'We want to go as fast as possible, sure, but the train ain't running off from any wagon in trouble. I still say the best thing is to borrow a wheel. We can get it here tonight, slap it on, and you'll be ready to start in the morning.'

Major looked at Ma.

'We're obliged, Mr Judson, but I reckon the boys want to fix the wheel,' Ma said. 'Like Major said, you folks go on. We'll catch up. There's some bad feelings already about us holding up things too often.'

Judson didn't deny that. 'I'll leave my horse for Major and Lafait. They can get the spokes from Marion's wagon quicker that way, and we'll all—'

'Won't need it,' Lafait said.

Judson gave Lafait a sharp look and then he glanced at Ma. 'You folks figure on going across the mountains with everyone else, don't you?'

Ma nodded. 'We do.'

'Well, then, us being all together and from the same state, mainly, it seems—'

'Won't need the horse,' Lafait said.

72

Ma shook her head at Judson. 'Thank you just the same.'

You could see that Marion was half mad, but maybe he was thinking of how Pa had saved his life because he didn't say anything. He and Judson rode away polite enough but you could tell they weren't pleased with the way the Whitlocks had acted. Major fancied he could hear Marion saying, 'Folks in a fix like them Whitlocks oughtn't to be so stubborn and prideful.'

CHAPTER SIX

At daylight Major and Lafait were on their way, making their breakfast of cold meat that they munched as they walked. They followed the wagon tracks until they came to where they could see the wide part of the valley, and then Major made a straight line toward Goodwin's store. When they crossed the Arkansas at the end of a deep canyon, the water was running clear and blue and low.

A half mile from the store Lafait said, 'Ain't no use to see Goodwin again.'

Instead of crossing the river to the easier going on the south side, they stayed on the hilly side and went past the old campground where the train had waited on the flood. There was a wagon at the store, a low-boxed one with a

73

heavy team. The sight sort of startled Major. 'There must be people living around here someplace.'

'Goodwin said so, didn't he?'

'I didn't hear him.'

'You was too busy mooning around Malinda.'

They plunged down into the willows where Major had run so hard when he thought Pa was tangled in Marion's wagon. How long ago was that? Only three nights ago but there was something far distant about remembering, even when they went along the river bank and saw the trampled place where everyone had gathered around Pa after he'd heaved himself out of the river.

They found Marion's wagon a long mile farther down the river. It was badly smashed, but they pried loose four unbroken front wheel spokes and knocked loose some long sections of the rim. For good measure they took the best of the back wheel spokes too, although some of them were broken. Two tires were left, bent and twisted, but Major dragged them ashore. When they waded to the bank for the last time and looked at their pile of salvage, Major knew they had more than they could carry, and yet they needed it all—and more.

They were figuring on just how much they could take when they heard the noise in the willows. A moment later Goodwin appeared on a horse. 'I saw you across the river. Figured you'd be down here.'

'What do you want?' Lafait asked.

Goodwin didn't seem to mind Lafait's surliness. He looked him over real careful and said, 'You ought to be glad I grabbed that rifle, son.'

'Don't you call me son!'

'You'd'a had four, five bullets in you,' Goodwin said. 'That's a fact, ain't it?'

Lafait knew it was the truth but he wouldn't say so. He spat into the river and looked at something on a far hill.

'You ain't fixing to carry all that stuff, are you?' Goodwin asked Major.

'I reckon we can.'

'Maybe you could, but it would be kind of a chore. What's the matter with taking my horse? We can fix up a drag—'

'Don't need your horse,' Lafait said.

Some kinds of stubbornness were plumb silly, Major thought. Goodwin wasn't trying to work out something for himself; he was just being neighborly. 'We'd be right obliged to use the horse,' Major said. Lafait spat into the river again.

Goodwin went to work like he knew what he was doing. Out of a tangle of stuff piled up by the flood he picked out two long, springy poles and began to tie crosspieces on them. Major noticed he didn't cut the rope but just kept using it in one long piece. Lafait didn't do anything to help. He sat down on a rock and

75

looked at the river, but Major noticed how he watched from the sides of his eyes and began to show interest when it became clear how the thing Goodwin was making was going to work.

Major and Goodwin tipped the long poles up and slipped them over the horse and tied the ends to the saddle. 'The Indians call this a travois,' Goodwin said.

Without saying anything Lafait began to help Major load and tie the wheel parts on the platform of crosspieces.

'Do you know a lot about Indians?' Major asked Goodwin.

'Not a whole lot. Mano's band—they're Utes—were camped where the store is when I came here this spring. I got acquainted with them a little.'

'Are they mean?' Major asked.

'Oh, they could be, I reckon. I'm not figuring on doing anything to test out how mean they are. I learned something about Indians from my pappy. He spent most of his life out here, from Taos to the Yellowstone—what you call a Mountain Man.'

'Where is he now?' Lafait asked.

'Dead. The Blackfeet got him, near as I know.'

Lafait grunted with disappointment.

'That was twenty years ago,' Goodwin said. 'He was getting old even then. I remember the stories he used to tell when he'd come back to St Louis about every two years. He'd been through the mountains from hell-to-breakfast. When he'd get a little drunk and start telling about some of the things he'd seen and done, it was some doings. In the old days this country was something. I guess I waited too long to come out here.'

'You can still remember some of them stories, huh?' Lafait asked.

'A lot of them. Thinking about them is what got me out here, though it's too late now to do the things my pappy did.'

All the wheel parts were loaded on the travois. Goodwin led the horse away. The load on the crosspieces dragged along as easy as you please. 'You can turn this horse loose when you get back to your wagon,' Goodwin said. 'He'll come home.'

When they reached the store, the wagon that had been there was far away toward the foothills near the fork of the river where Pa had killed his last deer. Lafait and Major avoided looking toward the cottonwoods where Pa was buried.

'Those folks live around here?' Major asked, looking toward the distant wagon.

'About six, seven miles up Little Creek there,' Goodwin said. 'There's four other claims made in the valley here and there. I got one of my own on Little Creek.'

Lafait took the bridle reins. 'We'd better go.'

'Just turn him loose when you get there.' Goodwin put his hand on Lafait's shoulder.

'What made you think Bill wouldn't shoot you the other night?'

'Knew he wouldn't, that's all.'

'Did you know where he was in the room?' Goodwin asked.

'Behind me,' Lafait said, 'a little off to the right.'

'Where was Major?'

'Holding onto the table, with his mouth open.'

Major might have sworn that when Lafait marched into the store with Pa's rifle, he had eyes only for Grove. Major himself couldn't have said where Bill was.

'You got a way of sizing a mean situation up, Lafayette.' Goodwin grinned.

'Nobody says my name like that,' Lafait said. He led the horse away.

'Good luck with the wheel,' Goodwin told Major.

'We're obliged for all—'

'Don't bother to say it.' Goodwin waved his hands and walked toward the store. He stopped in the doorway to watch the Whitlocks on their way.

The horse stepped along briskly. Dust streamed back from the dragging points of the travois. It was a fair thing to carry stuff. Major wondered what Jude would think of it.

Lafait said, 'Wish we'd had time to hear some of them stories about Goodwin's pappy.'

Any kind of tale with a fight in it was Lafait's

meat. Grandpa Whitlock had come into Kentucky when it was dark and bloody ground, and although Lafait and Major had never known him, Uncle Lafe had been full of stories about him. Lafait had sat by the hour, with his black eyes gleaming, listening to Uncle Lafe tell about how Grandpa Whitlock had fought Mingoes and Shawnees and cougars and bears and about everything else there was that was dangerous.

Ma always said that, to hear Uncle Lafe tell it, Simon Whitlock had taught Dan Boone everything he knew and then some. The fact still stood that Grandpa Whitlock had been a fearful man. He was real old when the axes got to ringing so hard in the Kentucky woods that he claimed they were deafening him, so he went out across the big river all by himself and spent the last of his days with the remnants of the Shawnees he had fought so hard when he was young.

He was one Whitlock that Ma couldn't say got himself killed in a useless fight, because he died of overeating after a big hunt with the Indians.

Major and Lafait got back to the wagon before noon. Jessup had brought tools and was ready to go to work on the wheel. He had it off the wagon and laid on some cottonwood poles with the broken parts already removed. He looked over the stuff on the travois and said, 'Good, good. That'll more than do it. Just give

79

me a hand, Major, and you'll be rolling in on time.'

Judson said, 'I'll go on back to camp and tell them.' He caught Ma's steady look. 'I'll admit they been a little restless, Mrs Whitlock, wanting to get on.'

'Wait just a spell, Mr Judson,' Ma said. 'Wait till I have a few words with Major.'

Puzzled, Major went with Ma as she walked into the grove, past a little spring, and on to the edge of the valley beyond. From here you couldn't see the torn up ground where the wagons had crossed. Tall grass ran down toward the river on both sides of willows beside a wandering stream. The meadows were wider running toward the mountains until they ended against the gray rumps of hills where nothing but piñons and rabbit brush grew.

Ma looked at the mountains for a long time, and then she turned her back to them. 'We can settle right here.'

'Here!'

'I know you got your mind set on going with the rest. And there's Malinda to think of.'

'I hadn't thought about stopping anywhere short of where Pa and Uncle Lafe said.'

'Pa and Uncle Lafe ain't in this no more, Major. I know one thing, you eat your own insides when you're obliged to somebody. You're like my Pa's folks, the Stuarts.' Ma's face was quiet and thoughtful. 'I'm going to leave the say to you about staying or going on.'

Ma went back into the grove and left Major alone.

What about Malinda? The Malones were going on. Malinda would marry Matt Pilcher sure as shooting if Major stayed here. Jude and Dorcas wouldn't like being here away from everybody. Lafait, he probably didn't care one way or another where he stopped. Ma herself didn't like the mountains; she'd said she'd never settle where they were looking down on her, all cold and cruel. But Major guessed she hated being bounden to anyone as much as he did.

She'd walked off and left him to make the choice.

Major went out into the meadow. It was fine hay, but what could you do with it? Even Goodwin didn't think the land was much good for growing anything else. After they ate what was in the wagon, there wouldn't be anything left but game.

All the problems Major had worried about would be the same here as if they went on with the others, only worse.

And Malinda would be gone forever.

Out in the deep grass, Major found himself staring at the mountains. All of a sudden they scared him. They were so enormous and grim. From up there on the high rocks this valley was likely no more than a narrow strip of green, and he wasn't even a speck. The mountains weren't jeering him; they didn't even know he was here, all tight and scared, trying to settle problems too big for him. The mountains made Major feel more alone than he had ever been in his life.

After a time he went back to the camp.

Jessup had stopped working on the wheel. He was puzzled as he stood by the logs with a scowl on his forehead. Judson was still on his horse, and anxious to be off.

'What have you got to say, Major?' Ma asked.

Major wished she hadn't put it all on him; but he looked at Judson and said, 'We're going to stay here.'

'How long?' Judson asked.

'For good.' Major heard Dorcas gasp, and he saw Jude starting to cloud up with protests.

'We're obliged for everything, Mr Judson. Major and me talked things over,' Ma said. 'Tell everyone good-bye for us.' She looked like she was at Pa's burying again, ready to cry but set so hard against it that no tears could come.

'Ma!' Dorcas cried, 'we're not going to stay here all by ourselves!'

'Hush,' Ma said. 'We are, and that's all there is to it.'

Jessup picked up his handsaw. 'Talk to her, Judson, while I fix this wheel.' He started to work again.

'Leave the wheel be, Mr Jessup,' Ma said. 'We're settling here.' She looked at Major.

'Now that's right, ain't it?'

It was Major's last chance to change his mind. 'We're going to settle right in this here valley,' he said.

Judson looked from Ma to Major. He was a shrewd man, and so he didn't make a big fuss, although he argued for several minutes in a reasonable way, and then he gave up. 'Get your tools, Jessup.' Judson went over to Ma. 'I can't deny it's a likely looking valley, Mrs Whitlock, maybe as good as we'll find on the other side, for all we know.' He worked the toe of his boot in the mold under a tree. 'My wife's got more dried fruit than she knows what to do with. Could I send some back before we—'

'Thank you, no, Mr Judson. That's kindly of you, but you'd do it and then others might want to send something.' Ma shook her head. 'We've plenty to do with.'

'I don't want to stay here!' Dorcas sat down on a log and began to cry.

Lafait gave her a disgusted look and said, 'Aw shut up.'

'You shut up yourself and leave her alone!' Jude shouted. His face was all lumped up like he was about to cry too. 'You leave her alone, you fawn killer!'

That didn't make Lafait mad, for once. He went over to Dorcas and patted her on the back. 'This is a good place.'

Dorcas wriggled angrily away from his touch and batted at his arm. 'You like any old

83

place where there's something to shoot!' she accused. 'All you care about is tromping the woods anyway.'

'Bawling don't help nothing,' Lafait said.

It wasn't often that Ma let her children bellow and storm around so without doing something about it, but this time she acted like she didn't hear them.

Jessup was wrapping his tools in a long roll of greased canvas. Now and then he shook his head as if to say that the Whitlock family was crazy.

Major went down into the willows to get the oxen Marion had sent back. Judson caught up with him and together they got the beasts started toward the camp. 'I'm not altogether clear on the rest of the way through the mountains,' Judson said. 'Your pa was some careful not to map out the whole trip at once. Did he tell you much about it?'

'No, he didn't. I remember Uncle Lafe said you went almost to the head of the Arkansas and then you had your choice of two ways.'

Judson nodded absent-like. 'I guess we'll find a way all right.' He cleared his throat. 'You coming up to the camp to say good-bye to anyone?'

'I reckon not.'

'Anything you want me to tell Malinda?'

'Tell her—' Major felt hurt and choked up as he thought about Malinda. 'Tell her we're staying here. That's about all there is to it.'

84

He helped Judson put the harness on Marion's oxen.

Jude and Dorcas were huddled together in misery, watching every move Major made, as if at the last second everything was going to change. Lafait was cleaning the long rifle, which did not need cleaning. Ma was sitting on the logs beside the broken wheel, with her back to the mountains.

The Whitlocks watched Jessup and Judson ride away, the oxen lumbering slowly in front of them. They dipped through the rich mud of the meadows and went up the hill on the other side of the valley. Judson turned his horse and waved and then all of them, the two men, the oxen and the horses, went from sight beyond the hill. The Whitlocks were alone in silence at the foot of the great, watching mountains.

Dorcas began to cry again.

'It ain't that bad.' Lafait sighted his rifle at something down the valley. His swarthy cheek lay flat against the stock, his eyes were quiet as rifle holes. You'd'a thought he was seeing a hundred buffalo down there.

Major tried to take charge of things. He said to Dorcas, 'Stop that bawling. You hear me, stop it right now!' Dorcas didn't quit but she did bring her loud wailing down to a gulping kind of sobbing.

Ma turned slowly to watch Major.

'The first thing,' Major said, 'is we're going to have to build a cabin. We'll start it this

85

afternoon, and everybody but Ma will have to help.'

Still sighting down the rifle, Lafait said, 'The first thing is I got to take Goodwin's horse back. I ain't going to turn it loose and have it wander off, no matter what he said.'

'The horse knows the way back,' Major said. 'You just want to ride it down there.'

'Yep.' Lafait lowered the rifle. 'And I think I'll take Pa's buffalo gun along.'

'You leave that rifle be,' Major ordered. He was only repeating what Ma had said.

'It'll be proper for him to have the rifle now.' Ma reached out and tapped the broken wheel. 'There ain't no blazing hurry, Major, to build a cabin. The first thing I want done is the fixing of this here wheel.'

Jude and Dorcas perked up. 'You mean we're going on, Ma?' Dorcas asked.

'I mean,' Ma said, 'we're going to have the wagon so it'll run. Other folks will be along this way. I won't have them saying we stopped here because we didn't have no choice.'

It set Major back and sort of jarred him, but at the same time he was relieved to know he wasn't running things just because Ma had let him have the say about staying or going on.

That afternoon the Whitlocks repaired the wheel. Jude knew more about what to do than Major and Lafait put together, for although they all had seen wheels fixed before, Jude was the only one who could remember the step-by-

86

step way the work had been done.

They finished the job before sunset and drove the wagon into the grove to the place where Ma and Dorcas were making a permanent camp. Dorcas had one last go at complaining. 'The wagon's all right now. Why can't we go on, Ma? We could catch up again, like we always did—'

'The others always waited,' Ma said. 'I'll have no more talk about going on. The say was left to Major because he had more to lose than any of us. From now on nobody in this family will make light of what he did.'

In Ma's presence no one ever did make light of Major's decision thereafter.

Lafait at once saddled up Goodwin's horse. He tried to mount with the buffalo gun in one hand. He dropped the reins and the horse shied away, and altogether Lafait made an awkward but determined spectacle of himself before he was in the saddle.

'You better shorten the stirrups,' Jude said.

'That don't matter.' Lafait rode away. The horse knew where it was going and it trotted briskly, bouncing Lafait in the saddle. It looked like he was going to fall off before he got up the hill.

'He'll make it—if he don't bust his neck first,' Jude said. 'Look at them stirrups a-flopping like a fish out of water.'

Major sort of expected Lafait back not too long after dark, but he didn't come then.

87

Sleeping under the wagon, Major didn't rest well.

After a while, he crept out quietly and went up on the hill. The land was all blue shadows, and the mountains were so big and quiet that a person got a feeling they were sneaking in toward him a little when he wasn't watching.

If Lafait had got dumped off the horse, the beast would have gone on home and Goodwin wouldn't have thought anything but that it had been turned free like he'd asked them to do. Jude had no business saying that about Lafait busting his neck. Major went back to the wagon to get the long rifle.

Ma was up, waiting in the trees.

'He's all right,' Major said, 'but I thought I'd stroll down toward Goodwin's to see what's keeping him.'

'If you think he's all right, you got no business going.'

'Well, he could've fell off and busted a leg.'

'A busted leg won't kill him.'

'My God, Ma! If—'

'You got to learn not to be worrying every minute about this family.' Ma drew the old blue greatcoat tighter around her shoulders. 'No great harm has come to Lafait, so leave things be and go back to bed.'

Major went back to bed but he didn't sleep. It was too easy to think about all the things that could have happened to Lafait. Maybe he was out there somewhere in the cold, dark night in mortal pain, hurt and trying to crawl back to the camp. Major knew Ma wasn't sleeping either, the way she kept scrooching around in the wagon. It was a strange way for her to act, telling him not to worry, when she was worrying herself.

At daylight Major got up to go in search of Lafait. Ma shook her head at him and said, 'Give him time.' When Jude and Dorcas wanted to know why Lafait wasn't back, Ma told them that he'd stayed all night at Goodwin's, rather than come trudging back in the dark.

Major held off until sunrise. Then without even saying a word to Ma he started out, and he had a feeling that he'd made a bad mistake waiting all night, and that it was too late now to set it right.

He saw Lafait coming before he was a quarter of a mile from camp. Major sat down and waited for him, running over all the angry things he was going to say. When Lafait walked up, all easy and unconcerned, the worst Major could blurt out was, 'Where in tarnation have you been all night?'

'Listening to Goodwin yarn about his pappy. I never heard such fine, exciting tales in all—'

'And us here fretted sick! What kind of man is Goodwin to let you stay, knowing we'd be worrying ourselves—'

'He didn't know. I told him you expected me

to stay all night.' Lafait yawned. 'That horse sure made my butt sore. I didn't wait for breakfast. Sure am hungry.'

Ma was watching from the cottonwoods when they went over the hill and started down into the valley. Major saw her stiffen and stand real still, as if she was making sure it was Lafait. Then she reached out and put one hand on a cottonwood and leaned against it for a minute.

By the time they reached camp, Ma acted like it was nothing for Lafait to be gone all night. She asked him if he'd had breakfast and he said no, Goodwin had asked him to stay but he'd thought he'd better be getting back.

'After all night, you finally thought—' Major said.

'Leave him be,' Ma said. 'He's here.' She asked Lafait, 'What did Mr Goodwin think about us settling here?'

'He didn't seem to mind none.'

Ma gave Major a wry look.

'Mostly he talked about his pa,' Lafait said.

'I wonder why?' Major had to grin.

'Goodwin's pa was a great hunter. In the old days out here it must have been some doings.'

'Some doings,' Ma said. 'The old days. What kind of days are they right now, I'd like to ask? All Mr Goodwin said about us settling was he didn't mind, is that it?'

'I guess so.' Lafait frowned. 'He did mention something about coming up one of these days

90

to survey the land for us. He said something about doubling the size of the claim because Pa was a soldier.'

Ma looked at the valley. 'There's a God's plenty of land right under our feet, without doubling anything. I'm only wondering what we can do with it now that we're on it.'

'Me too,' Major said. The wagon train was far away by now. No doubt Matt Pilcher was acting big man around Malinda.

CHAPTER SEVEN

For several days Dorcas was mean and bitey. Nothing suited her. She even snapped at Jude like a sick hound, and she pretended she wasn't hungry when it was time to eat, but when she thought no one was looking she gnawed away like a fox pup on the food Ma set aside after every meal. Major got tired of such behavior.

'No use for you to be pining after all them younguns that went on with the train,' he told her. 'None of them Pilchers, including Luke, was any bargain, I can tell you.'

'I didn't ask for none of your fat advice,' Dorcas said. 'And who are you calling younguns?'

'Ain't going to do you no good to flounce around,' Major said. 'We're settling here and the train's gone.'

'And Malinda's gone too,' Dorcas said, all spiteful. 'You making out like you cared a lot about her and then—'

'You stop such talk!' Major felt hurt inside. Dorcas didn't know how much he'd tried not to think about Malinda and himself when he was making up his mind after Ma gave him the say about staying.

'You stop telling me what to do, Major!'

Dorcas was madder than she had need to be, Major thought. Her face was all hot and her eyes shining with anger and her chest was heaving under her old linsey woolsey gown as she fired right back at Major. She'd always been as fair and bright as a frisky young pup from the time she was able to toddle along the floor back home by holding onto the benches.

Jeem's Cousin! She wasn't a pretty child any more, or even a girl; she was a woman, and a mighty fine looking one too. It startled Major to know that she had grown up right before him, and him still holding her to be a youngun. No wonder Luke Pilcher had looked so hound-dog foolish dancing with her. And that Bill— likely he had come to the train to tell Ma he was sorry about Pa's killing, but just the same, he'd wanted to have another look at Dorcas too.

'You got to be watching out for men,' Major growled before he thought, and instantly he knew he'd put his foot into the butter. Dorcas cut loose on him with such a blast that all he could do was stand there blinking like a bullfrog in a hailstorm.

'I can look out for men a pile better than you can look out for women,' Dorcas said. 'You let Malinda wind you around her little finger, always with her talk about how Pa was no good—'

'You shut up!' Major yelled. First she was on Malinda's side and then she was against her, but she sure did know some of the things Malinda had said. He might have expected such, for when a young couple strolled away from the train, there were younguns slinking around in the grass like wild Indians to overhear anything they could.

Ma came back from the spring. 'What's the big fight about this time?'

'Nothing,' Major said.

'Dorcas was yelling bloody murder just for fun, huh?' Ma shook her head at Major. 'I won't have you jumping on her, young man. Dorcas is a grown woman.'

'I know.'

Dorcas turned away from them both and went into the trees.

'You're mad because Jude and Lafait don't seem to take no interest in building a cabin,' Ma said. 'They will. Give them time to get used to the place.'

'It'll likely be winter before that happens.' Jude was off somewhere hunting arrowheads and Lafait was chasing deer, in spite of Major telling them they ought to stay here and help him get a cabin started.

'You can't worry up a cabin,' Ma said, 'and you can't shout it up either. You'll get all the help you want from Jude and Lafait if you don't try to rush them around. Never was anyone with a drop of Whitlock blood in him that would let folks, even his kin, rush him around.'

Major took the advice. When Dorcas and Jude came wandering back to eat along about noon, Major began to ask them about where they thought the cabin ought to be, and how it should be built, and how big it should be. They were both suspicious of him at first, until Ma pitched in to help him. All Dorcas had to offer was that the cabin should be up on the hill. When they ruled her down on that, she got mad and said she didn't care where they built it, or if they ever built it at all.

Jude said they ought to go clean up in the mountains to get their logs, because there were better trees there, not a lot of twisty, thick-barked things like the cottonwoods.

'You been up there?' Ma asked.

'Way up,' Jude said.

'You're traipsing too much, Jude.' For a while Ma forgot all about the cabin.

Dorcas made one more suggestion, the cabin ought to be made of chipped logs. When Major said that was a heap of work and not necessary, she walked off from the conference, calling

94

back over her shoulder, 'About all you'll be able to build is some crookedy, crumbly thing like the Hurlbuts got back home.'

The Hurlbuts, back on Blue Run, had about the worst cabin in all Kentucky. It was so bad that one night Tessie Hurlbut had fallen through the floor and crippled a tan hound bitch with six pups. Major was going to say something hot to Dorcas, but Ma touched his arm and shook her head. She was smiling at mention of the Hurlbuts.

'Too far to drag logs from the mountains,' Major said.

'Take the box off the wagon and haul 'em,' Jude argued. He went over to sight up a cottonwood and you could tell he was disgusted with the look of it. While he was telling what was wrong with cottonwoods as building logs, Lafait took the long rifle and wandered off. Jude went on strolling through the grove and the next thing Major knew both him and Dorcas had disappeared.

'Never mind,' Ma said. 'Let them all have a little fun while the sun is bright.'

'Seems to me I never had much time for playing.'

'The truth is you didn't, Major, so maybe that's why you shouldn't mind so much about Jude and Dorcas. Lafait—' Ma shook her head '—ain't nobody, not even me, going to make him do anything he don't care about. He ain't lazy, he's like his pa and your Uncle Lafe.'

95

Major was chopping a tree at the edge of the grove when he saw Jude and Dorcas looking for arrowheads on the south hill. They laughed about something and the sound came clean and clear to Major. He guessed Ma was right. You couldn't expect everybody to be as heated up as him about working; but in time the others would help him if he didn't try to boss them around.

He swung the axe hard. The dead cottonwood was the meanest thing he'd ever tried to chop. Tarnation on such stuff. He'd use cottonwood for the fire and take Jude's advice about hauling buildings logs from the mountains.

Major was trimming away on his third tree when Ma called to him from the camp. Her voice wasn't real loud and it wasn't exactly scared, but still it said there was no time to fool around saying *what*. He dropped the axe and ran.

It looked like the whole world was made of Indians. They were everywhere in the grove, on foot and on ponies. Ma was smack in the midst of them with a stern look on her face, but you could see that she was scared plenty.

'Don't get excited, Ma, don't get excited!' Major stopped running and tried to stroll up as if it was nothing at all for him to see a few hundred Indians every day. That was his first guess about the number of them. Then he decided there was about a hundred, and a little later, when he wasn't swallowing so hard, he guessed maybe a third of a hundred would be about right. Splitting things up like that left just part of an Indian somewhere in the deal. *I'm thinking crazy*, Major told himself. *I got to be real calm and show them I'm not scared.*

They were the darkest looking Indians he had ever seen. You didn't have to have a gill of brains to catch on that they weren't the raggedy, begging kind the train had met on the prairies. These were solid, wide, tough looking Indians who acted like they hadn't given up their country yet. Major pushed his way through them, taking care that he didn't bump any of them around, but still he had to get over to Ma and stand beside her.

Tarnation, how dark they were. There was one who was a pile bigger than Shad Hurlbut back home, and that was some big. He was an ornery looking Indian too, not with a sneaky, little-meanness look, but with a bold, big-meanness expression standing on his wide face. He watched Major with hard, dark eyes all the time Major was working his way over to Ma.

'Where's the younguns?' Ma asked real quick.

'Way up the valley.'

'Good.'

And then Major saw Lafait.

Major's first wild thought was that Lafait had been captured. He was over in the midst of a bunch of ponies and bucks, with his back to

Major. Then he turned to the side and Major could see he still had his long gun in one hand. With the other hand he was making signs to the bucks, but they didn't seem to understand.

Lafait turned around and yelled, 'They're hungry, Ma!'

'Heathens always are,' Ma said. She was more angry than scared when she said that.

The enormous Indian looked at Major and then he looked at the big pot bubbling over the coals of Ma's fire. It was full of deer stew, thickened with a little flour. Major held his arm toward the pot and nodded his head.

At least they didn't kick the pot over in their rush and then fight over what was spilled on the ground, like one bunch of sneaky looking Pawnees had done. One Indian took a stick and lifted the pot off the fire. Then a whole bunch of bucks squatted around it and stabbed at the pieces of meat with knives. They ate the pieces so smoking hot that Major wondered how they kept from burning their mouths. A squaw edged in and dipped out some stew with the smoke blackened half of an army canteen. She gave it to the big Indian, who kept dipping his fingers in it and licking them.

Lafait came strolling up about the time the pot was empty. He looked like he was pleased as punch with the whole business. 'They'll have to have more to eat than that,' he said.

Ma gave him a dark look. 'You're mighty free with our food, young man.'

'Got to feed 'em,' Lafait said. 'That's the custom.'

'We'll change that custom after this,' Ma said, but she went back to the spring and got what was left of the last deer Lafait had killed.

The Indians had plenty of time. They wandered around the camp, peering into the wagon, poking their fingers at anything that interested them, making themselves at home. Major noticed that they didn't bother anything, not like the miserable plains tribes he had seen, the ones that would steal the pegs out of your boots while you were standing talking to them.

The big Indian sat down on the crib of logs where Jessup had laid the busted wheel. Major guessed he was the chief, although there was nothing in his dress to show it. He asked Lafait, 'They're Utes, huh?'

'Sure,' Lafait said, as if he had known them all his life. 'That's Colorow there on the logs. He's the chief.'

'Colorow.' The big Ute nodded. He looked from Major to Lafait. 'You brother?'

'Yep.' Lafait poked his own chest, then stabbed Major with his finger and then pointed at Ma coming back with two cloth wrapped haunches of deer meat.

Colorow grunted. You couldn't tell what he meant.

Some of the squaws gathered around Ma as she began to fry meat in the big pan. The steaks

99

were still dripping blood when the squaws speared them with knives and carried them over to their men. Most of the bucks were now lounging in the shade, talking and scratching. You could tell that Ma was fit to murder somebody. When anyone butted into her cooking, she was like a sore-nosed bear; but she went right on cooking until all the meat was gone.

Lafait was strolling around, enjoying himself. He tried all kinds of sign talk but most of it just made the Indians grin at each other. He got into one deal where it was clear enough that a wide-mouthed, pockmarked buck was trying to trade him out of the long rifle. The buck kept pointing at the ponies and then at the rifle and holding up fingers. He got up to three ponies but Lafait grinned and shook his head.

'That meat was just a mite tainted anyhow,' Ma said. 'Now they've eat, get 'em out of here, Lafait.'

'Oh, you can't do that, Ma. You got to be slow and easy with Indians. Goodwin told me his pa—'

'I've had enough of Goodwin's pa, young man.'

Colorow got up and said something. He kept pointing toward the wagon. Lafait made a sign and Colorow nodded. 'He wants something else to eat.'

You could see that Ma was ready to explode,

but maybe Lafait was on the right track, even if it did cost some food. The Whitlocks were going to stay here and the Utes could come by any old time they pleased. It was a good idea to be friends with them.

'Give them some dried apples, Ma,' Major said.

'My dried apples! I will not!'

'Better do it.' Major talked a little sharper than he meant to. It sounded like he was mad, but he was only trying to tell Ma that it was the smart thing to do. Colorow looked at him and grunted approval, and the old devil's eyes gleamed with a tickled look, as if he had understood every word that was said.

Ma got a whole double handful of dried fruit from the wagon. You could see it was like taking her heart's blood, but she marched over to Colorow and gave him the apples. He knew what he had, sure enough. He sniffed at the brownish, wrinkled slices and then he began to chew away. Some of the bucks got up and came over. As if he had a whole wagonload of stuff to give away, Colorow tossed off pieces of fruit to the other Indians until he had only what was left in his mouth, which was a-plenty.

With his cheeks bulging he pointed at the wagon again. Major shook his head and spread his hands. 'That's all.'

Colorow said something in Ute. Part of a chewed slice of apple spun out of his mouth and stuck to a log and a young boy wandering

101

past snatched it up as quick as a minnow darting at a tiny bug. As he leaped away Colorow boosted him along with a kick from the side of his moccasined foot.

The Utes laughed as easy as white men. An old squaw showed her toothless gums in a wide grin and said something quick to the women near her that set them all to giggling. For all the world they reminded Major of a benchful of women back home at a square dance after one of them had said something funny.

He felt some easier about the Utes. They were savage enough, he didn't doubt, and they had strange ways, but they were people just the same. Even the broken remnants of tribes he had seen on the plains, before he learned to look down on them, had scared the daylights out of him because his whole picture of Indians had been based on stories about the Shawnees and Mingoes of Kentucky a hundred years before, massacres at lonely cabins, blood-curdling warwhoops in the woods, children captured and taken far across the Ohio, torture by fire at the stake—the tomahawk and blood.

It was hard to believe but maybe the Shawnees, too, had been people and not painted fiends.

Major walked over to Colorow and stuck out his hand. The fierce dark eyes stared back at him. For a moment those stories of long ago told Major that he was making a mistake, for Colorow went on steadily chomping dried

102

apples and paid no mind to Major's hand. It was an insulting thing. Major felt foolish and angry and he was just going to jerk his hand back and walk away, when Colorow reached out and took it in a powerful grip.

'Good!' Colorow said.

It wasn't much and all it did at the moment was relieve Major's feeling that he had made a silly mistake, but many times in the long years afterward when white miners went into the mountains and never returned, when rumors of Ute savagery perched terror on the ridgelogs of lonely cabins in the high valley of the Upper Arkansas, Major was thankful that the Whitlocks had blundered their way into, not friendship, but a feeling of mutual tolerance with the war chief of the Utes the first time they met him.

Today, Major was grateful for no more than the fact that the Whitlocks were getting away with their lives and property.

The Indians were in no rush to go wherever they were going. You could see that hurry was no great part of their lives. Since the Whitlocks wouldn't give them any more to eat, they began to cook their own food. The squaws built fires and began to roast deer meat. When Colorow's squaw had some lumpy chunks of meat seared black on the outside, the chief gestured for the Whitlocks to come over and eat with him.

Ma's lips were tight. 'That meat is bloody red inside.'

'You got to eat some,' Lafait insisted. 'Wouldn't be polite not to. Indians always—'

'Don't tell me what's polite, young man. You think you know an all-fired plenty about Indians, don't you?'

'Goodwin's pappy told him—'

'Goodwin's pappy! Where is he, I'd like to know?'

'Been dead twenty years,' Lafait said. 'The Blackfeet got him.'

'Good for them,' Ma said, 'but they ought to found some way to shut him up after they killed him.'

'We'd better eat with them,' Major said.

Ma was real bitey. 'Another one that must have been listening to Goodwin's pappy.' But she went over with Major and Lafait and ate some of the meat.

She was right, it was bloody inside and hot enough to make your teeth jump. Lafait didn't seem to mind. He tried to eat as much as Colorow, which was a big chore. When Colorow belched, Lafait let out a fair blast himself. Ma looked at him in horror. You could see that Lafait was going to be in for some talking to when all this was over.

Lafait, he knew it too, but he was having himself a time. After he ate he got in with a bunch of bucks who were having a sort of argument over in the trees. He trooped away with them and a short time later there was a shot.

104

'Oh, Lord!' Ma said.

Major squatted down to look through the trees toward the hill. 'They're having a shooting match, it looks like. It's all right, Ma.' He could see Lafait standing there with the long rifle.

The shooting went on for quite a spell. When it was over, Lafait had a bow and a hide quiver of arrows and about four pairs of moccasins. The Utes he'd been shooting with seemed to think he was a big thing.

'Their rifle guns ain't much good,' Lafait said, 'so I given 'em a chance by setting my target twenty steps farther out.'

Ma looked at the things he had won. 'Gambling with heathens,' she said, but you could tell she wasn't mad. She always had bragged about how good shots most of her folks were.

If there was one thing Pa had not skimped on, it was cartridges for the buffalo gun and powder and shot for the long rifle. Sometimes when the wagon had been stuck Ma had said it was because there was such a load of shooting stuff in it. Lafait got some powder out of the wagon and passed it around to the Utes. He gave some first to Colorow, and then to the men he had been shooting with.

'You ain't supposed to do that,' Ma said, and maybe she was thinking back to some of her kin killed long ago by trade muskets given the Delawares by Frenchmen.

The Indians stuck around for quite a spell longer, and then all at once they up and left like they had a heap of busy things to do. They were on their ponies and straggling away without anybody giving orders, so it seemed.

'They're going down to Goodwin's to camp,' Lafait said. 'I better go along and—'

'You'd better stay right here, young man.' Ma's mouth was thinned down and her eyes were snapping.

Lafait was wearing a buckskin shirt Colorow had given him. It was too big and you could see it wasn't brand new made, but he was busting proud about it. And yet when Ma bore down on him the way she could, Lafait just shrunk down till he looked like a youngun with his pa's night shirt on; and he didn't argue with Ma.

Ma didn't leap on him any more right then. She waited till Jude and Dorcas came in along about sundown. They had to know all about the Indians and they were real put-out because they'd missed seeing them. Ma let everyone gabble on for a while and then she said, 'Every one of you set down over on them logs.'

Major sat down with the rest.

'There's been too much traipsing around since we settled here,' Ma said. 'Starting when the sun comes up in the morning, this family is a-going to build a cabin.' She pointed at Lafait, then Jude, and then Dorcas.

Dorcas said, 'I suppose Major is too

good to—'

'Major done started the cabin,' Ma snapped. 'The rest of you was traipsing. Everybody hear me?'

No one said anything, but you knew they heard, and they weren't going to argue. The chances were, Major thought, if Ma hadn't got upset-mad about the Indians, she would have gone on for a while letting the younguns come around to working without orders from her.

That seemed to be all she had to say, but when Lafait started to leave with the rest, Ma pointed at the log and made him set down again. 'That big heathen of a Colorow, he can belch the lining of his stomach loose for all I care. He don't know better, but you, Lafait Whitlock, don't you ever do a thing like that around your family again.'

'Yes, Ma.' Lafait started to rise.

Ma made a whacking motion with her finger that set him down again as quick as if somebody had pushed him.

'Seems to me you were almighty thick with them Indians, Lafait. Not that they weren't coming this way anyhow, but you had 'em eating our food before they asked, I'd say.'

'Goodwin's pa—'

'You say Goodwin's pa to me one more time and I'll whack you with a stick!'

Lafait gulped. 'I was skeered when I first met 'em.'

'I'm right pleased to hear that. Go on.'

Lafait looked miserable. He wriggled around on the log some. He scratched his head. 'I was skeered and I wanted to make some signs, like Good—like I'd heard about from Mr Goodwin. The only one I could think of was *are you hungry?* They understood it too.'

'I'll say they did.'

Lafait was so silly looking that Major turned away so Ma couldn't see him grinning. Dorcas and Jude were ready to bust out laughing, too.

'It's a good thing to be friends with them,' Ma said, softening down some, but she was real bitey an instant later when Lafait scratched his head again, this time real brisk. 'But you been too close friends with 'em, Lafait. You're lousy!'

'No I ain't, Ma.' Lafait pulled his hand away from his head real quick. Ma just stood there watching him until you could see him getting red in the face from wanting to scratch.

'Bring me Grandma Ripley's scissors out of the chest, Dorcas,' Ma said. 'I'm going to slash Lafait's hair down to a scalplock, since he loves Indians so much. Get the big kettle on the fire, Jude. We're going to boil Lafait's clothes, and maybe we'll boil him a little too while we're at it.'

'You can't boil this here shirt, or my moccasins neither,' Lafait said, all alarmed. 'It'd ruin—'

'We'll sulfur those hides and then we'll hang 'em over a smoky fire,' Ma said. 'If that don't work, we'll sprinkle gunpowder in the seams and light it.' She shook her head. 'To think a child of mine would wind up wearing deerhide clothes.'

'I ain't no child,' Lafait said, but he was pretty weak in declaring so. It was a sight, the way Ma had him cornered. 'We can't use good gunpowder just to scorch a few little bugs.'

'You made free enough with it with the Indians,' Ma said. 'I reckon we can spare some to burn out some of those little presents they gave you that you didn't figure on, young man.'

'Gosh darn it,' Lafait said. To look at him now in his sloppy shirt and all beat down by Ma, you'd never think he could march into a place with a rifle and face a whole pile of tough men. He was sheepish as could be, and he kept wiggling and scratching.

Watching him, Major felt like doing a little scratching himself. He wondered if the lice the Utes had given Lafait were like dog fleas that could jump like the devil. Major couldn't help it; he started scratching a little.

The way Ma swung her eyes toward him was like the pointing of a rifle when a hunter hears game moving in the brush. 'You too, huh?'

'No!' Major said. 'It was just the thought of it.'

'Some of them thoughts might bite,' Ma said sternly.

Dorcas came back with the scissors, clicking

109

them and eyeing Lafait's long black hair with a happy look on her face.

'We'll do the shearing clean away from this camp,' Ma said. 'Some of that hair might up and crawl into our beds.'

'I seen one way the squaws was getting them,' Jude said. 'They just picked 'em out of the men's hair with their fingers and then cracked them between their front teeth and spit 'em out. I think they spit most of them out.'

'Jude Jefferson Whitlock!' Ma said. 'Stop that kind of talk!'

'That's the way they done it,' Jude said. 'I didn't know what it was at first and so I leaned real close to have a look. A squaw like to put my eye out when she spit one of them—'

'Shut up!' Ma said.

Jude and Dorcas and Major began to laugh heartily.

Lafait got up from the log. 'You ain't really figuring to waste good gunpowder, are you, Ma?' His voice was so serious and pleading that even Ma began to laugh, and then, scratching like mad, Lafait had to grin.

Ma took him out of camp and cut his hair down as close as she could with the scissors. He pleaded for her to leave him a scalplock, just for fun, but all she left him was little bunches of hair here and there that she couldn't get real close with the scissors. She made him go down to the creek and scrub with soft soap. She brought his clothes back to camp on a stick like

110

she was carrying a dead copper snake. The buckskin shirt she smoked over a fire, but that didn't seem to be enough, so she made Lafait carry it on a stick over to the hill and lay it on an ant hill. There he stood looking silly, with a blanket around him and his hair cut down to uneven patches, watching red ants swarming like mad on his prized shirt.

Maybe Ma had said that not even she could make Lafait do anything he didn't want to, but just the same when she got wound up over the lice business, there was some doings, as Goodwin's pappy would have said.

CHAPTER EIGHT

They all went to work on the cabin the next day. Ma told Lafait when he could go hunting, which was only when they needed meat. Since you could see deer almost any dawn in the upper end of the meadows, Lafait didn't get to do much tromping.

It was Jude who had the most ideas about how to build the cabin, and most of his ideas worked. To start, he wanted the base logs put down on rocks, instead of just being plunked against the ground to rot. Sixty-five years later, when all the family but Major was gone, the cabin was still being used as a storeroom, and sometimes Major went out to stand by it,

111

remembering with clear poignancy young faces and young days.

They saddle-notched the logs because that was the only way they had ever seen them put together. Getting the bark off the logs was worse than husking a green black walnut, but Jude said the bark had to come off or it would rot and carry away all the daubing.

Sometimes Major got mad at Jude's wanting to do things his way. 'For somebody that never built nothing but a stick house, you know a hell of a lot about making this cabin.'

'It's only natural sense,' Jude would say in defense of whatever idea they were arguing about, and Ma always backed him up.

To Major the building of the cabin was a step by step thing. After you finished one thing, you puzzled out the next move. Although he admitted it made sense and saved time, he was suspicious of the rope Jude used for measuring; Major would rather lay pieces where they were going to go, and see with his own eyes that they were long enough and the right shape, before the final cutting was done on them.

To Lafait the cabin was a pile of work that he wasn't much interested in. He did insist that the ridgelog stick out in front far enough so you could hang a deer or two on it for skinning, but Dorcas said it would be a terrible thing to have your doorway always blocked with game, when you could just as well hang deer somewhere in the trees out of sight. 'You're getting too particular,' Lafait told her. A teepee would have suited him fine. He grunted and complained but he did what was told him. One log at a time was enough for him to understand.

Jude saw the whole thing in his head right from the start, clean to how every piece of the roof would go together. It was easy enough for any of them to draw with a stick in the dirt and make a picture of the finished cabin, but when Jude made pictures, they were always busted down into different parts and sections, something like a skeleton. Once he made the pictures in the dirt, Major could understand them clear enough.

They hauled the logs from the mountains, green, heavy trees that they couldn't have handled if Jude hadn't figured a way to roll them up on the wagon by means of slanting poles; they used the same method to get the logs in place on the walls. From the oak of the wagon box they cut framing for the door and the window holes.

Jude was most particular about the rafters and the joists to hold a loft where Ma and Dorcas would sleep. He picked the same kind of poles the Utes used for their lodges. Sometimes even after they were cut, he said they wouldn't do. They were having an argument about that the day Lafait ran into bear sign. Lafait just up and disappeared. He didn't get the bear but he managed to stay

113

away until the wagon was loaded.

Goodwin was visiting Ma and Dorcas when they got back. He said the Indians had been camped at his place until the day before, so he hadn't had a chance to come up sooner. You could see he was surprised by the solid look of the cabin, and from the way he kept asking Jude questions, it was no trick to tell that Ma had been bragging on Jude.

'How you going to roof it, Jude?'

'So it'll stay put a while,' Jude said. 'First, we'll pin the rafters from the sides to the ridgelog. Then we'll run long pieces clean across them rafters and pin the shakes.'

'Purlin pieces,' Goodwin said.

'I don't know what you call 'em. Anyway, I don't aim to have a lot of logs on top to hold every row of shakes. We'll fix them shakes so they'll stay by theirselves.'

'Uh-huh.' Goodwin nodded. 'You know anything about cutting shakes?'

'Saw it done,' Jude said. 'We got a froe. We left the mallet somewhere when we was driving wedges under the tires, but I can make one.'

'What kind of wood will you use?'

'I don't know,' Jude answered. 'We'll have to try different kinds.'

'Get cedar,' Goodwin said. 'We ain't got it too big out here, but it'll work. Cut your shakes about an inch thick.' He got up and walked all around the cabin, and the Whitlocks watched him anxiously, but he didn't say anything about their work. 'If you boys can spare the time, I'll survey some of your land this afternoon.'

Some of your land... It had a fine sound to Major. They went to work at once cutting stakes as Goodwin directed. Goodwin set up his compass out from the grove, against the hill. He made Jude and Major the chainmen, with Jude on the front end. Lafait was the axeman, driving the iron tally pins, and then replacing some of them with wooden stakes when Goodwin told him to.

Major didn't understand what was going on, except that they measured their way up the valley pretty fast, and that the line was one side of their property. *Property.* That was another word with a fine sound.

The first time they had to wait for Goodwin to move and set up his compass again, Jude asked, 'How do you know where this land is?'

'It's right here before our eyes, ain't it?' Goodwin grinned.

'Sure.' Jude frowned. 'But how do you know where it is from some place else?'

'You've touched the whole secret of surveying, Jude,' Goodwin said. 'The truth is I'm doing things backward. First, we'll mark the land. Later, it can be tied into a government survey. Right now you want to know what you own, so you can put up markers and maybe start fences.'

'That's good enough,' Lafait said. 'This is

Deer Valley and we know where it is.'

Goodwin laughed. 'That's a fair name, Lafait.'

Deer Valley it became forever afterward.

Goodwin didn't finish his survey that day; he came back several times afterward while the Whitlocks were still working on the cabin, and each time Jude and Major and Lafait went out with him, measuring, driving stakes, and marking rocks. When he finished his survey, he told them they owned 480 acres, running up and down the valley from the piñon trees almost to the Arkansas River.

On that first afternoon Goodwin surveyed they went back to camp when it was too dark for him to read his compass. Ma had cooked a fine meal, including two great big apple pies. She had used, too, some of their precious store of coffee.

Lafait sulked some because they didn't give Goodwin any chance to talk about his pappy. Ma wanted to know all about the settlers in the country. The Whitlocks were surprised to find out that some of them had been here six or seven years already, the Burnines over on Little Creek, the McAllisters about three miles from the Burnines, the Shermans up against the hills about eight miles away, and some others scattered around in the valley without their families.

'What kind of crops do they raise?' Major asked.

116

'It ain't a crop country,' Goodwin said. 'The McAllisters did raise some potatoes one year, they told me, and sold some of them up the river to the miners in California Gulch for a dollar a pound.'

'Jeem's cousin!' Major had visions of getting rich.

'They ain't many miners there now,' Goodwin warned, 'and I'm not sure you could raise potatoes here on your land.'

'There's some sandy stuff close to the hill,' Major said.

'You better get your cabin built.' Goodwin looked at Ma and she nodded. 'You figure on lining the inside with something?' he asked.

'With the wagon top, far as it'll go,' Ma said.

'I got some alum. I packed it in here for the McAllisters, and then Katy didn't want it,' Goodwin said. 'You soak cloth in alum water and it won't catch fire from fireplace sparks or tipped-over candles. I'll bring it up when you're ready to line the cabin, Mrs Whitlock. Lafait can leave a deer at my place now and then to pay for it.'

'I'm right obliged,' Ma said. 'Back home we had a cloth ceiling under the loft to keep the younguns from pushing stuff down on us, and I was always a-worrying lest that cloth catch afire and roast 'em alive some night.'

Dorcas wanted to know if there were any young folks at the places Goodwin had mentioned. His eyes sort of twinkled in the

117

firelight when he answered. 'The Burnines got two girls. The Shermans got some young girls, about eight to twelve, I'd guess.'

Lafait said, 'She means boys.'

'You shut up, Lafait!' Dorcas cried.

'Oh, yes, there's some boys around too,' Goodwin said. 'I reckon they'll come calling in time.' He looked at Major. 'That girl you walked around with some there at the crossing—she went on over the mountains, I suppose?'

'Yeah.' Major got up and put more wood on the fire and turned his back to the flames.

*   *   *

'There's a fine man,' Ma said, after Goodwin had left.

'He'd 've been finer if we'd let him tell some stories about his pa,' Lafait said grumpily.

The next morning Lafait thought he had discovered a terrible error in the cabin. 'Where's the fireplace going to go, Jude?' Aside from the doorway and window openings, there was no other place cut out in the logs.

'All of it inside, at that end,' Jude said. 'It's bad enough to weaken the logs where we have to, without having a whomping big fireplace hole.'

'I never seen a fireplace built that way.' Lafait shook his head.

'You never looked at a fireplace, Lafait,'

118

Major told his brother, 'unless there was something cooking on it, or you wanted to scrooch up and warm your hind end at it.'

Ma and Dorcas whittled the pins they used to drive into auger holes to fasten the joists to the top logs. They fastened the rafters to the ridge logs the same way, and then Jude ran light, straight poles across the rafters, leaving a big opening at the back end of the cabin for the chimney. That would put the fireplace off to one side, instead of smack in the middle of the wall. It didn't seem right, but you couldn't run the chimney through the ridgelog.

With the roof framed, they went to the mountains again to find cedar for shakes. It took a power of cutting and sawing to find pieces that suited Jude. Sometimes Major and Lafait got only two sections out of a tree that were good enough for shakes, for knots had a way of twisting clean through the white of the wood into the rich red center. Back home one man could whack out shakes with no trouble, but Jude didn't have the strength to do it alone, so he held the froe while Major hit with the maul Jude had made of cottonwood and deerhide.

Sometimes the shakes came off the block as clean and true as could be, but sometimes they wedged off into thin ends and were worthless. But no matter how they split, the clean, rich smell of the fresh cedar was always there. When the cabin roof was gray and old and

Major was the same way, he could still remember the smell of the cedar.

Day after day they walked to the mountains, starting at daylight, and coming back to the camp at dusk. The stacks of shakes grew until Jude said they had enough, and then they hauled them down with the wagon. Dorcas insisted that Jude was wrong as stealing when he started laying the shakes at the eaves instead of at the ridge. He selected the thinnest ones for the bottom row, and then he laid a second row on top of the first to cover the joints. Major and Lafait weren't sure that Jude knew what he was doing, either, but they followed his orders.

When they began the second row of shakes, it became clear enough. Jude had them put two small auger holes through each shake, about two inches from the edge and a little above middle on the long run of the shake. The holes went on into the light timber crosspieces that the shakes rested on, and then they tapped small, wedged pins tightly into the holes. The next row of shakes overlapped the pinning holes. It was a surprising thing to Major that everything came out just as Jude had planned.

When the roof was finished you could see a million holes from the loft inside, because the rough shakes didn't lay tight against each other, and yet the roof never leaked. It was a fine thing to look at, that red-brown roof standing up toward the sky, but it didn't stay colored very long; the sun soon faded it to silver and then to dull gray.

Before that happened the Whitlocks were hard at work on the fireplace. They hauled flat stones from a place Lafait had seen in the mountains and sticky clay from a bank Major and Jude discovered near the river. The mantel was one huge, long stone that they dragged to the doorway with Fawn and Steuben, whose feet were now healed and sound. The boys rolled the stone across the floor and worked it into place on skid poles.

They were as proud as punch when the fireplace was finished. It was the very heart of the house. Jude had set pieces of iron from Marion's wrecked wagon into the stones for Ma to hang pots on, and above the mantel he had worked deerhorns into the rock for the buffalo gun and the Pennsylvania rifle to lay across.

Goodwin was up on one of his surveying trips the first time they built a fire. Ma put some water in the big pot and hung it on one of the irons. The fire was laid with sticks and wood on cedar shavings.

Goodwin gave Ma a match. 'The honor is yours, Mrs Whitlock.'

Major noticed that Lafait was hanging back, with a funny grin, but he laid it to the fact that they were making such a ceremony over lighting the first fire.

Ma touched the cedar shavings with the match. The whole inside of the fireplace blossomed with a loud *poof!* Ma let out a yell. Major knocked Jude flat as he jumped back.

Lafait had sprinkled the gunpowder on the wood.

'I'll be danged!' Goodwin said, and then he laughed as loud as the Whitlocks.

Once the fire took hold, Major couldn't take his eyes from it. As much as the roof overhead, it meant that the Whitlocks were settled at last. Lafait put the rifles on the deer horns and stood back admiring the picture they made. Ma said, 'Once the ashes build up, them pot hooks will be about the right height.'

Jude got down on his hands and knees to see how the chimney was drawing. He was satisfied, and after that he was ready to start building something else.

While they were helping Goodwin survey that afternoon, Goodwin said that he had talked to Shad McAllister and that Shad would be glad to blacksmith some hinges for them from the iron they had salvaged from Marion's wagon. 'It would be a good idea if you had him make enough hinges so's you could have plank coverings over the two windows too. You got enough wagon boards left for that, ain't you, Jude?'

'Who's going to be bothering us?' Lafait asked.

'I didn't say anybody was.'

'Then why do you want us to cover the windows?' Lafait asked.

Jude said, 'To keep the heat in, for one thing.'

'That ain't what he meant.' Lafait shook his head.

You could see that Goodwin knew now there was no use to try to say things in a 'round-the-bush way to Lafait. 'This country ain't settled and civilized yet,' Goodwin said. 'There's some tough, irresponsible people go up and down this valley. Put some heavy shutters on them windows.'

'You thinking of people like that bunch at your store the night they killed Pa?' Lafait asked.

Goodwin hesitated. 'Not that bunch in particular. Sort of like them, yes.'

'Bill wasn't so bad,' Jude said. 'What does he do to make a living?'

'He's got a little place on up the valley.' Goodwin got busy with his compass. 'Let's get to work.'

'How are we going to pay for all this surveying?' Major asked.

'Don't worry about it now,' Goodwin said. 'When it's all tied in properly—maybe years from now—we'll talk about paying.'

'We don't like to owe for things,' Major said.

'That's something you'd better get over,' Goodwin said. 'Anybody always owes somebody else for something, and there ain't always ways to pay.'

That was the day they ran out the last corner

of their land, far down toward the river where the valley dwindled off into rocky washes. Only the stream that ran all the way through their land left any greenness down here, and that was at the bottom of a narrow gulch where the creek plunged over one little waterfall after another.

They owned a stretch of ground, sure enough, but still Major couldn't figure out what they were going to do with it to make it pay.

He went hunting with Lafait a few days later. All the heavy work on the cabin was done, but they were lacking deer hair to put in the daubing. That was Jude's idea and even he didn't know where he'd got it, but he was sure that deer hair mixed with the clay would make it hold much better. Jude and Dorcas had left early that morning to walk to the McAllister place with some iron strap to be made into hinges.

From high in the mountains the Whitlock valley was a narrow green streak between gray mesas. You could see the grove but there was no way of telling that a cabin was there. When you were down on the meadows, you were sure you owned a lot of the earth, but from up here, the whole layout sure didn't amount to much. Major wondered how small things would look from the top of one of the mountains.

Lafait was not interested in the view. He had found fresh bear sign again and that was enough for him. The bear was going up and Lafait was going after it and Major couldn't argue him out of it.

'What do we want with a bear?' Major asked.

Lafait was shocked. 'That's a terrible foolish question to ask. Anybody likes to kill a bear, for the grease and the hide and the meat and things like that.'

'The hide wouldn't be any good, and Ma don't like bear grease nor meat either.'

Lafait kept right on going. Major grinned and stayed with him. 'You've never killed a bear, Lafait.'

'That's one reason I need one.'

They found almost enough tracks to make soup of, but they never did find the bear. In the afternoon they were skirting a timbered hollow when they heard a heavy crashing in the trees below them. Lafait raised the buffalo gun and waited. It sounded like great animals were busting out every which way down below.

'Deer—a whole slough of them,' Major whispered.

They saw only one of the beasts. It came lunging like a horse to the rim of the hollow across from them, and there it stood among the rocks and trees for a few moments, looking in their direction. It was a kind of tan color, an enormous animal, much taller than a buffalo. Its horns were in velvet, and they looked like great tree limbs branching up from its head.

'By Ned, by Ned!' Lafait kept muttering, and his rifle came no higher than it was.

The big beast, long striding and awkward looking, ran away over the rim suddenly. Lafait just kept staring where it had been. 'What was it?' he asked. Major shook his head. He had the long rifle, but he too hadn't even thought of shooting.

They went down to look at the tracks. The animals had been bedded all through the hollow. In their flight they had busted small limbs and kicked pine needles all over the place. Some of the tracks were as big as the hooves of a cow.

'Let's go home,' Lafait said suddenly. He didn't say anything more until they were clear down on the piñon flats. 'I figured out what it was. Them were elk.'

'That big?'

'Yeah. That one looked even bigger than what Uncle Lafe said.' Lafait walked on and then he stopped and faced Major. 'You ain't going to tell that I got all scared and forgot to shoot, are you?' Even when he was little, Lafait hadn't been one to beg for anything, but he was begging now, and what was left of the boy in him showed on his face, in spite of his deep-set black eyes and heavy features.

''Course I won't,' Major said. He didn't talk about it until years afterward, when Lafait himself brought up the subject and laughed about how he had been frozen and awed at the sight of his first bull elk.

After-sunset coolness lay on the valley when from the south hill they came in sight of the cabin. Smoke was rising straight up from the chimney. Fawn and Steuben were wandering in from the meadows for their daily rub against the rough-barked trees. They looked contented and at home, and the wagon in the trees, with its top gone, belonged close to fields and houses.

'What's wrong?' Lafait asked. 'What are you staring at?'

'Smoke—and things.' From that moment on Major began to quit thinking of Kentucky as 'back home.'

CHAPTER NINE

To save leather Jude and Dorcas carried their shoes slung across their shoulders and walked barefooted on their way to the McAllister place. It had been a great saying of Pa's that feet healed up from cuts and wear but shoe leather ground away was gone for good. There would be time enough to put on their shoes when they were in sight of the McAllister place.

'You reckon they got much of a family?' Dorcas asked. 'Mr Goodwin didn't say.'

'We'll see when we get there. All I'm hoping is McAllister knows something about blacksmithing.'

'You and that old iron. You'd think it was jewels in that pack.' Dorcas looked at Jude too long, not watching where she was stepping. Her foot came down on a cactus. She howled and hopped around on one leg before she sat down. 'Pull 'em out, Jude!'

Jude's hands were long and tapering and his fingers were deft and sure as he plucked the cactus spines from his sister's foot. 'They don't work in. They're made like icicles hanging from a roof.' He examined the last spine critically. 'That's the very shape we should've had the pins we drove in the shakes, tapered so—'

'All you think about is roofs and things like that,' Dorcas said angrily. She drew up her foot and peered at it to be sure Jude had pulled out all the spines. 'All Lafait wants to do is go hunting, and all Major wants is to own things.'

Jude grinned as he flipped the spine away. 'And all you want is to get married.'

'I will, too—if there's any decent men in this whole country.'

They got up and went on, skirting the foothills at the high, dry edges of the valley.

'Bill?' Jude asked slyly.

'Bill! I don't even know his last name. Besides, he's a bushwhacker. Anybody can tell that. Because Lafait thinks he's a prime wonder is no reason for me to give him a second thought.'

Soon the long reaching hills ran out so far across their path that they had to cross them, or go miles down the valley to get around them. Jude chose to cross over the hills. 'I hope you know where you're going,' Dorcas told him.

Jude knew. He had an instinct for direction as sure as Lafait's, and in some cases, much better. Long before noon they came out of the piñons and looked down on that part of the valley where Little Creek ran. It appeared to be all meadowland, with cottonwoods standing high and green to mark the flow of the river.

'There's somebody's place,' Jude said.

They could see a log fence and several buildings in a grove of young cottonwoods. 'They planted those trees like that,' Jude said, 'all squared off pretty.'

At the foot of the hill they ran into a marshy stream. Dorcas stopped to wash the dust from her face and from her arms. She smoothed her fair hair as she stood looking across the meadows at the grove. She sloshed her legs in the deepest part of the stream again and then jumped from hummock to hummock to reach dry ground without getting all muddied up. She started to put her shoes on.

'Looks like more water on over there,' Jude said. 'No use to put your shoes on yet.'

Dorcas followed his advice, but it turned out there was no more water between them and the grove. At the last moment, when they saw a woman churning in the shade, they stopped to put on their shoes.

'Now she's seen us!' Dorcas said. 'She knows what we're doing.'

'She's probably barefoot herself. The only reason I'm putting on my shoes is in case they got chickens around that yard. I can't abide stepping—'

'Shut your mouth, Jude!'

The woman in the yard wasn't barefoot. She was a tall, husky looking woman with a red face. She went right on churning away as the visitors walked toward her.

'How'd do,' Jude said. 'Are you Mrs McAllister?'

'I am.' The churn plunger kept going up and down as the woman eyed them sharply.

'We're Whitlocks, from over that way.' Jude pointed.

'Oh, yes. I do believe Goodwin mentioned something about you folks the other day. You're settled, huh?'

'Yep.' Jude's eyes went up and down with the plunger.

'That's fine.' Mrs McAllister nodded in company with the churn strokes.

'I was a-wondering if your husband could do a little heating and hammering on some iron—'

'You'll have to ask the mistopher about that. He's down at the crick with the boys.' Mrs McAllister looked at Dorcas. 'What's your name, girl?'

Dorcas told her.

'All right, Dorcas, you just grab this here churn handle so I can straighten up a minute. Get it quick now, so we won't miss a stroke.' They made the shift and Dorcas found herself churning. Mrs McAllister stood up and yelled at the biggest cabin, 'Bessie, oh, Bessie! Come out here. We got visitors.'

Jude started toward the creek.

'No use to take that pack with you, boy,' Mrs McAllister said.

'I guess not.' Jude hung the pack on a corner log. As he was doing so, a plump girl about his own age came out. She was wearing a clean dress, he noticed, and her eyes were bright blue or gray. He gave her a glance and walked off toward the creek, thinking that it wouldn't be no trouble at all to make that churn work a lot easier by fixing up some pulley wheels and a treadle for it. But like as not Mrs McAllister was the kind who'd rather pound her butter out the hard way.

He found Shad McAllister and his two sons busting beaver dams on Little Creek. They'd sure caught themselves a job. Jude knew how those dams were put together because, before Ma blew up about building the cabin, he'd spent a good many afternoons and early evenings watching beavers in the upper part of the meadows on Deer Creek, and he'd wound up pretty well satisfied that the beavers knew their business.

McAllister was as red-faced as his wife. He

was a bone and muscle man, just a little stooped. There didn't look like there was enough fat on him to grease a burned thumb. His sons, both of them as old as Major, or maybe even a little older, were a whole lot like their father, bony faced and tall, with thin lips and heavy chins. Their eyes were a real sharp gray.

McAllister said he reckoned he could make a hinge or two, and then him and his boys went right back to prying and picking at the beaver dam. You could tell that the whole tribe was the working kind, and the chances were they did everything like a bull busting through a log fence. Jude didn't figure it was his business to tell them how to bust a beaver dam, but if he was doing it, he'd start at the bottom and chop his way in, instead of fighting the top. Most all of the busted dams he'd been showed that the water had gushed out at the bottom.

He took off his shoes and went out to help the McAllisters. They chopped away with sod hoes and pried with long poles, and Jude had to allow the McAllisters could bring a lot of power to bear on things when they all three got on a pry pole. Of course they had to stumble around in the flood they were making, since they were going down from the top.

They didn't do much talking. They worked like they were burying the devil.

They had the dam busted by the time Mrs McAllister came to the top of the hill and bellowed that it was time to eat. For a while Jude thought they weren't going to pay any attention to her. They were eying the next dam downstream. Then Shad said, 'I guess that'll do for a minute or two, boys. Let's eat.'

'How far do those dams run?' Jude asked. He began to put on his shoes.

'Two miles up, three miles down—right close to Goodwin's store,' Shad said. 'We don't own that far but we got plenty of water covering good hayland where we do own.' He started away in a long, shambling stride and the sons, Jake and Toby, were right with him. Jude had to trot to catch up after he got his shoes on.

'Your Pa was the one got killed by Grove, huh?' Shad asked.

'Yep.'

'That Cy Grove ain't no good. Never worked a day in his life, I'll bet,' Shad said. 'I can tell a worker the minute I lay eyes on him. Even you, Whitlock, little and puny as you look—I knowed you was a worker the minute I seen you. What do you folks figure on raising up your way?'

'We don't know yet.'

'Better get cows. Them's the things that'll make this country go, you can bet.'

They passed a fenced garden plot. It sort of startled Jude to see vegetables growing way out here. He got hungry just glancing at the tops of turnips.

133

'I got two hundred and six, counting everything,' Shad said. 'That's a start.'

It took Jude a moment to understand that Shad was still talking about cows. Two hundred and six. Some start. Back in Kentucky the Whitlocks had been lucky to have two milk cows, which the Rebs had got during the second year of the war. Maybe the McAllisters did go after things lickety-split and head-on, but you couldn't say they wasn't getting somewheres.

When it came to eating, they were hard workers too. Mrs McAllister set out deer steaks, fried fish, a vegetable stew, loaves of bread that you picked up and tore apart in hunks as big as your fist, pale yellow butter piled in a dish lop-sided, as if Mrs McAllister knew it wouldn't be there long enough to matter how it looked—Ma always made a neat mound of it—and coffee enough to refill the busted beaver pond.

Now and then Jude noticed Bessie watching him. Her round face was kind of damp from the heat of cooking. Her eyes were real bright and inquiring, and you could see she wasn't no bashful girl at all. That was fine with Jude because he was pretty busy eating and wondering about whether or not Shad was going to spare time to make the hinges before he busted about twenty more beaver dams. Bashful girls or brazen ones—none of them bothered Jude.

Shad didn't taper off his eating, he just quit all at once when he was done and got up like the house was on fire. His sons jumped up too. 'I'll make them hinges,' Shad said. 'Where at is the iron?'

Jude was still chewing when he got outside to give Shad the straps and short pieces of rod from Marion's wagon. 'If you could make a square bend in the rods and a loop in the straps—'

'I've made a hinge or two before.' Shad was already on his way across the yard. Jake was headed back to work at the creek, but Toby was hanging back a little.

'Show you something, Whitlock,' he said, as Jude started to follow Shad. He said it sort of wistful-proud, like he'd be disappointed if Jude didn't see what it was. Inside the house the women were banging pans around and cleaning up like they were getting ready for a visit from the preacher.

Jude went with Toby through the trees to a log fence. Out in the grass a buckskin horse was grazing. It came walking over when Toby whistled. Toby pulled a handful of grass and held it out and the horse wrinkled its lips and took the grass just as if it didn't have a whole pasture on its side of the fence.

'Hey, that's sure a pretty horse,' Jude said.

'Got a saddle of my own for him too.'

'What's his name?'

'Robin Hood.'

135

'That's a good name.'

'Sure is.'

The way Toby twisted his feet around and kept busting big splinters from the fence, you could tell he had something on his mind. He didn't say it until after he'd started off without warning to go back to work on the beaver dams. Then he turned, still walking, and said, 'Your sister sure is a pretty girl, Whitlock. You tell her I said so.'

'I sure will.' Jude grinned. He went over to where Shad was firing up a stone and dirt forge under a rough pole roof built among the trees. 'How many pair?' Shad asked.

'Three. The long straps for the door.'

'You got just about the right amount of iron.'

Jude worked the bellows. Shad wasn't as good as Troy Harkens back in Kentucky, but he knew what he was doing just the same, and he sure whaled away fast. 'You got some big nails to fasten these straps?' he asked, and when Jude said no, not mentioning that the Whitlocks didn't have nails of any size, Shad said he would give Jude some.

In the house, Dorcas had never seen such a slamming and banging around when it was time to clean up after eating. You'd have thought the next meal was going to be served ten minutes later. She plunged in to help but it left her a little short of breath the way Katy McAllister and Bessie went at things. They sure weren't ones for fondling dishes when it was time to dry them, the way Dorcas did some of Ma's things. The McAllisters just gave them a swipe and slammed them at the cupboard.

Mrs McAllister had bread rising on the warming oven of the stove, a pile of dirty clothes heaped in the corner of the room, and a whole tableful of smoked trout that she was going to salt and pack in a keg. She said she was going to do all those things this afternoon, as well as hoe in the garden and make a fence jumper for Tom Moore, whom the mistopher swore was going to break a leg if she wasn't stopped from jumping fences.

'Tom Moore?' Dorcas asked.

'Oh, we name cows and things for anything that strikes us,' Mrs McAllister said. 'Her calf's name is Bull Run. I named it myself because that's where the mistopher got shot in the butt during the war.' She punched carefully at the dough on the warming oven. 'I need a bigger stove. Four loaves I can bake in this one, and they eat that much at a meal. What kind of stove did you folks bring?'

'We ain't got none,' Dorcas said.

'It's just as well. All stoves does is make men expect more food and quicker. I notice your brother don't eat hearty. Is he sickly?'

'Lord no!' Dorcas said. 'Ain't none of us ever been sickly.'

Mrs McAllister began to slap fish around as she salted them. 'Get me a keg, Bessie. Like as not you'll find them full of nails or scrap iron or something else the mistopher stored in 'em, so dump one out and bring it here. You got a young man, Dorcas?'

'No.'

'Oh, sure, there ain't scarce been time since you got here. Did you have one in the wagons that went on?'

'No.'

Mrs McAllister marched over to punch the dough again. Her foot dragged a pair of heavy pants out of the pile of wash as she was coming back across the room. She kicked the garment against the logs with a swipe of her foot and went back to salting fish. Bessie returned with a keg. Her mother sniffed at it suspiciously. 'Is that the one the mistopher left full of fish and forgot for a week?'

'No!' Bessie said. 'Besides I renched this one out.'

'Wouldn't matter, I guess. The McAllisters don't taste the food they eat anyhow.' Mrs McAllister dusted the salt from her hands and lit up a short stemmed pipe. 'Your Ma burn a little weed now and then, Dorcas?'

'No, she don't.'

'It's a filthy habit, I always say. I'm thinking of making the mistopher quit.' Mrs McAllister smoked as hard as she worked. 'Bessie, why'nt you show Dorcas your room.'

Your room? What in tarnation was that? Dorcas followed Bessie across the stifling kitchen and into a room with a real glass window. One glance was enough to know that the furniture was none of your homemade, knocked-together stuff. There was a pink coverlet on the bed and a pillow with a lace-trimmed edge, and on the floor beside the bed was a rag rug, a fine thing to put your bare feet down on of a bitter morning.

A low rocking chair of polished wood was about the size grannies sometimes used when they were sewing. In one end of the room was a big drawer chest with an oval mirror above it. The window was trimmed with dabs of pink cloth that made an eye-catching splash against the whitewashed logs. Except for one of the drawers that stood half pulled out, the room was in apple-pie order. A colored picture of Jesus walking on the water was on one wall.

'This is just for you—the whole room?' Dorcas asked.

'Pa built this on for me when the boys made themselves a bunkhouse. I used to sleep in the same room with Pa and Ma.'

A woman having a room all to herself ... Dorcas had never heard of such a thing, except the time back home when the judge's wife ran him out of the house and made him sleep in the barn because he'd been after nigger wenches. But that had been for only a week or two before the judge went back to the house, and back to chasing nigger wenches too.

Dorcas looked sharply at the half opened

139

drawer, remembering the soiled dress she had seen smack on top of the pile of wash. Sure as the world, after Bessie saw the Whitlocks coming, she'd jumped around and changed quick into a clean dress.

Her and her fine room. Huh!

From the corner of her eyes Dorcas looked at herself in the mirror. Her hair was straggling and her face was still red from the heat of the kitchen. Her old dress was just something to cover her, frizzly around the bottom hem and streaked with dust.

All at once she hated Bessie McAllister.

'Don't you like it, Dorcas?' Bessie tried to sound timid and concerned, but she wasn't fooling Dorcas one bit.

'Oh, it's fine. My own room back home was something like this, only bigger.' The loft had been bigger, maybe, if you didn't figure how much the slope of the roof cut down the space you could use, and if you didn't count the herbs hanging from the rafters and all the junk four generations of Whitlocks had piled in it.

'Ma said I ought to have a room like this. You're the first girl I've showed it to. I was afraid the others would laugh at it.'

Bessie was trying to make light of it, and her eyes were sort of disturbed, as if she wasn't sure of herself. Oh, she was a sly one, sure enough.

'It's all right—for a place so far out in the mountains,' Dorcas said. She stepped over to the mirror. Her face had been dusty when she reached the house, and then the heat of the kitchen had made her sweat, so now her skin looked all dirty smudged, like the faces of the wagon men when they'd been struggling with wagons stuck in the sand.

'How old is Jude?' Bessie asked.

'Sixteen. Him and me's twins. Why?'

'I just wondered.'

Huh! Bessie would soon find out that Jude had no more interest in girls than Lafait had in patching a torn shirt. 'I think we'd better be starting home,' Dorcas said.

'Can't you stay all night? You could sleep here with me. We could talk.'

'Ma wants me back. Likely we'll have company. Folks are always dropping in on us.' Dorcas stepped back from the mirror. She would have given a tooth to own one like it.

Dorcas felt better when she saw Mrs McAllister again, puffing on her pipe and slapping away at the fish. Mrs McAllister wasn't one to put on airs. 'What did you think of Bessie's room, Dorcas?'

'It was fine.'

'It's not much, but I suppose silly young girls ought to have things like that. The Lord knows I never did.'

Jude came to the door with his pack. 'You ready to go, Dorcas?'

Mrs McAllister was outraged. 'Why, you just got here. Seems to me you could stay a day or two, at the very least.'

141

'Got to finish the cabin,' Jude said.

Mrs McAllister allowed that building a home was important work, sure enough. She said the McAllisters would be over for a visit just as soon as they could catch up a few chores, and then she loaded Jude's pack with smoked fish.

Bessie walked with the Whitlocks to the first marsh. When Jude took off his shoes, Dorcas paid no mind. She waded right in with her shoes on, like she had a dozen more pairs of them at home.

At the top of the first hill, Jude stopped to look back. He grinned and shook his head. 'I'm tired just from watching them McAllisters work. Old Shad, he made some pretty fair hinges though.'

'Hinges! Is that all you thought about while we were there?'

'That's why we went, wasn't it?'

'That Bessie, I've never seen the likes of her. She acts like she thinks she's a lady.'

'I thought she was all right. You know, the way they was busting them beaver dams was—'

'Dams!' Dorcas shouted. 'There you go again. That Bessie was making sheep's eyes at you and asking how old you were and if you had a girl and all sorts of questions—'

'That reminds me,' Jude said. 'Toby said to tell you he thought you were a mighty pretty girl. He's got a horse named Robin Hood.'

'Which one was Toby? I never paid enough attention to tell one from the other.'

'Toby is the bigger one, the one with his shoulders kind of stooped like the mistopher.'

Jude grinned. 'The mistopher. Ain't that some name for her to call him all the time?'

'Toby wasn't either the slouchy one,' Dorcas said. 'He was the one that looked—' She stopped suddenly.

Jude began to laugh. He took off at a fast walk and Dorcas shouted after him, 'Think you're smart, don't you!'

On their way home they went through the hills on a short cut Shad had told Jude about. Lafait and Major were out hunting when they got home. Ma wanted to know all about the McAllisters and it was a funny thing how little Jude and Dorcas could think to tell her, except about the things they had been interested in themselves. Jude could have talked a long time about the tools Shad McAllister had around his place, and how they went about breaking beaver dams the wrong way, but Ma said, 'Oh, for heaven's sake, Jude Whitlock! What I want to know is what kind of folks are they.'

'The mistopher—' Jude had to grin '—he's a hard worker and so are the boys. I'll bet you when it's time for his cows to take up with the bulls, they're all out there a-yelling at the bulls to get busy and—'

'That's enough!' Ma said. She shook her head and looked at Dorcas. 'Do they have a good house?'

'I guess,' Dorcas said.

Ma sighed like she had a mortal pain. 'I see I'll have to go over there myself, if I want to know anything.'

Jude was busy fixing the hinges on the door made of wagon boards. 'Shad is a fair blacksmith. I can tell you that much.'

'That's fairly wonderful to know,' Ma said. 'I was awful curious about that.' She smiled. 'I got some news of my own to tell, but now you two can just wait until your brothers come back.'

It was after sunset when Major and Lafait came in. Lafait was as silent as if he had missed a shot at a deer. When he put his rifle above the fireplace, he stood a while staring at it and he didn't even hear Ma ask how-come he had got no game.

Major said, 'We didn't see none, that's why.'

After supper Dorcas and Jude managed to think of a few things they had noticed at the McAllister place that Ma wanted to hear about. Lafait sat on a stool by the fireplace and didn't seem to be listening until Jude mentioned Toby McAllister's horse. Lafait swung around quick enough then.

Dorcas wanted to know what it was Ma had to tell them.

'Oh, nothing much,' Ma said. 'Just that Mark Pilcher was here today.'

'The Pilchers are clean over the mountains

by now!' Major said.

'No,' Ma said. 'They turned back. They're settled on the river about ten miles away. Matthew went on. He's working for Marv Wright.'

'And fixing to marry Malinda,' Jude said.

Ma gave her youngest son a bitey look, and then she glanced at Major. 'They met some folks up the river that told them everything across the mountains was Indian land. I wondered about that when your Uncle Lafe spoke so high about that country.'

Dorcas said, 'It makes a body feel better to think someone you know is settled real close.'

Lafait spat into the fireplace. 'The country's getting crowded up,' he grumbled.

CHAPTER TEN

For as long as he lived Major could date some events in Deer Valley from such things as 'the day Goodwin finished the surveying' or 'about a month after we seen the Indians that first time.' The Rusks came when 'we were finishing the daubing.'

They had three wagons, the Rusks. They camped near the house and the Whitlocks were glad at first of the company, even if the Rusks were from Ohio, which was nothing real bad against them, maybe, but not quite the same as

145

if they had been from Kentucky, or even North Carolina. Like the Whitlocks, they had come up the river—the hard way. By now the Whitlocks knew that most of the other settlers had come to the valley by much easier routes.

That was superior knowledge that the Whitlocks could hold over the Rusks. Major found it possible, too, to be a little sorry for them because they weren't fixed for the winter yet; in fact, the Rusks weren't even sure where they were going to light.

The Rusks were parts of two families. Amos had some grown boys and Lonzo had two grown sons, and then there was a mixture of younguns that Major never had time to get straight in his mind. They were a dark looking bunch, as if they had a fair dash of Indian blood in them. They were hell for borrowing during their four-day stay, until Ma clamped down on them, but that still didn't stop them from asking for everything from flour to gun-powder.

Lafait left the best axe sticking in a cottonwood one night, and the next day it was gone. He was ready to march over to the Rusks' camp and do some shooting to get the axe back, but Ma made him behave. 'You ain't sure they got it,' she said. 'You're always leaving tools laying around somewhere. We'll let Major ask 'em if they seen it, but we're not going to say they stole it unless we know they did.'

'I know they did,' Lafait said.

Major asked Lonzo if he'd seen the axe.

'Sure didn't,' Lonzo said. 'No sir, none of us around here seen it.' He looked at his brother and his sons and nephews and they all shook their heads solemnly.

And they were all lying, Major was sure. They looked like that bunch in Goodwin's store that had told all the big lies and then bust out laughing after he left.

Lonzo dropped the subject as if it had been settled, with everybody happy. 'You sure got a fine piece of property here, Whitlock.' He looked up and down the valley. 'Clear from that pile of rocks down there to the piñons, huh? Where do you go to make papers on land out here?'

Major didn't know. The Whitlocks had left all that up to Goodwin. 'In Denver,' Major said.

Lonzo shook his head. 'That's a long haul, I swear. Well, I guess we'll be leaving in a day or so to find our own selves a piece of property.'

That was welcome news, but Major was still feeling hot inside about the axe. He was sure they had it, but they had lied, and what could he do? He went back to the cabin.

'They got it?' Lafait asked.

Major nodded.

Lafait cursed under his breath so Ma wouldn't hear him. That night he drove the other axe into a tree and fixed to sit out and

147

watch it with his rifle across his knees. Ma caught on to what he was doing and made him bring the axe in. 'Maybe they got it,' she said, 'but it's worth it to get rid of them. We don't want trouble.'

'I'll take it any old day, to letting people steal from you and run over you,' Lafait said.

'What you gave them Indians was just bribery,' Ma said. 'Let's call the axe the same thing.'

'No, sir! Giving to Indians is being neighborly. Letting them Rusks steal our axe is being damned fools!'

Ma acted like she was going to whack him, and then she turned away as if she knew the day of whacking her kids was gone.

The Rusks didn't steal anything else, maybe because the Whitlocks made good and sure nothing was left lying around loose. When the three wagons pulled out one morning, Major was relieved, although he still knew he hadn't done very well about the axe.

He noticed how easy the wagons made it across the meadows, fairly well dried out now. That one big rain that had caused the wagon train all the trouble at the river crossing had been just about the last real rain of the summer. Still, Major knew the meadows were good and wet down deep.

He went to work alone setting posts about fifty feet apart along the south side of the valley. It wasn't fencing the way he would have

148

liked it, but it would serve to show where Whitlock land was.

The way Lafait and Jude came trotting up with the rifles about two hours before noon, Major knew something was bad wrong.

'Them sneaking Rusks went over the north hill and then turned down toward the river,' Lafait said. 'They're below the bend of rocks, fixing to settle in our valley.'

'Did you say anything to Ma?'

'Nope,' Jude said. 'The Rusks are just off our land, but there ain't no good ground between them and the river, so you know what they got in mind. They'll start scrooching this way the minute they think they can make it stick.'

Major worked spittle around to wet his mouth. It was a mortal bad thing anyway you looked at it. Folks like the Rusks wasn't going to be put off that ground by talk; and there were enough of them to eat the Whitlocks if it came to a fight. He kept trying to figure the best thing to do. 'Maybe if we talked to Mr Goodwin and got him—'

'Goodwin, hell,' Lafait said. He shoved the buffalo gun into Major's hands. 'Goodwin ain't got nothing to do with it. Come on.'

'What are you going to do?'

'Run 'em off.'

It was all there was to do and Major knew it. He was scared every step down the valley. They crossed the meadows and got behind the north hill so Ma and Dorcas couldn't see them.

The Rusks had their stuff spread all over the ground and their oxen turned loose as big as you please in the tall grass. Some of them were fixing up a canvas, and a batch of younguns was out in the middle of the valley hand-fishing trout like they owned Deer Creek and everything it touched.

Major walked down the hill with a tight feeling in his chest. The Rusks saw them coming and stopped everything they were doing and talked low for a minute, and then went on with their work.

Jude said, 'Uh-huh! There went our axe into the wagon.'

Lonzo was all smiles. 'Well, boys, going hunting?'

'Yep,' Lafait said. 'Get off our land.'

The smile sort of faded but then Lonzo wrassled it back in place. He looked up the hill where the pile of rocks marked the northeast corner of Whitlock property.

'We know where it is,' Major said. 'We know what you're aiming to do, too.' He saw a fine looking repeating rifle leaning against a bedding roll close to where Amos Rusk was standing with his sons. If one of them started to grab the rifle real quick, what was Major supposed to do? He wasn't mad; he was scared, and he doubted he could shoot anybody just from being scared.

The thing of it was, nobody paid much

attention to Major. All the Rusks, some standing right where they had been from the start, were watching Lafait. God, there was a pile of them and they looked as mean as skimmed cat piss. Major didn't have his rifle pointed exactly at any one of them, and Lafait, he had the long gun slanting across his body easy like, as if he didn't have no intention of using it; but Major knew that Lafait could snap the rifle around from that position and pick off a sparrow bird sitting thirty feet away.

'You damn' fool kids—' Amos said.

'It's all right, Amos.' Lonzo had his smile working good again. 'These boys got the idea we're trying to move onto their land, but after I talk to 'em a little—'

'Don't need the talk,' Lafait said. 'Just git.'

'You don't own this land, no more than nothing,' Lonzo said. 'Them rock piles don't mean nothing. You folks are just squatting here trying to get the whole valley because you happened to fall into it first. You said you filed in Denver, but that ain't so. I asked there and the man said nobody knew the particulars about getting land up this way, and I heerd your Ma say herself none of you been out of here since you lit. Who you trying to tell you own this valley?'

'You.' Lafait moved his rifle a little. It pointed straight into Lonzo's face. 'I think I'll take an ear off you.'

You could see Lonzo was scared but he

wasn't going to give up and yell for the Rusks to start packing. His eyes slid toward Amos and the others standing close to the rifle leaning on the bedroll. 'If I was you, I'd be a little careful of that weepon, boy,' he told Lafait.

Major saw one of Amos' sons reach toward the repeater. 'Hey!' Major said, and started to swing the buffalo gun to discourage the grab, but he was too slow.

Lafait tipped his rifle down and shot like he was in a bet with Jude on a sparrow bird. The bullet whacked the stock of the repeater and knocked the rifle over. The man reaching for it jumped back like he'd started to pick up a rattlesnake by mistake. 'Christ a'mighty!' he yelped.

For an instant Major didn't know what to do, and then he swung his rifle back and held it on Lonzo, not on his face, but on the middle of him.

Lonzo's wife yelled, 'Those boys are crazy, Lonzo! I told you not to come down here. There's other places—'

'Never mind.' Lonzo wasn't quitting yet. He watched Jude skin over and grab up the repeater. 'You boys fool around and kill somebody and we'll hang you and burn you out.'

'It'll be you that's dead.' Lafait's ramrod was clanging in the barrel as he reloaded.

'There's too many of us,' Lonzo said. He

spoke real loud like he was trying to make the others get some starch in their backbones and help him.

'I dunno,' Amos said. 'This ain't such a fine valley as we thought, maybe.'

'I ain't leaving,' Lonzo said. 'No bunch of whey-faced younguns is running me off.'

Lafait smacked the ramrod back into the keeper under the barrel. He primed the long gun and snapped the pan lid down. 'You tell your folks to git.'

Out in the valley Major saw the younguns that had been fishing running like the devil toward the camp. One of the women yelled for them to stay away, but they kept right on coming.

'I ain't telling nobody to git,' Lonzo said, 'and I'm warning you Whitlocks to get out of here right now. You don't own the land, you got no right to make threats or tell decent, law-abiding folks what to do. I'm warning you.'

His voice raised all the time he was talking, like he was trying to build up enough steam inside him to do something besides talk.

'I done warned you already,' Lafait said. The long rifle flicked up and he shot. He wasn't much more than fifteen feet from Lonzo. The way Lonzo grabbed his face and howled, some of the burning powder must have hit him. The side of his neck began to turn red from the blood running down from his torn ear.

153

'Ma!' he howled. 'I'm shot!'

His wife ran to him, cursing and wailing at the same time. 'I told you! I told you!' she yelled. She grabbed Lonzo's hands away from his face to see how bad he was hurt. His eyes were running water and he kept blinking like an owl. 'It's just your ear, you crazy fool!' his wife shouted, and then she looked at Lafait and yelled, 'You murdering bastard!'

Afterward it was funny, her telling Lonzo it was just his ear and then calling Lafait a murderer in the same breath, but at the time Major was too stirred up to think about anything funny. He saw that Jude was standing beside him now, holding the captured repeater. It was shaking. But the Rusks didn't have time to pay that no mind. They weren't waiting for Lonzo to give any orders; they were scurrying around gathering up their plunder and throwing it into the wagons. Some of the younguns went scooting to the meadows to get the oxen.

Lafait was reloading his rifle. He got that done and looked the Rusks over without any worry or strain. 'Let's get back on the hill,' he said, big as you please.

The Whitlocks sat on the hill and watched the Rusks getting ready to leave. All at once the rifle across Jude's knees fell to the ground and he lowered his head and began to puke.

'Don't let 'em see you do that!' Lafait said angrily.

You could see that Lafait was some shook up himself but he wasn't going to let anybody know it if he could help. Major didn't feel so well himself as he looked at Jude's bent back tightening and jerking. Major didn't see how it ever would be possible to go around pointing rifles at folks and shooting their ears off without feeling pretty shaky afterward. Down there at the meadow he hadn't been sure from one minute to the next what he was going to do. But Lafait, he'd known all the time what he was going to do.

'Suppose old Lonzo didn't scare out even after you shot his ear,' Major asked, 'what would you've done then?'

'They was trying to scrooch in on our land, wasn't they? They was—' Lafait scowled and let it go. He never was one to use a lot of words to make something come out reasonable. Lafait just did things.

The Rusk wagons started up the hill, with about half the Rusks walking. They kept watching the Whitlocks. At the top of the hill Amos stopped and yelled, 'You stole that rifle, and we ain't going to forget it neither!'

'Give it back to them, Jude,' Major said.

'Hell with 'em,' Lafait grunted.

'No,' Major said. 'Give it back.' He shouted at Amos, 'Give us our axe and you can have the rifle.'

A wagon stopped, a young Rusk stuck his head out and shoved an axe blade-first at

155

Amos. With one eye on the Whitlocks, Amos reached for it. He cursed as he cut his hand.

'Right there is the reason people like that ain't no good,' Lafait said, and laughed to himself. 'They can't watch two things at the same time.'

Amos came walking toward them with the axe. Jude went out to meet him. 'Stay off to the side, Jude!' Lafait said, and Jude instantly made a little swing away from the direct line between Lafait and Amos.

Jude's voice was shrill and outraged when Amos started to toss the axe toward him after they stopped. 'Don't you throw that down in the rocks!' Jude walked over and took the axe and gave Amos the rifle.

For a half mile or so the Whitlocks followed behind the wagon at a distance. There wasn't much doubt that the Rusks were leaving, but part of the following, Major guessed, was because he and Jude and Lafait weren't very anxious to go back home and face Ma. She always knew when something had happened and she could generally get it out of Major because he wasn't much good at lying.

'Maybe we ought to go down by the river and get a deer,' Jude suggested.

Major knew that wasn't apt to fool Ma, not even if they carried back a half dozen deer. She'd heard those two shots, and she knew darned well Major wasn't in the habit of giving up work to go hunting all of a sudden. 'No use,'

Major said. 'We'd just as well go back now.'
The axe was evidence against them, too.

As they went back along the hill toward home, they didn't laugh or make jokes about how the Rusks had scooted. Major kept remembering how scared some of the ragged younguns had looked as they trotted up the hill beside the wagon. Using guns against people, unless you were in a war or fighting Indians, which was a kind of war too, was a damned poor thing. He remembered himself with his hands clawed against the table in Goodwin's, staring at Pa on the floor. He'd seen about all he wanted of shooting right then.

And yet he was glad the Rusks were gone, and he guessed Lafait's way was the only one that would have worked.

Ma and Dorcas met them when they came close to the cabin. Ma looked at the axe Jude was carrying. 'I heard two shots.'

'Turned me a couple of prairie dogs inside out,' Lafait said. He ducked into the cabin.

'I'll cut some kindling, Ma.' Jude hurried off into the grove.

'Better get back to the posts, I reckon.' Major started away but it didn't work.

'Major!'

'Yeah, Ma, what do you want?'

'What happened? How'd you get that axe back?'

Ma could afford to let the others escape because it took a heap of doing to squeeze a

157

story out of them when they didn't want to tell it. 'Traded a rifle for it,' Major said, and that was the mortal truth.

'Whose rifle?'

'Their own rifle. They left it laying around.'

'And the shots?'

'One went in the air and the other hit the ground.'

'He's lying, Ma,' Dorcas said.

'You shut up, Dorcas.' Major glared at his sister.

'He's telling the truth, as far as it goes,' Ma said, 'but it ain't going as far as I'd like to know.' She watched Major for a minute and then, surprising him, she went back inside the cabin.

Lafait popped out of the cabin like he had a lot of business. He and Major went to where Jude was skulking behind a tree. 'What'd she say?' Jude asked.

'Nothing,' Lafait answered. 'Major just told the truth—sort of—and she let him go. I guess she knows we're growed up now.'

Growed up. That was about the size of it, sure enough, and Ma must have known it a long time before her sons did. Lafait's upper lip and chin were sprouting dark, silky whiskers. Like as not if he started shaving, in no time his beard would be as black and thick as Pa's. Two times now he'd stood up against men, just as sure of himself as could be.

Even Jude wasn't no youngun any more. Oh,

158

he still went skipping off on trifling things when it pleased him, and his ragged fair hair and long face still had a boyish look, but the strong things inside him, which were different from his brothers' wants and knowing, had been cropping out more and more since the Whitlocks started west. Jude was the one that had showed them how to build a proper cabin. The dreaming in him was developing into doing things.

All at once Major was sad inside himself. There wasn't going to be a Whitlock family in this country like there'd been back in Kentucky, close living and holding strong to their kinship all their lives. Back in Kentucky you could trot across a few ridges and visit Whitlocks all the way, and a good whoop and a gunshot from Turkey Knob would bring Whitlocks swarming from all directions. They had their own burying ground where there were Whitlocks and Hubbells and Horns and Berwicks and others that even the old grannies couldn't rightly name any more.

Out here it wasn't going to be the same. Someday this family would start scattering, and when it did there was no telling how far apart they would wind up.

Major couldn't say what Dorcas and the others wanted, except he knew Deer Valley wasn't going to hold them like it was going to hold him. This was his home now. There might be better places, maybe over the mountains

159

where the rest of the train had gone; but Major would never jump around like a flea on a hot skillet trying to find a better place.

Suddenly he was scared a lot deeper than he had been down there arguing with the Rusks, for he realized that for all his shakiness and not wanting to use his rifle, he had been more dangerous than Lafait. Lafait could shoot a man in the ear and scare the daylights out of him. Major couldn't do anything fancy like that, but he knew he would have killed old Lonzo if that had turned out to be the only way to keep the Rusks from grabbing any part of Whitlock land.

The Rusk version of the quarrel came to Ma a week later when Luke Pilcher rode down to see Dorcas. The Rusks had gone up the valley telling how the Whitlocks, all of them dressed in dirty buckskin clothes and looking savage as Shawnees, had started blazing away at the Rusk camp without warning. Some of the Rusk younguns had been in danger of their lives and a bullet had glanced off a wagon wheel right close to where Amos Rusk's wife was standing. And all this just because the Rusks had camped near the Whitlock cabin to rest their tired oxen. On top of that, they Rusk side of the tale said the Whitlocks had stolen a rifle—and an axe.

Major had to tell Ma the straight of things then. She didn't like it, but all she did was stare hard at Lafait.

CHAPTER ELEVEN

All the rest of the summer Major put posts in the ground to mark Whitlock land. The McAllisters, the Burnines, the Pilchers and others who came to visit admired his energy, but they couldn't see the sense of a lot of posts with nothing between them. Goodwin didn't say it was a waste of time.

'You'll have a good line to go by,' he told Major, 'when you get around to building real fences someday.' He seemed to understand how it was with Major.

When Major stepped beyond the line between the posts, he thought, 'Now I'm off the place,' and when he stepped back he thought, 'This is home ground,' and there was a prideful feeling in it, although he knew well enough that the Whitlocks didn't have any kind of paper to show real ownership; but Goodwin said that would come in time.

During the summer wagons went up the river and a few came down the river, all folks looking for a place to settle. Sometimes riders, alone or in bunches, came by the Whitlock place. Some of them were miners from Cache Creek and Oro City, where it was said men had taken water buckets full of gold out of the gulches before the war. The miners generally stopped to eat at the Whitlock place and they always insisted on paying for their meals. Sometimes it was money but more often it was in pinches of gold dust, which Ma regarded suspiciously until Goodwin told her it was as good as any money there was.

That interested Lafait. He went up to the Pilchers, who were settled under a hill on meadowland against the Arkansas, and talked Luke into going up to the mines of California Gulch. They took turns riding one of Ross Pilcher's horses. They were gone a week. When Lafait came back he said mining appeared to him to be the most horrible kind of work there was. 'You got to shovel gravel all day and roll boulders out of the way, and even then I didn't see nobody with a bucketful of gold. I might've worked there long enough to get me a pistol, but nobody needed any help.'

'And what do you need with a pistol, young man?' Ma asked sharply.

'Everybody needs a pistol,' Lafait said. 'A young fellow let me shoot his and I could see right away I could do pretty good with it, saying I had more practice.'

'A young fellow, was it?' Ma asked.

'Maybe twenty, twenty-one,' Lafait said, and looked silly when the other Whitlocks laughed.

'He was from Missouri,' Lafait added solemnly.

Afterward, Lafait told Major and Jude that everybody up the river knew about Cy Grove and the bunch with him. They had tried mining but it proved too hard for them, so they had drifted into bushwhacking, which was the only name Lafait could think of to describe their life. They went where they pleased on good horses, gambled, stole horses and cattle and raised hell in general. One fellow had hinted that they had killed a couple of miners who had some gold.

'You ain't aiming to go after that Grove, are you?' Major asked.

Lafait gave him his dark stare. 'I might, if it comes handy.'

'It won't help Pa none to get yourself killed.'

'Nope,' Lafait said, and refused to talk any more about it.

In spite of his dark feeling against the men who had been with Grove the night Pa was killed, Lafait was friendly enough to Bill when he came to the Whitlock place a few days later. Bill Gifford was his full name. He was going down to Goodwin's after food, he said, but all the Whitlocks could see he was cleaned up considerable for a man making a dusty ride to get a little bacon. Jude teased Dorcas about that afterward.

You could see Ma wasn't settled in her mind about Bill. She asked him a lot of questions, what kind of land he had, what he figured to raise on it, and if he was up there all by himself. He said he had a place up on Indian Creek, which was back in the hills somewhere between

163

the Whitlocks and the Pilchers. He'd have some cattle in time, but meanwhile he was just there by himself getting along.

When Bill went on to the store, Lafait decided to go with him. Lafait said he owed Goodwin a deer or two more for the alum Ma had got for the canvas ceiling under the loft, and maybe he would pick one off beside the river on the way. It was getting so Lafait went about where he pleased and Ma didn't argue much with him about it any more.

Jude said, 'I guess I'll go along too. Goodwin wanted me to come down two days from now anyway, to help him put a roof on the store, so's he could get rid of that canvas. It won't hurt if I'm a little early.'

'You'll go down there when he said, not now,' Ma told him.

Jude squirmed around and grunted about it, but that was the way it stood. The two days didn't make no mind, Major guessed; Ma was making sure only one of her sons at a time had a chance to get into mischief. What mischief you could get into at Goodwin's was more than Major could see, but he guessed Ma was taking no chances.

One thing about Jude, he never sulked much. As soon as Bill and Lafait were gone, he grinned and began to tease Dorcas about Bill. 'You'd make a fine couple, Dorcas.'

'Him with that clean shirt and the same old ragged pants? Hah! What makes you think I'd even look at him a second time if he was the last man on earth?'

'Because he wears pants.'

'Oh, shut your mouth, Jude.'

'I like Toby McAllister's horse better, I think, than Bill's,' Jude said, 'but Toby, he don't hardly talk as much as the horse himself. He just looks at you like a lost hound dog, and when he stays to eat he fumbles around so much I don't see how he hits his mouth.'

'Never was a McAllister born that didn't know the way to his mouth,' Ma said.

Major grinned. The McAllisters were hearty eaters, no mistake about that. They had visited the Whitlocks twice and Ma had busted herself to see that they had plenty to eat. Afterward she'd said that Colorow and his whole bunch couldn't have eaten one lick more than the McAllisters. There was nothing mean in the words, though, because she liked Katy McAllister and Bessie a whole lot. In a day or two she was going over to visit them.

Jude and Dorcas went on jawing at each other, both enjoying themselves. Unless they got mean with each other, Ma always let them go their best. It was a fine thing to sit a minute or so in the cabin after eating, listening to the family and watching Ma's quiet smile as Jude and Dorcas tried to get the best of each other. The walls were clean and solid, the roof was about the best there was in the country, and the furniture Jude and Major had made was good enough for anybody. Grandma Ripley's chest had a place of honor against one wall, sitting there on a little stand Jude had fixed for it. From a distance you couldn't see the scars and scratches on it because Jude had rubbed the juice of some berries into them and Ma had shined the wood with a little deer fat.

Although the chest was about the only big thing that hadn't been made right on the spot, it was proof that the Whitlocks hadn't just dropped out of the air without any respected folks or history behind them.

Major didn't waste too much time sitting around feeling proud. He had more posts to set. When he had the whole valley enclosed with them, he would work up a pile of wood to last all winter, and build a shelter for Fawn and Steuben, who were fatter and stronger looking than he'd ever seen them. Goodwin sure hadn't been wrong about this bottomland grass being good.

As he went across the valley to resume his digging, Major studied the mountains. Like as not the weather would always show first up there and in time a man could learn just what to expect by watching the mountains. They were friendly things to Major now. Ma still didn't set any store by them. Sometimes Major would see Ma looking at them with a strange expression, as if she regretted settling right under them, the thing she'd vowed she never would do.

Someday Major would climb clean to the top of the highest mountain in sight, just for the fun of seeing the world from up there.

It was twenty years before he ever took time to do that.

He went to the toe of the north hill and began another post hole. Jude and Lafait weren't much help on digging, but you couldn't say that they didn't keep him well supplied with posts from the mountains.

He wondered how Matt Pilcher and Malinda were doing by now. No doubt Rawls Judson, who was a kind of preacher, had married them up and by now they would have a baby started. Major dug hard at the gravel. He no longer had any doubt that he had done the right thing for the Whitlocks when he made the decision about staying here, even if he had hurt part of himself. He guessed he should have gone to the wagon camp, instead of just letting Malinda go away with a second-hand goodbye, and told her what he was going to do and asked her....

But that was dreaming about something that was done and finished. Major kept driving his bar between the round, slippery rocks, prying, getting down on his knees to reach the loosened stones. He could have moved ten feet out, into the meadow, and had easy digging; but this was where the line was and this was where he would build a strong fence someday.

The day he put in the last post was another

day to mark time by. That was the day the two wagons camped not over a quarter mile from the cabin. They came over the hill and stopped at the cabin first and Major saw the people talking to Ma and Dorcas, and then a little later the wagons went down valley along the bottom of the hill and camped near a spring seep where Lafait often killed deer late in the evening.

Jude and Lafait were in the mountains getting poles to make a shelter for the oxen. When Major went to the cabin to eat, he asked Ma, 'Who are those folks down there?'

'I didn't catch their names.'

'Did they ask you about staying on our land?'

'Yes,' Ma said, slow-like. 'They said something about staying a while here while they was looking around for a place to settle.'

You could see that she was some worried. Major said, 'You know what Goodwin told us—anybody that lights and stays very long builds up a kind of right to the ground.'

'I know.'

'They didn't really ask, did they?'

'Well, they didn't deny this was our place.'

Ma was worried about something happening that might be worse than the Rusk thing. Major looked at the buffalo gun. He wanted to take it with him but he was afraid of what he might do if he got in a real bad quarrel with the folks down the valley. He walked away without it.

The two wagons were in good shape. The oxen, ten of them, weren't worn down; and from the stuff scattered around the camp, Major could tell that these folks were pretty well off. He talked to the first man he saw, a fellow with a face that sloped out like a beaver's. 'How long you folks figure to camp here?'

'Well,' the man said, 'we don't rightly know yet. Maybe all winter. We want to scout the country to find a good place to settle.'

'In that case, there's places farther up the river that will be just as good, maybe better.'

It was like the Rusk trouble all over again. People got real quiet. Some of them sidled up beside the slope-faced man.

'We kind of like it here.' The man looked around him slyly, and then he studied Major as if he was seeing just how much there was behind his words.

'We like it too,' Major said. 'The difference is—we own the place. We ain't aching for trouble with you or nobody else, so I guess the best thing you can do is move up the river.'

'Got to rest our beasts,' the man said.

'Rest 'em up that way.' Major pointed. 'You got lots of time before dark to reach a good camping place on Indian Creek.' He'd said enough. There was no sense in making threats or standing around arguing. He turned and walked off.

The man said, 'Hey, there, just a minute,' but Major kept going. He didn't know whether he had done any good or not, and it worried him while he was eating. Afterward, he sat outside the cabin to see what would happen. It was an almighty temptation to make some kind of threat with the buffalo gun, but he left it right where it was on the deer horns set into the fireplace.

'You think they'll leave?' Ma asked.

'I don't know.'

'You can't scare folks like that just by walking down there real big and talking to them,' Dorcas said. 'You should've waited until Lafait—'

'No! He did just right.' Ma put her hand on Major's shoulder, as if she knew how he was arguing inside himself about what he had tried to do.

The folks at the wagons started to move just before Lafait and Jude came back with Bill, who had met them in the mountains. Major was glad it was *before* the trespassers saw three more men at the cabin; it made him feel solid and strong inside to know he'd done the job by himself and without having to wave a gun around.

Lafait made one of his quick shots and blew a bird to pieces on a cottonwood branch. The sound made everybody jump. 'I think we'd best go down there and hurry 'em along.'

'That ain't necessary.' Ma gave Lafait and

Bill a bitey look. 'A gun is going to get you in bad trouble one of these times, Lafait Whitlock.'

'And likely out of it too.' Lafait began to reload.

Bill dropped his eyes when Ma kept staring hard at him. Major wondered how true it was what the Burnines had hinted about, that Bill's place on Indian Creek was one of the hidey-holes where Cy Grove's bushwhackers hung out sometimes. It was danged funny how took Lafait was with Bill, considering Bill had been one of the men with Grove the night Pa got killed.

That evening Dorcas and Bill wandered outside and sort of kicked around the woodpile. They laughed and talked but the Whitlocks inside the house couldn't tell what they were saying.

Jude was cooking a bubbling mess of deer hooves to make glue for a rocking chair he was building for Ma. The hooves were bad enough but he'd added manure and a few other ingredients which he thought might strengthen the mixture. 'Like Goodwin says, this is sort of experimenting,' Jude explained.

'Sort of stinking up the place, you mean.' Ma was sitting where she could look out the glass window at the mountains. Goodwin had packed that window all the way from Denver, and Ma had paid him for it with gold dust. 'Mind you boil that pan out good, Jude,'

171

she said.

Major could tell she wasn't really paying much attention to Jude; she was staring at the mountains and listening to Bill and Dorcas talking outside.

Lafait was flat on his back on his bed, pretending to shoot arrows from the bow he'd won from the Utes. He was forbidden to touch an arrow to the string inside the house, ever since an arrow had slipped and he'd almost shot Dorcas while she was cooking at the fireplace.

Major said, 'Maybe it's time Dorcas came inside.'

'Let her be.'

'I just thought—'

'Let her be, Major! Dorcas is old enough to know what she's supposed to do and how to behave.'

It was clear that Ma didn't like Bill courting Dorcas, but she wasn't going to make a big fuss over it, unless maybe she knew for sure that Bill was as thick with Grove as some hinted. When things displeased her she lots of times looked hard at the mountains like she blamed them for the bad that had come about.

Major caught her mood. He strained when he couldn't hear his sister and Bill murmuring outside, and then he eased off when they started in again and he knew they were still close outside. There was a long silence just before they came inside. Bill said he guessed

172

he'd be getting back home.

'You're welcome to stay,' Ma said. 'Riding by night ain't good for a man.'

She meant something darker than just the words, Major knew, and he could tell that Bill knew that too, but Bill wasn't put out. He grinned and said he didn't mind riding in the dark, considering he had several things to do around his place early in the morning.

When he was gone, Dorcas turned on Ma. 'You don't like him, do you?'

'Didn't say so,' Ma said. 'Oh, I like him well enough. Maybe I wouldn't like some of the things he does.'

'And what are those things, I'd like to know?'

The way Ma looked at Dorcas, you'd have thought Dorcas was six years old. 'You get on up that ladder to bed,' Ma said. 'I ain't in the mood for a big jangle tonight.' She went back to looking at the mountains.

Dorcas flounced around the room, daring Jude or Lafait to start an argument; but for once they didn't care to tease her. 'I'm more growed up than he is,' she said of Jude. 'I don't waste my time cooking stinks at the fireplace.'

Major and Jude and Lafait all grinned at each other when Dorcas at last gave up and started climbing the ladder to the loft. From the top she yelled back at them, 'When I get married, I'll have a room all to my own, just like Bessie McAllister!'

173

'And where'll your husband sleep—out in the barn?' Jude wanted to know. Almost in the same breath he said, 'Whew! I think I got too much bark scrapings in this glue.'

'The stuff you got too much of in there didn't come off no tree,' Lafait said.

Ma didn't pay any attention to them. It wasn't often that she was broody; but Major reckoned she had reason enough, worrying about Bill and Dorcas, hating the mountains the way she did. He sensed, too, that she missed Pa something awful, for every now and then some little remark about him would pop out in her talk to prove that she was thinking back a whole lot more than you might figure.

Major could see now that it had been foolish for him to worry so much about his brothers and Dorcas; they would get along all right. It was Ma that he was bounden to take care of. He vowed that he would see to it she had as few worries as possible the rest of her life. She didn't seem so awful old—but thirty-seven was no young age for a woman. Major remembered women back in Kentucky who had been gray and stooped and nearly ready for the grave when they were no older than Ma.

Yes, he would do the very best he could by Ma for the rest of her life.

The Whitlocks were surprised as all get-out to see Matt and Luke Pilcher ride up to their place a few days later. Major had been getting used to Luke and figuring that maybe he was about the best of the Pilcher tribe, but Matt didn't look any better to Major than he ever had. The first thing Major wanted to blurt out was, 'Where's Malinda?' He wouldn't give Matt that much satisfaction although he was dying with curiosity to know why Matt was here, while Malinda was clean over on the far side of the mountains.

Ma acted happy as could be to see Matt. She had him inside in no time for a bite to eat, and then he started talking about what had happened to the train. They had got clean to the top of the mountains after a fearful trip, and there a bunch of Utes had met them and pointed them back the way they had come. That was all there was to it, the Indians claimed the land where they were headed.

'Wright was fit to be tied,' Matt said. 'He wanted to go right on in spite of the Indians, but the others they wasn't so sure it was a good thing. We camped a week and jawed about it, and then we turned back after some miners come along and told us, sure enough, the government said everything over the mountains was Ute land.'

'Where'd everybody go?' Ma asked.

'Here and there.' Matt acted like he didn't want to talk about it. 'Some of them come back and settled way up high in this here valley. The Marions and Wright and the Jessups and the Malones went to South Park.' Matt glanced at Major. 'I went along but I come back.'

Jude asked, 'What about Malinda?'

'Oh, her?' Matt pretended that he had to think on it to remember who she was. 'She up and married some fellow over in South Park. I don't remember his name.'

He remembered the name, Major didn't doubt, and a whole lot more than that. 'Had his own place, I suppose?' Major asked.

'Yeah, he did,' Matt said. 'She didn't know him very long, but—' He shrugged as if it didn't matter, but the way he looked at Major was like saying, 'I guess the two of us ain't much good.'

Major felt a little more toward liking Matt Pilcher after that; they shared a common failure. Still, it was a jar to Major to know that Malinda had just up and married somebody she hardly knew. It was years before he ever saw her again, and then there was no pain in the meeting.

Outside, Dorcas was flirting for all she was worth with Luke.

CHAPTER TWELVE

Jim Goodwin was pretty busy all the time, running his store, having trouble with freighters that hauled his goods, and trying, late in the summer, to get a cabin built on the claim he had on Little Creek; but still he found time to come up and visit the Whitlocks about every week. Once Jude, grinning and sharp-eyed, tried to tease Ma about Goodwin showing up so often, but she just looked at him and shook her head. 'You ain't talking to your sister, Jude. I was married twenty-one years ago.'

'I remember Uncle Lafe telling about a woman who was a grandma and five times married, but still her comb got red every change of the moon. Uncle Lafe said—'

'Young man, it seems to me your Uncle Lafe did a power of talking to younguns who didn't understand half of what he was saying.'

'Oh, I understood,' Jude said. 'The way he explained it—'

'Never mind, Jude Whitlock. You get that rocking chair built and forget the things Uncle Lafe said. Mr Goodwin is a good friend and I'm glad to see him drop by and that's the size of it and don't you forget it.'

'Yes, Ma.' Jude still had an ornery twinkle in his eye.

Goodwin came visiting the very next evening. He said that the government had picked his store as the place where supplies were to be given to the Indians, and that he was going to help in handing out the stuff. But there was a mixup and the Indian agent was being very stubborn about it.

He gave a letter to Major. 'The Indian agent sent one of his assistants over with that

177

yesterday.'

What Major had learned of reading had come hard but surely from Cousin Jonas Hubbell, who had reached out from his sick bed to rap ten-year-old Major across the head with a stick every time he stumbled over a word he should have known. Major read the letter aloud slowly. When he mumbled or slid over some of the most bristly looking words, his scalp still cringed under the threat of that long ago stick.

'... Certain supplies, herein enumerated, to be distributed to Ute Indians now dwelling in the general area of the Upper Arkansas Valley, to be delivered under Army escort to the store on the ranch of one James R. Goodwin, on Little Creek, in the Territory of Colorado, he to assist in the distribution of said supplies...'

'What's wrong with that—if I read it right?' Major asked.

'The agent says he won't deliver the supplies to the store because it ain't at a ranch on Little Creek, and he won't deliver them to my place on Little Creek because there ain't a store there.'

'The Jesus Christ!' Lafait said. 'Ain't that something!'

Goodwin smiled as he folded the letter and put it back into his buckskin shirt. 'It's not unusual when you're dealing with the government. I've fallen into worse holes

178

working for the government as a surveyor. If the Utes don't get those supplies here, they'll have to ride a hundred miles or so to get them somewhere else. They'll be sore, and they might take it out on any white men that fall handy. Besides, I've already told them that the stuff was coming here.

'That's why I came up to see you folks. I need some help. I figure to move the store to my place on Little Creek within ten days. It had just as well be there as where it is. In fact, it'll be better to have it on my own land because I'll be in legal residence on the claim and won't have to worry about somebody contesting my right to the ground.'

'That's a heap of work,' Lafait said, 'just because of a little old letter. Looks like it'd be easier to change the letter.'

Goodwin laughed. 'Not with the government. You boys want to help me? I'll pay you and pay you for your wagon and oxen too.'

'We'll take it out in food,' Major said.

'We'll mark every piece with a hot iron,' Jude said. 'We'll take it apart and haul it away and put it back together in no time. We used nails on them shakes but I got a way figured out to get 'em off without splitting. Then we'll—'

'You're making my back ache already,' Lafait grumbled. 'I still can't see how it makes a difference where the Indians get their stuff.'

No matter what he thought, Lafait worked

179

as hard as the rest when they tore the store down log by log. Jude was in his glory as he marked the pieces with a red hot length of wagon iron.

Major was glad to see the place come down; it stood on bad remembered ground.

He stayed behind when Lafait and Jude went away with the last wagonload of logs, and then he walked over to Pa's grave. Goodwin had dragged a big stone to the head of it even before he knew that the Whitlocks had settled in the country. Across the river Major could see the ruts made where the wagons had come down to the flooding Arkansas. Later trains were now using crossings farther down the river.

Only the past was here now. Major hurried away to catch up with the wagon.

Goodwin had a fine stretch of land a mile below the McAllisters' on Little Creek. Close to the stream, cottonwoods and flooded beaver ponds took up much of the best meadows, but Goodwin said all that could be changed in time. All he'd had time to do so far was survey the land and get a cabin started.

In three days they reassembled the store, with Jude doing most of the directing, and once more Goodwin was impressed by Jude's keen mechanical skill. 'Put some mathematics with that natural bent of his,' Goodwin told Major, 'and there's no telling where that boy will wind up. You send him down here as much as possible during the winter and I'll teach him some surveying.'

'Jude can figure some but he can't read a lick.'

'Teach him to read!' Goodwin said.

The very idea scared Major. He himself had had a hard enough time learning to read and write, without trying to teach someone else. 'I don't know. It was just an accident that I—'

'You can do it,' Goodwin insisted. 'With a mind like Jude's, half the battle is won when you make the first start. You the only one in the family that can read and write?'

'Yeah.' The mention of that always embarrassed Major, maybe because Pa had been hell to brag about how good his oldest boy could read and write.

'I'll talk to you more about it later on,' Goodwin said.

When the store was completed, except for the fireplace, Goodwin said he had to go to Denver at once to see the Indian Agent. He asked the Whitlocks to take charge of things while he was gone, to build the fireplace and to finish the cabin for him, if they had time. Major and Jude were eager to take on the extra work but Lafait wasn't near so happy about it. He told Goodwin he'd like a pistol for what he had done so far.

'You don't need one,' Major said. 'We'll take our pay in food.'

'Ain't worried about food. I want me a pistol.'

181

'We can't afford it.' Major shook his head. 'We got to think of other things.'

'Want a pistol,' Lafait said.

'Wait a minute.' Goodwin studied Lafait a long time. 'What do you need with a pistol?'

'I want one, that's all. If my share ain't enough for one, I'll work for you some more—later on.'

Goodwin looked at Major. 'He'll get one, one place or another. I've got one here, but it ain't no Colt by any means.' He dug into a chest and came up with a long-barrelled revolver. It was a Prescott Navy pistol, six shot, rimfire, a .36 caliber, which was about the same as the Pennsylvania long gun. As a pistol it didn't look near enough heavy to Major to be much good. 'I've got three hundred rounds for it,' Goodwin said. 'They go with it, but after that I don't know where you'll ever get cartridges. In fact, I don't think you will. That's why I've still got the pistol.'

'I'll take it,' Lafait said. 'How much?'

'You've paid for it.'

Two minutes later Lafait was shooting at a tree. For a minute Major thought he was missing it completely, and then he saw a small limb stub snap away, no bigger than a man's finger. Goodwin got a worried look, as if maybe he'd made a mistake. He cleared his throat. 'Maybe you'd best not say anything to your Ma about having that pistol, Lafait.'

'Didn't figure I would,' Lafait said, and

182

sprayed bark very close to a tiny, brittle limb. 'You got some traps there. How about letting me use a half dozen and going shares on what I catch?'

'That's one thing my pappy told me never to do.'

'Give your traps out on shares?' Lafait asked.

'No, go trapping on shares.'

'It's me that's going, not you.' Lafait began to unload the empty cartridges from his pistol.

'That's what I mean,' Goodwin said. 'I'll sell you the traps and you can pay for them out of what you catch. If you don't catch anything, I'll just take the traps back.'

'I'll catch something.'

'You ought to,' Jude said. 'The crick's full of beaver.'

'Ain't interested in beaver,' Lafait said. He reloaded the pistol. 'I'm going up in the mountains, come winter, and catch me wolves and things like that.'

'All right,' Goodwin said, 'I'll make the deal—if you stay here and help your brothers finish the work.'

Lafait thought it over. 'Guess I'll have to.'

You could tell that Goodwin figured he'd done one good thing to sort of offset what might be bad about selling Lafait the pistol. The fact that Goodwin didn't want Ma to know about the pistol showed that he was some worried about it.

Goodwin went to Denver, and the Whitlocks finished the work while he was gone. When he came back, the dangdest bunch of Utes the Whitlocks had ever seen were already trailing along with the six soldiers escorting three wagonloads of supplies and thirty lean looking steers. Colorow was in the bunch. For a while he acted like he'd never seen the Whitlocks before, and then he got friendly. He picked Jude up and slapped him on a calico pony and gave the pony a solid whack with his hand. Away it went toward the river with Jude hanging to its mane for dear life. The nose rope was swinging and Jude didn't have any control at all, except yells which the pony didn't understand.

It looked like they were headed clean out of the country, but at the edge of the beaver ponds the pony stopped suddenly and Jude slid up on its neck. He tried to push back but he couldn't make it. He flopped under the pony's neck and there he hung as upside down as a possum. The pony was backing up and jumping around and it finally dumped Jude *kersplash* in the shallow water. The Utes were yelling and laughing fit to kill.

Major saw that Jude was all right, he was getting up with the nose rope in his hand. Danged if he didn't scramble back on the pony and come racing toward the store. He was bouncing something awful but he managed to stay on, and all the time he was yelling like a

184

wild man, so Major knew he was about half scared and about half mad. Jude headed straight for the Indians. When he yelled *whoa!* the pony didn't pay no mind, and Indians fell over themselves getting out of the way.

The pony went between the cabin and the store. It knocked over a squaw and scattered yelling children and ran clean to the top of the hill before Jude got it stopped. The Utes were whooping and laughing like they'd seen the greatest thing that ever happened. After he saw that nobody was hurt, Major had to laugh himself.

The Whitlocks stayed three more days at the store. Major knew they ought to be going home but it was pretty hard to break away, considering the fun they were having. One of the clerks the Indian agent had sent along couldn't write worth a darn when it came time to put down the things the Utes were getting, so Major took his place.

Jude was everywhere around the Ute camp, learning sign language, seeing how the lodges were made, poking into a hundred things that interested him. The Indians all seemed to like him and hardly an hour went by that some buck didn't try to get him to ride a horse again. Lafait was always with a bunch of bucks, trailing his long rifle around and wearing his pistol in his belt. Wherever a big game of hand was going on, with the Utes betting practically everything they owned, Lafait was always an interested watcher; but he never got in the games.

It seemed to Major that the Utes were determined to stay until they had eaten up all the food the government had given them. They ate at all hours, slept when they pleased, had horse races and gambling games, and got along with each other with scarcely any trouble at all. When Goodwin gave out the cattle, each family knew just which steer it was getting. A bunch of riders would run it along the meadow and then two or three men would skim out on their ponies, shooting bullets and arrows into it. Mostly they used bows and arrows. After the steer was dead the women would go out and start butchering.

Lafait couldn't stand still for watching that kind of sport. He talked Colorow into letting him have a try at a big brindle steer, along with two Utes. Having seen Lafait shoot the long rifle, Colorow cut him down to a bow and arrow.

Away Lafait went with the two Utes chasing the steer along the edge of the meadow. It looked at first like Lafait was fair outstripping the two Indians, until Major decided they were holding back to see how Lafait was going to make out. Lafait was bouncing something fierce but at least he was staying on. He got in close to the steer and then Major saw he was having trouble staying on and getting an arrow on the string at the same time. When Lafait tried to lean out and shoot, the arrow went end over end above the steer's back, and Lafait went smack on his head on the ground.

Major thought he must have busted his neck, but when Major got to him, Lafait was staggering up, pretending that he hadn't even been jarred. 'It ain't like shooting an arrow when you got both feet on the ground, I can tell you.' Lafait wobbled away.

The Utes were laughing their heads off. Lafait just grinned and let them go their best. A little later he got some of them into a shooting match. Those who had shot with him before didn't bite, but they were willing enough to let their friends try. Lafait won two ponies and four blankets and he was piling up some other loot until he got cocky and tried to match his new pistol against two Utes with rifles. The Indians liked him all the better for being a wild gambler.

The Whitlocks might have stayed as long as the Utes camped near the store, but Toby McAllister came by one day on his way back from visiting Dorcas and said that Ma was wondering what had happened to her sons. Major felt a little guilty. He still hadn't built a shelter for Fawn and Steuben and there were some other chores that needed doing.

Lafait said right out flat that he wasn't going home just yet. Some of the Utes had invited him to go hunting with them after they left the store. He gave his brothers one of the ponies he'd won. They loaded it with supplies in exchange for the work they had done for Goodwin, whose own stuff had been hauled in one of the three wagons under Army escort.

* * *

From the top of the south hill Major and Jude stopped to look down at the cabin in the grove. It was a clear, warm day, although high on the mountains the first new snow of coming winter lay like fine white dust. Smoke was rising straight up from the fireplace. There was work to do and it was good to be home.

Going down the hill, Major said, 'Maybe we'd best not tell Ma how we come by this pony.'

'She can guess without no trouble.'

They had been away for more than two weeks. That didn't make Major nearly as uneasy as the thought of something else that was sure to come when they faced Ma. She and Dorcas were right glad to see them return, and Ma didn't get mad about Lafait staying with the Utes; but still you could see she had a thing or two on her mind.

Major and Jude rattled away about what they had in the blankets on the pony.

'You done real well,' Ma said. 'I'm proud of you.' When they started to carry the stuff inside, she said, 'You can leave it be for a while. You're lousy, ain't you, both of you?'

Major and Jude looked at each other.

'Some, I guess you might say.' Jude wriggled a little.

'Some is quite a bit,' Ma said.

They slept out in the grove for two nights until Ma was satisfied that they had got rid of all their little visitors.

CHAPTER THIRTEEN

In a way it was the shortest winter Major ever spent in the valley. The snow came early but it never lasted long on the meadows, although the mountains grew solid white and stayed that way until April. Until the snow grew too deep in the timber, they hauled poles to build fences. Fawn and Steuben had a snug shelter in the cottonwoods and they never wandered farther than the meadows. The two ponies, which Jude named Warty and Smoke, were kept in a corral at night and turned loose to forage during the daytime. They soon learned that they had a good home and the Whitlocks forgot their fear about the ponies striking out to rejoin an Indian camp somewhere.

The Indians were gone. Some of them had ridden up the Ute Trail to winter in the warm hills near Manitou Springs near the base of Pike's Peak, and others had gone somewhere down the Arkansas. Lafait, who had spent two weeks hunting with them after the gathering at

Goodwin's place, said he saw no reason why he shouldn't have stayed with them all winter. It was no secret among the boys that Jude had had himself a time with some of the Ute girls, and Major guessed he wouldn't have minded some of that fun himself, since he'd got lousy anyway.

Goodwin didn't forget his idea about having Jude learn to read, and Ma agreed with him. She said the whole family, including herself, might as well learn to read and write a little, since they'd have to listen to the lessons anyway. Jude was all for it. Dorcas was interested too, mainly because Bessie McAllister could read. Lafait declared the whole business sounded to him like a mortal waste of time.

The Whitlocks had only a Bible, with print so small that it was hard to make out by candlelight. Goodwin brought up the only book he had, a brown-covered volume called *The History of the American Privateers* by a man named Coggeshall. The only reason Goodwin had the book was because one of his ancestors had been a sailing master and was mentioned in it.

'The first thing, I suppose, is to learn the ABC's,' Goodwin said. 'After that—well, after that, you sort of pick up words from the sounds the letters make. Major can show you.'

'Yeah.' Major would rather have been out building fences. About all he could remember

190

at first of Cousin Jonas' teaching methods was the rap on the head with the stick. Before the winter was over he knew why Cousin Jonas had used the stick.

It had been a funny thing, him learning to read and write. Cousin Jonas, barely known to only a few of the older Whitlocks, had been a school teacher and a sort of lawyer over in Virginia. One time he got a man off in court for stealing pigs, when everybody in the country, including Cousin Jonas, knew the man was guilty. Some of the kin of the man who had been robbed of the pigs didn't care about such goings on in court, so they burned down the schoolhouse where Cousin Jonas lived and shot at him a good part of the way across the Cheat Mountains.

He got to Kentucky just when the Hubbells were having a little trouble with the Weldons. Danged if Cousin Phleg Hubbell didn't up and shoot Cousin Jonas the very day he arrived mistaking him for some kin of the Weldons. You couldn't much blame Phleg because Cousin Jonas did look a little like some kind of flatlander cousin to the Weldons.

That was when Cousin Jonas spent most of the winter with the Whitlocks, getting well, cussing, hitting Major on the head with a stick and teaching him to read and write.

After three minutes as a teacher, Major had to allow that a stick made a lot of sense. He started right in with the story of the privateers.

'What's them?' Jude asked.

'How do I know?'

'You're the teacher.'

'Well, I don't know everything that's written,' Major said.

'If you can read, you ought to.'

'Damn it, I *can* read, but there's things I don't know about.'

'How did you know the word then?'

'Jesus Christ! Shut up!'

'That's a good idea,' Ma said.

Major shifted to the Bible. At least he had read that and wasn't so likely to get confused with words like privateers. 'We'll start with the letters, like Goodwin said.' The Whitlocks leaned close, peering over Major's shoulder. 'Now this here is an A.'

'That's easy,' Lafait said. 'It looks like an Indian lodge with a band around the middle.'

Major felt that he was making progress. 'Now this here is a little A.'

'You sure?' Lafait asked. 'It don't look nothing like the lodge.'

'It's the same, only—'

'The hell it is,' Lafait said.

'They're the same, I tell you! One's a capital and the other's a little letter.'

Lafait shook his head. 'They ought to look alike then. Even a baby looks like a man, only smaller. You trying to mix us up?'

'No! If you *write* an A, it looks even different again.' Major demonstrated with pen and ink and the tablet Goodwin had left. 'See there?'

'Three ways to make just one letter.' Lafait shook his head. 'It don't make sense.' He put his finger on a capital Q. 'That looks like a possum with his head ducked. Where's a little one?'

Major showed him a small Q.

'That don't look like no baby possum.'

'It sure don't,' Dorcas agreed.

'See there?' Lafait went to his bed and lay down, as if he had proved the worthlessness of the whole effort.

'No, you don't,' Ma said. 'You ain't getting out of learning something just by starting a quarrel. You come back here to this here table.'

'Ain't no use,' Lafait said. 'There's too many ways to read and write. Think how mixed up the Indians would be if they had three different signs for everything.'

'We ain't talking about Indians!' Ma said.

Major closed the Bible. 'I don't think it was a good idea to try it in the first place.'

'It would have been easy if you knew what you was trying to do,' Dorcas said.

'I quit.' Major shook his head.

'No, you don't.' Ma shook her head too. 'Just don't try to do everything at once. Go easy and slow.'

'Let's start with just one kind of letter,' Jude said. 'How many are there altogether?'

'Twenty-six.'

Lafait groaned.

'We'll adze some poles down smooth and write the letters with charcoal. I'll peg the boards to the wall and you can point to each letter with a stick.' Jude was ready and eager.

That would help, Major thought, and he'd wind up with a stick in his hand after all. He began to remember how Cousin Jonas had made him learn combinations of letters that didn't make sense, only sounds. That lesson had been pounded into Major's head until he was able to figure out and say almost any ordinary word, though often not understanding its meaning.

He nodded to himself. 'Sounds. It's the sounds...'

Lafait sat up quickly and grabbed at his belt, where he carried his pistol when he was out of Ma's sight. 'What sounds?' He looked toward the door.

Major began to laugh. 'The sounds words make!'

Ma watched Lafait with a narrow look. 'You got a pistol hid around here somewhere, young man?'

'Yep,' Lafait said, big as you please. 'I got a place fixed for it under the roof of the ox shed.'

'Uh-huh.' Ma nodded. She turned away from Lafait and looked down at the table. 'You might as well bring it inside, Lafait. Since you got it, there's no sense in it getting rusty or stole by somebody.' You could see she didn't like it but was thinking there wasn't much she

194

could do about it. 'That's what comes from stringing with Indians, I suppose.'

Lafait went out right then and got his pistol. Ma never did say any more about it, and since she'd hinted that it had come from the Indians, her sons were willing to let it go at that.

There were weeks of cold and wind when the tall, curled hay sticking above the short-staying snows on the meadows twisted crazily and made whispering noises. It was no joy to be outside on such days, but Major stuck stubbornly to the fence building. His brothers helped him, more because they hated to stay inside than because of any other reason. Major watched the mountains every day. The cold hadn't run long enough yet, he said, to make furs prime.

Shivering in the wind as they built the fence, Jude said, 'If I had a fur it'd be prime right now, I'll tell you.' All their faces were dark from the cold. Their hands were scarred and rough from work, and their eyes and noses ran in the biting wind.

They stayed with the work until all the poles they had hauled were used. 'It'll take one million years to fence this land,' Lafait said, for when they had used all the poles, less than one half of one side of the land was fenced, starting from near the house and running toward the bleak pile of rocks that was the southwest corner.

'We'll finish it next summer.' If the wagon

held together, Major thought.

During the evenings Major taught. There were times when he didn't want to, but Ma never let up. The long adzed plates pegged to the logs grew until one wall was almost covered with them, charcoal marked with capital letters, small letters, combinations of letters and simple words. Major used a willow stick as a pointer. At first he broke two or three every night, whacking them on the table because of stubborn arguments with Lafait, until he learned that Lafait was cooking up silly problems just to see Major lose his temper.

After that Major tried to pay no mind when Lafait made animal howls and wails out of the combinations of letters that all the Whitlocks chanted together. It looked like Lafait was resisting learning as hard as he could but he picked up considerably before the winter was over, although all his writing thereafter, except his name, was made print style with small letters; right from the start he ignored capitals.

Ma was the one that surprised Major, until he realized that day after day she had heard about everything Cousin Jonas had said when he was teaching Major, and now a lot of it came back.

Jude made shallow writing boxes with canvas bottoms. With sand sprinkled lightly in them, a finger stroke marked through to the canvas, which was stained brown with deer blood. A shake of the box wiped out everything and returned the sand to a clear writing surface. On these crude slates the Whitlocks learned to write. Often as not Lafait was dabbing out a picture of a deer or a bear when he should have been making words, but still he learned. Jude just naturally soaked up everything that came his way, while Ma and Dorcas were steady and careful.

Time after time Major was baffled by his own ignorance but he always admitted the fact, and then they had to wait until Goodwin could settle the troublesome point.

The lessons went on even after Lafait left to go trapping. Jude, too, was gone a great many evenings, staying at Goodwin's place, where Goodwin was teaching him arithmetic and things about directions and the use of a compass.

When visitors stopped by, Bill riding down from Indian Creek, or Toby McAllister and Bessie, or some of the Pilchers, Ma always tried to get them interested in the work. Major figured it was because she didn't want things interrupted by visiting. Bill tried a little but he said he reckoned he was too dumb to learn. Toby spent his time sitting next to Dorcas and dabbing away in one of the extra boxes Jude had made, but Major could see he wasn't learning much. None of the Pilchers even tried.

Bessie could already read and write but she didn't make any show of it. She sat next to Jude when he was home and acted like she didn't know any more than anyone else. More often than not she stayed all night when she came, and although Dorcas still said bitey things about her, Major noticed that they were becoming pretty good friends. You could hear them giggling and whispering together in the loft long after it was time for everybody to be asleep.

When they tried to tease Jude about Bessie, he'd grin and say, 'Sure, she likes me. I can't say as I blame her, either.'

Before Lafait left in the dead of winter to go trapping, the Whitlocks had read aloud *The History of the American Privateers* and the Bible. From Goodwin they knew now what a privateer was. They took turns reading, sometimes stumbling and overrunning punctuation marks, sometimes laughing at each other, sometimes growing furious at each other's jibes.

Major gave them all he had. After that it was up to his pupils to go ahead or to rest where they were. Jude lit into learning like he was building something. He pestered Goodwin with endless questions. He scoured the country on Warty to borrow reading material. From the Burnines he borrowed one by one the six books they owned, and read them all before spring.

Bill Gifford brought a prize bundle one day, a dozen newspapers from various parts of the country. Some of them were old and worn from much folding, as if they had been carried in someone's pockets for a long time; but there were two copies of the *Rocky Mountain News* not yet a week old. Since Bill couldn't read, he didn't know the difference in the dates. Ma asked him if he had been somewhere lately, and he said no he hadn't, that somebody had left the papers at his cabin last fall.

Ma didn't push him into a corner, but the Whitlocks knew what she was thinking. People that Bill didn't want to talk about had visited Bill's place lately. Back in Kentucky it had not been unusual for somebody who had been in a scrape to drift into the Whitlock cabin and stay a while, but they were generally kin who had done nothing worse than wound somebody with a bullet, or maybe used a knife a little careless in some strange county where the law folks had a narrow view of such goings on.

The Whitlocks had grown up believing that their kin couldn't be too awful bad, no matter what they done; and if they did something that was pretty bad, there was always a good reason for it. But it was a little different about Bill. He had been with Grove's gang when Pa was killed, and even if he had acted decent afterward, you still had to remember that people said Grove used his place as a hidey-hole, and so, although the Whitlocks liked Bill well enough, things like these two recent newspapers made them silent and thoughtful after he left.

Major guessed that he'd better go up to Bill's place one of these days and see what he could find out. He didn't like the idea but the Whitlocks would have to know for sure about some of the things they'd heard. If Bill was really thick with Grove, Major would just have to tell him not to come see Dorcas any more. . . .

The clear sunlight was warm out of the wind on the day Lafait declared furs must be prime. He got his sack of traps out of the ox shed and said with a grin, 'I'm going to luff-to and fire me a broadside at some varmints, and begat myself a few furs. Verily I say this.'

Major and Jude and Lafait were standing out of the wind on the sheltered side of the shed. They had to laugh at the way Lafait mixed up what he'd read in the privateer history with what he'd read in the Bible.

'You ought to trap beaver on Little Creek,' Major said.

'Hell with beaver.'

The wind stung Major's face as he peered around the corner of the shed. Up there on the mountains the snow was blowing six ways from the middle. 'It's a long ride every day.'

'Ain't riding. I'll walk, and I'm going to stay up there.'

'With Bill?' Jude asked.

'Nope. Just here and there, once I get my traps strung out.'

'You'll freeze your ass off!' Major said.

'No, I won't. I ain't tramping along no tame

crick catching beaver. I want something wild and tough.'

When Lafait made up his pack Ma kept shoving food at him, but he wouldn't take much, mostly a little flour, salt, and some bacon. He didn't short himself on shot and powder for the long rifle.

They all went outside to see him off.

Lafait didn't hesitate. 'I won't be too far away,' he said, and headed for the south hill. He went around the start of the fence and up the hill and struck out straight for the mountains. The blankets he'd won from the Utes were tied on top of his pack. The long gun was aswing at his side, and he was wearing Pa's old coonskin cap.

Goddamn, he looks like a little boy, Major thought; but he knew it wasn't so, he was only thinking back to a sturdy, square built youngun who was gone forever. Long after Jude and Dorcas went back to the cabin, Ma and Major stayed on in the bleak wind that stiffened their faces and made their eyes run.

Ma's look kept shifting from the figure growing smaller on the long run of the hill to the snow blowing wildly on the mountain she hated.

'He'll be back,' Major said.

'This time—and now and then at other times.' Ma's shawl fluttered on her shoulders as she went back to the cabin. She stopped at the door to wipe the wind moisture from her eyes before she went inside. Major guessed he'd always known it; Lafait was her favorite. Maybe because he was more like Pa than any of the rest of them.

CHAPTER FOURTEEN

Scattered all through the cottonwoods close to the Burnine place were the lodge poles of the Utes, who had used the grove as a camping place long before white men came into the country. Carl Burnine, a Texan who was the first settler in the valley, never disturbed the poles, and he always welcomed the Utes back every summer when sometimes as many as two hundred of them camped at his place.

Jude and Major rode past the skeleton framework and on to the small cabins where Burnine lived with his wife, two small sons and two daughters. Five long-snouted, vicious dogs charged out to greet the Whitlocks. Warty kicked one of them rolling and then all of them withdrew even before Burnine came out of the house to shout at them.

He was a short, wide, dark man with cold gray eyes. Shad McAllister said he'd been a Rebel colonel who had pulled out in disgust after things went to hell in Texas following the war. If Burnine held any grudges about the fighting, Major didn't know about it, for all the

Burnines had been friendly to the Whitlocks from the first, although Burnine knew that Pa had been a Union man.

'Put your ponies ahind the corral there and come in,' Burnine said. 'This is a day to freeze the ears off a brass monkey.'

Inside, he poured the Whitlocks whiskey. The first time, Jude, who hated even the smell of whiskey, had nearly strangled, but he'd learned to sip away real easy after that. Major could take a drink at a gulp, like water.

'You boys just ramming around?' Mrs Burnine asked. She was short and heavy like her husband, and she was generally full of cheerful jokes and drawling stories.

'That's about it.' Major watched Susan, the oldest girl. She was about Dorcas' age, with straight black hair and eyes the color of her father's, only not so cold and settled like. Jake McAllister fancied Susan considerable and came a-visiting at least once every week. Major guessed if he didn't live so much farther away, he might be over here more often himself.

'You boys catching up on your work?' Burnine asked.

'Not lately.' Major told him about the fencing they had done, and about Lafait going trapping. He had something else on his mind and he was wondering how to get at it easy. 'I guess the winter slows everything down, including men like Cy Grove.'

'Not much,' Burnine said. 'They was two

stages robbed in South Park a short while back. That was Grove's work.'

'How do you know?' Major wondered about those Denver papers Bill had brought to the Whitlock place.

'I just know.' Burnine gave Major a hard look. 'That Bill Gifford still hanging around your place some?'

'Some,' Major said uncomfortably, for Gifford was the subject he had come to talk about, although he hadn't expected Burnine to get at it so quick.

'I wouldn't have him here,' Burnine said. He glanced at his daughters.

'He acts all right,' Jude said.

'Yeah.' Burnine changed the subject to cows. Some of the coldness went out of his eyes when he talked about how well his hundred head was doing.

An hour later the Whitlocks rode down Little Creek to see the McAllisters. Jude was in a hurry to get on to Goodwin's because Goodwin had promised to let him do some practice surveying with his compass. Jude wouldn't have stopped at the McAllisters at all but Major said it wouldn't be polite for him to ride around the place, and besides, Bessie would feel put out.

'She don't worry me none,' Jude said, 'not like the way Susan Burnine gets to you. Sometimes you didn't even hear what her Pa was saying. Now that's a funny thing, you was going to die because Malinda got away, and then a few months later—'

'She's a fine girl, Susan. When I get the time I just might up and marry her.'

'You better warn Jake McAllister about that. Them McAllisters don't wait to get time, they just go ahead.'

They ran onto Toby almost a mile from the McAllister place. He had already laid up a few logs of a small cabin and was chopping more cottonwoods. He was glad to see them, but you could tell that every moment he was idle was fretting him. 'I took up this land, all along the river toward the Burnines,' Toby said. 'I'll have me a cabin here in a few days more.'

'You going to live here?' Jude asked.

'Naw. Not much, that is. I'll stay home mostly, but the cabin will prove I'm squatting on the land.' Toby was chopping hard again before the Whitlocks got started away.

'Them McAllisters—' Jude shook his head. 'If work will do it, they'll own the whole country in time. What good is owning a piece of land that keeps you held tight to it?'

That was just what Major had feared, but this was the first time Jude had come right out with it. 'What do you *want* to do when you're growed up, Jude?'

'Hell, I'm growed up now. I want to build me something—like a bridge that runs from one mountain to another. I want to make something real big and strong and pretty. I want to go from one place to another, doing something, not to stay in some little old valley watching hay grow.'

'Just running around ain't no good.'

'I won't be just running around. I'll know what I'm after—once I see it.'

The valley was wild and lonely, with only the square of young cottonwoods that marked the McAllister place showing that white men were settled here. The tall trees and the dense willows that were to grow along ditches built in Major's lifetime were not here now on the benches above Little Creek, so Major could see without obstruction across the miles of meadows and sage to the steep tumbled piñon hills on the north side of the Arkansas.

It made him lonely to think of Jude going away into the vastness that lay unknown behind the hills and mountains; but Jude would do it when the time came, with a grin and a good-bye wave, with his mind leaping ahead to dreams that were beyond the other Whitlocks. '... Not to stay in some little old valley watching hay grow...'

Well, that was good enough for Major. Maybe it was the best he could do. As he rode on toward the McAllister place he was suddenly discontented, unsure of himself. He was a young man and maybe he was missing great, exciting things by staying in Deer Valley. The Whitlocks had held land for generations in Kentucky, and it had grown poorer every year, until during the years of the war the young Whitlocks had made it pay meagerly only by terrible effort. Major had been real proud of what they had done, but Pa, returning from far places where he had beheld things his sons didn't know about, had seen that land as it really was.

Maybe Lafait or Jude, coming back to Deer Valley sometime in the future, would look upon the things that Major had worked so hard to make, and think he had wasted his time.

Hell, they ain't even left yet, Major told himself; I'm mourning ahead of time for things I'm making up out of my mind.

Shad and Jake McAllister were slamming up a calf corral. They said hello while they worked, and it made Major ache to see the way one or the other of them, unable to wait for help lifting a log, would grab it in the middle and strain and grunt to lift it in place by himself. They stopped to rest a minute only when they ran out of cut logs.

'How's the dam busting been going?' Jude asked.

Shad cussed. 'Them beavers build back faster than we can wreck the dams.'

'Trap 'em,' Jude said. 'Clean 'em out.'

'They breed too fast,' Jake said. 'There's two being born while you're skinning one. Next spring we'll get some black powder and blow up the high dam just below where Toby's building his cabin. Maybe enough water will come down to carry out everything below it.' He wiped his forehead on his sleeve. 'You happen to see Toby?'

Major nodded.

'He's got ideas, that boy has. He's spreading out. Guess you know he figures to marry up with your sister.'

'He acts that way, sure enough,' Major said. 'Bill Gifford, he's around our place quite a bit too.'

Shad and his son looked at each other.

'How about Bill Gifford?' Major asked. 'We don't know much about him.'

Shad looked at the ground for a spell. 'The old lady's got some coffee. Let's go over to the house.'

Jake picked up an axe and went to work.

Summer or winter, Major never was in the McAllister kitchen when it wasn't blazing hot. Mrs McAllister was baking bread. Bessie was sorting carrots out of a pile of sand in the middle of the floor. Mrs McAllister said, 'Howdy, you young Whitlocks. Glad to see you.' She slammed tin cups on the table and grabbed a huge coffee pot off the stove. 'How's your ma?'

Major had just time to say, 'Fine,' and Mrs McAllister was off again. 'Look at them damned carrots,' she said. 'The mistopher didn't bury 'em deep enough and they got nipped. Let 'em go for a spell, Bessie, and make eyes at Jude.'

'Ma!' Bessie protested. Her plump face colored as she rose, dusting sand from her hands.

'Maybe you better try Major,' Mrs McAllister said. 'That Jude, he don't get rattled none at all by girls. I remember when the mistopher was his age—'

'For Christ's sake, shut up a minute, Katy,' McAllister said. 'Major just asked me about Bill Gifford.'

Mrs McAllister got her pipe from the top of the warming oven and sat down at the table beside Major. 'Well, what did you tell him?'

McAllister raised his cup in both hands and made a slurping sound. 'Nothing.'

'Of course, of course.' Mrs McAllister lit her pipe. 'Bill Gifford ain't no good. Oh, maybe he don't exactly run everywhere Grove's bunch of murderers do, but he treats 'em big as kings around his place. I wouldn't be surprised but what there was thousands of dollars of buried gold and jewels around his place.'

'Oh hell, Katy!' McAllister slurped again.

'Why not? They've robbed everybody from Betsy to Besheba. They've—'

'From Beth to Besheba, Ma,' Bessie corrected.

'From hell to breakfast then! Does that suit you any better, young lady?' Mrs McAllister yelled. 'Tell these boys about that time you were up there, Mistopher.'

'No,' McAllister said.

Mrs McAllister looked at Major. 'He quit work and brought you to the house so I could tell it, so I will.' Her story was that her husband had happened by Gifford's place one day when his corrals were full of stolen horses from South Park. McAllister had even recognized a two-year-old bay he'd sold that spring. The cabin and the trees behind it were swarming with Grove's men but McAllister had pretended not to notice anything. He'd visited a minute or two with Bill and ridden away.

'There you are,' Mrs McAllister said. She puffed on her pipe. 'I'm glad you finally asked. Now you can tell that Bill Gifford to stay to hell away from your sister.'

She made it sound real simple. Jude and Major talked about it when they rode away. 'Maybe it ain't so,' Jude said. 'Sometimes the looks of things fool people.'

Major didn't doubt McAllister's story, even though the mistopher had let his wife do the telling. He didn't go on down to Goodwin's store with Jude, but turned across the hills and went home.

Ma came out to the corral when he was putting Smoke inside. She was wearing the Army greatcoat and her skirts were flapping as she helped Major rustle some hay. She asked about the Burnines and the McAllisters and then she said, 'Bill was here today.'

'Yeah?'

'He asked me about marrying Dorcas.'

'What'd you say?'

'I put him off. He knew why.'

'Did he get sore?'

'No. I wish he had. He said he'd just wait a spell and the next time he'd ask Dorcas herself.' Ma shook her head. 'She's took with him. She'll say yes in a holy minute.'

'Can't have it,' Major said.

'The more fuss any of us makes against Bill, the more she'll be determined to marry him. Just remember that.'

Major told her what Burnine had said about Bill and what the McAllisters had said. 'I guess I'll go talk to him direct. That's what I should've done in the first place, instead of going around asking people what they thought about him. All this time I've sort of liked Bill, but now—'

'I reckon it's a good thing you did go about asking folks what they thought of him. If he marries your sister, no matter what he turns out to be, there's one thing I'll still never be able to get out of my head.'

'Yeah,' Major said, 'I know.' He turned toward Smoke. 'I'll go see him now.'

'No. Wait till morning. It's better to let things like this roll around in your head for a spell. Tomorrow you can find Lafait and take him with you.'

During the evening Dorcas had nothing to say. She hummed to herself while she was washing the dishes. Afterward she sat by the fire in the rocker Jude had made for Ma, just looking at the flames and now and then smiling about something. It fair tore Major apart to think of his sister throwing herself away for a man who might be no good at all.

Tarnation! Why didn't girls have sense enough to pick good men when it was time to get married! There were worse fellows than Luke Pilcher, even if he did come from an ornery, loud-mouthed family; and Toby, though he had the McAllister habit of working like a horse all the time, no doubt would make Dorcas a fine husband.

But Dorcas, she had to put her sights on a man who ran with bushwhackers, no matter how agreeable and polite he acted. It must be a fearful thing to be a real parent and have a passel of younguns to worry over.

CHAPTER FIFTEEN

It was storming on the mountains when Major set out the next morning to find Lafait. Clean down to the foothills the storm covered everything like dirty gray smoke, and Major had a feeling that he would be stumbling around lost as soon as he rode into the first aspens. The pony didn't like the looks of things ahead; it sniffed and tried to lag, but Major kicked it on and went straight into the great pall that blotted out the mountains.

It was not as bad as it looked. Fine snow, boiling and drifting, filled the air after the piñon trees began to thin away, but he could still see the valley behind him. He struck the stark and leafless stands of aspens and there the snow was heavier underfoot. There didn't seem to be much more of it in the air but now he could no longer see the valley.

He had an idea that Lafait's camp would be somewhere close to where they had seen frequent bear sign while cutting fence logs. Lafait was hell bent to kill himself a bear. Jude had told him they would all be snugged away in holler logs by this time, but Lafait had said there wasn't a holler log in the whole land big enough to hold a bear, so the chances were they had to stay out all winter in this country.

Sure enough, Major found a camp near the edge of heavy timber by a spring where they had cut poles the summer before. It was a cold, dead place now and it gave Major a bad feeling. Lafait had cut pine boughs and piled them up to make a shelter under a leaning dead tree. Snow had blown inside now. The place looked long deserted.

Deep in the snow the Indian pony humped its back as it turned to look toward the valley. Major waded around until, under the soft new snow, he felt an uneven hardness, like a trail where Lafait had come and gone when he was camped here. Maybe something had happened to him; but no, that wasn't likely. He hadn't left anything in this camp; he'd just picked up and moved.

The grayness was all around Major as he went north, the way Lafait's trail seemed to point. After a while he struck thickets of fallen timber where he had to get down and lead the pony. The lay of the country, narrow, steep gullies that forced him to follow certain patterns, led him to Lafait's second camp, another bough shelter set under the wide spreading limbs of a group of spruce trees. Major would not have seen it, for he was following along a small frozen stream where you could hear the water singing softly under the ice, except he found a place where the ice had been chopped away.

The hole had froze up again and again and it was solidly covered now but the chunks of ice that had been chopped away still made a little basin. All Major had to do was to feel out under the soft snow the trail that led away from the waterhole. It took him straight to the second bough shelter. It was another cold, deserted place, without even a scrap of patching from the long gun to show that Lafait had been here.

The trails that led away from it seemed to go in all directions. Major kept feeling around with his feet, but he couldn't find one frozen carcass of a skinned animal. Outside of elk

214

tracks and a passel of wolf tracks, Major hadn't seen much sign of wild things in the deep snow. Maybe Lafait had given up and gone lower. It would be just like him, though, to head deeper into the mountains.

It was well into the afternoon. Major couldn't go into deeper snow with Smoke, and he didn't have time to look for Lafait in the lower country—and still get to Bill's place today. He set out across country to go to Indian Creek; he knew where that was, at least where the end of it dumped into the Arkansas. It came from the west. He was going north, so he couldn't miss hitting it even if a terrible storm came up.

He struck Indian Creek three hours later, coming off a sage mesa where the wind was bitter, dropping down into narrow meadows thick-choked with cottonwoods. The gloom of restless snow was thicker, although it was much warmer in the trees. Up or downstream? Major guessed he was above Bill's place, so he followed the flow.

For a mile beaver ponds, frozen and snow covered, forced him to ride along the edge of the hill. Air holes around the huge mud and stick lodges of the beavers were the only openings in the ice. Against the snow the water looked deep and black.

At one place, rather than backtrack to find an easy way up the hill, Major put Smoke out on the snow and ice where a dam crowded clean against the hill. The pony knew what was underfoot; it felt its way careful like, and they were almost across when rotten ice broke without warning. Smoke went down so quick and hard that Major flew over his head. Major landed in a sprawl but he broke through the air-bubbled ice and fell into shallow water.

He staggered up with his breath shocked out of him. The pony's forefeet had dropped into a beaver run and the animal was struggling violently. It was on its feet and trying to climb the steep bank when Major grabbed the nose rope. Its legs were skinned and until the blood froze, the pony left red in the snow as Major led it on downstream. His clothing was frozen stiff. The wind moaning in the tops of the leafless cottonwoods felt ten times colder than it had been before.

He came unexpectedly to Bill's place. One moment he was in the aspens, head down, walking stiffly, and the next moment he was against a corral with a rough pole shed across one end. On beyond was a cabin with a dull glow of light showing through an unchinked place between the logs. Major fumbled the gate poles back and put Smoke in the corral. It was then he saw that the shed held five horses.

It was a lot bigger corral than Bill needed, unless he had stock that Major didn't know about. Dimly seen against the trees across the meadow was an even bigger corral.

Major went on to the house. He remembered

to call out just before he reached the door, and then he went inside.

It wasn't real bright but for just a little bit, after the heat and the smell of tobacco smoke and the strong odor of men hit Major, he couldn't see very well. He saw two candles on a rough table, with a man's hand resting close to one of them.

'Hellsfire, it's Major!'

That was Bill, standing at the table. His hand moved away from the candle. 'You look froze, Major.'

'Yeah.' Major could make out everybody then. There were three others beside Bill, and they all had pistols in their hands, or were just putting them away. The lean man against one of the bunks wasn't wearing a Union blouse now, and his sandy beard was gone, but there was no way to forget him ever. It was Cy Grove.

He hadn't forgotten Major either. They stared at each other a long time, and then Grove quietly slipped his pistol back into his waistband. 'He needs a drink, Bill.'

Major started to say he didn't need nothing from any of them, but he knew that wouldn't get him anywhere. He took the drink that Bill poured and then he moved over to a small cooking stove that sat on a rock stand so low that a person would get a crick in his back doing much cooking on it.

The whiskey blasted its way down his throat.

It made his eyes bulge but it began to warm him a little. His frozen garments were beginning to soften, to sag wetly against his body. Bill was bustling around, talking all the time. He shoved wood in the stove. He picked up the coffee pot and shook it. 'Empty. It's always empty. How'd you fall in the crick, Major?'

'Horse busted through a beaver pond.'

'Happened to me once. I damn near froze before I got a fire going.' That was a man called Limber Jim talking. He'd been there when Grove killed Pa.

Major had never seen the fourth man at all, a tall, beardy fellow with small, sharp eyes. That one went outside suddenly. He sort of slid through the doorway. Major thought, I hope he freezes sneaking around out there to make sure I came here alone.

'I'll make some coffee,' Bill said, 'and fry you some meat.' He dipped water into the coffee pot.

'I ain't much hungry.' Major was starved but he didn't want anything from this outfit. He'd seen all he wanted to know. What he needed now was a chance to say a few words to Bill and then he'd leave. He couldn't keep his eyes off Grove. Grove was just a man, and he didn't look near as mean and vicious as the picture of him Major had held in his head all this time; but there was no forgiveness in Major—and no forgetting.

He knew he'd shoot Grove dead if there ever

was a good chance. The sure way was to sight down on him from the rocks or from behind a tree, and knock him right off his horse with the buffalo gun.

Grove pulled a stool up to the table and sat down. He watched Major steadily. 'How's your brother doing with his traps?'

'I don't know.' So they knew Lafait was trapping.

Limber Jim said, 'That shirt'll dry faster if you take it off, bub.'

'It's doing fine right where it is.'

'Guess so, it's steaming plenty.' Limber Jim smiled a little as he glanced at Grove.

'Coffee pretty quick,' Bill said cheerfully. 'How's your ma, Major?'

'All right.'

'She expect you to be gone all night?'

'I won't be.'

'No use to go out in the storm in those wet clothes.'

'I'll be all right.'

'Seen Goodwin lately?' Bill asked.

'No.'

After that Bill sort of gave up on talking. Major held close to the stove. Pretty soon the fourth man came in, rubbing his hands. 'Storm's breaking a little, I think.' He lifted the coffee pot as he stood across the stove from Major.

'That's just starting,' Bill said. 'Leave it alone.'

219

It was a pretty big cabin but it was so crowded with bunks that it seemed small, and it was about as dirty a place as Major had ever seen. The blankets on the bunks were twisted and ragged, dirty dishes with meat scraps were shoved in a pile in the middle of the table, and the dirt floor was littered with cigar butts. Wood was piled along one end wall under a crooked box cupboard and saddles were laying along the other end wall.

It sure wasn't the kind of place that Major had pictured as the nest of wealthy robbers.

Major stayed till the coffee was boiled. He had a big cupful and it helped warm him up. His clothes weren't dry yet but they would have to do. Bill offered to lend him a buffalo overcoat. Major said he didn't need it. 'I'd like to see you a minute, Bill.'

'Sure.'

They went out together. Grove and the rest were talking about steamboating. It was close to dark now. Major found Smoke making himself at home with the other horses in the shed, chomping hay out of a long manger. Since he had no saddle he was ready to go as soon as he had the nose hitch on.

'Glad you come by,' Bill said, 'but you'd just as well stayed the night, unless you're figuring on going over to Lafait's camp.'

'You know where it is?'

'Sure.' Bill gave him directions. Lafait was camped about three miles south, in the piñons at the base of Buffalo Hill.

'Has Lafait been over here?'

'Not since he's been trapping, he ain't.'

Major said, 'It ain't going to work, about you wanting to marry Dorcas.'

Bill laughed easy like. 'I could see that on your mind for a long time—you and your ma. You've been listening to the talk around the country.'

'I don't have to, I've been here.' The wind was coming through the cracks in the shed. Major hadn't dried out completely and now he knew it for sure.

'Sure, they're my friends,' Bill said. 'They come by here and stay sometimes. What do you expect me to do—throw 'em out because they're a mite rougher than pious folks like the Burnines? Come right down to it, did you ever hear why Carl Burnine had to leave Texas?'

'I ain't interested in Burnine. It's you and Dorcas.'

'All brothers are the same. Nobody is good enough for their only sister.' Bill laughed.

'It ain't you so much, it's the people you're running with.'

'I don't run with them. I haven't been ten miles from here with 'em.'

'You were at Goodwin's,' Major said darkly.

'That was an accident about your pa. Grove didn't like it any more than you did. He felt bad about it.'

'He felt bad. Jesus Christ!'

'It's the truth. We all did.'

'That didn't help Pa any.'

'You got to believe me, Major. Your pa got sore and started taking Grove apart with his hands. Grove's a bad one to fool with. He—'

'I know what happened! All that's over. It's you and Dorcas we're talking about now. I guess you'd best not come to our place any more, Bill.'

'*You're* telling me not to?'

'Yep.'

'That beats all. You think some more about it,' Bill said.

'I've already done my thinking.' Major swung up on the horse. His damp clothes pushed against his legs and thighs. He rode away.

'You'd better talk to Dorcas about this!' Bill called cheerfully.

There was the rub, Major admitted. Dorcas was as hard-headed as any Whitlock. With the wind at his back he went down the valley.

He was walking and leading the pony long before he ever got close to Buffalo Hill. Parts of his clothes were frozen stiff again. The bottom of his pants made a thumping against his boots at every step. He went clean past Lafait's camp before he began to yell. Lafait's voice came back strongly on the wind a few moments later, and Major turned up into the piñons.

'Who's hurt?' Lafait yelled.

'Everybody's all right. I'm on my way back from Bill's.'

'Oh.' After that Lafait seemed to think it was nothing unusual for Major to be ramming around in the freezing night. 'Got me a cougar yesterday, the biggest cat I ever seen. He's been hanging around the deer herds and I knowed—'

'Hell with the cougar. Build a fire.'

Lafait had made a windbreak of poles and brush and boughs behind his hut, and the shelter itself was close held by bushy piñons. Once he had a fire going, the place began to look right comfortable. Major huddled over the flames and rubbed his hands. An elk hide frozen like a sheet of iron was pushed aside at the entrance to the hut. Inside Major saw the Indian blankets. 'I'm staying here with you tonight.'

'Sure.'

'I see you got an elk.'

'Right between the eyes. I was afraid to hit him anywhere else.'

Major flexed his stiff fingers. 'Trapping been any good?'

'Some. I got me wolves—they're smart. I caught five, six bobcats, and I got a passel of little wolves—I don't bother to trap them, I just shoot 'em. The cougar was my big catch. You hungry?'

'Not for any damn cougar meat.'

'I mean elk.'

'Then I'm hungry.'

Lafait began to chop with a small axe on the frozen loin of an elk which hung from the trees in pieces. 'Come to think on it, I am too, getting up like this in the middle of the night. Funny thing, I was going home tomorrow to get the horses to pack this elk in. I'll tell you for sure you don't carry one of these on your back. They're bigger dead than they are alive.'

'How long you been out here, Lafait?'

'Couple of weeks, I guess.'

It was nearer five. Lafait looked bigger, heavier, than when he'd left home. His face was burned Indian dark and his beard was really beginning to sprout. 'I seen your other camps back in the mountains.'

'Wasn't much to trap back there.'

They roasted chops on sticks, the frozen meat popping and sputtering as it thawed. While he was still eating the first one Major began to roast another one. 'Seen much of Bill?'

'He come by with another fellow one day.'

'I guess you know about that bunch, don't you?'

'It don't take much guessing, considering what Goodwin and others have hinted.'

'All right,' Major said, 'what do you think about Bill being thick with 'em?'

'I don't know as Bill's been with them in their devilment. He didn't pull no gun on me down there at Goodwin's that time.'

224

When Lafait was taken with a man, a rocking of the world wouldn't change his mind. It was a fine thing in him, and at the same time, it was to cost him dear all his life, particularly after he became a man whose name was known and feared throughout the West.

'Bill's thick as can be with a bunch of robbers and murderers,' Major said. 'Cy Grove is over there at his place right now.'

'I ain't surprised.' Lafait gnawed the last meat off his chop and tossed the bone into the darkness. 'He's been around there before.'

Major was angry. 'After what he done—'

'Don't I know what he done? Don't you think I started to kill him that night?' Lafait picked another loin chop from the stones of the firesite and worked a green stick into it. 'Last summer I had my sights on Grove for three hundred feet when he was riding across an opening above Bill's place. All I had to do was pull the trigger and he'd never knowed what hit him—and that would've been the whole thing that was wrong about it.

'Afterward, I told Bill about it and I told him to tell Grove. He did.' Lafait smiled. 'You know the saying about shooting being too good for a man. That's the way it is with Grove, but I want him to know anytime he comes into this country, he might be riding past a place where I'm looking at him through my sights. He ain't sure whether I'm going to pull that trigger or not.'

'Hell! You think that'll bother a man like him?'

'Yep, it will.'

Suddenly his own brother looked like a half wild man to Major, with some kind of darkness inside him that Major didn't understand. He guessed he'd be pretty uneasy himself if he knew a man like Lafait was always waiting for him somewhere. Major knew what he'd do in a case like that. 'He might decide to come after you, Lafait.'

'I'll be waiting for that to happen too. He done sent that Jeff over here to see what he thought of me, and I guess he's pumped Bill too.'

'And you still think Bill's all right?'

'You think Goodwin's all right, don't you? He sells stuff to Grove and his men. They've stayed at his place. That's where we first seen 'em, remember?'

'That's different,' Major said. 'Anyway, Goodwin don't want to marry Dorcas. Bill does. Ma and me are against it.'

'What does Dorcas say?'

'She ain't got no sense about such things!' Major shook his head. 'You'd want her living up there in that filthy place, with a bunch of outlaws coming in any old time?'

'That's mainly up to her, ain't it?'

'No! She don't know what she's doing.'

'You always was like an old mother hen,

Major. If Dorcas wants to up and marry Bill, I can't see you got any right to try and stop her.'

'He's no good! That's enough reason.'

'What do you do if she runs off to him—shoot her husband just to prove he ain't no good?' Lafait grinned.

'He wouldn't be her husband. They can't even get married proper out here in the wilds.'

'Old hen stuff again,' Lafait said. 'How does anyone get married where there ain't no preacher handy? Hell—'

'I swear you been running too much with those Utes.' Angry and puzzled because of Lafait's stand, Major tried to make a crime of the Indian business. 'How many woods colts you got started, Lafait?'

'All I could, you bet. I ain't no mother hen.'

'You sure ain't.' Major tried to shake his head sadly over Lafait's behavior, but right in the middle of it he began to grin. 'All this ain't getting us nowhere about Dorcas marrying Bill.'

'That's right.' Lafait rose and stretched. 'Let's go to bed. You know, I still got near fifty rounds left for my pistol. I can hit with it close up about like the long gun, but it ain't heavy enough. The other day I shot a little wolf on the run and it didn't even roll him. He just kept scooting till he dropped dead. Got to have me a .44, I reckon.'

'What for?'

'Why, for anything.'

227

Major tied the pony where it couldn't trample the shelter in case some varmint came prowling during the night and spooked it. He crawled into the shelter with Lafait. He guessed he ought to take his boots off but if he did, they would be froze so stiff in the morning he couldn't get them on. Lafait pulled the elk hide in place and it shut out the light from the dying fire.

When he began to warm up under the blankets Major could smell the different odors on Lafait, hides and animals, smoke and forest. The hut itself smelled of piñon needles and the pitchy, bleeding ends of cut branches.

'About Dorcas,' Major said, 'maybe we could talk to her and tell her about Bill.'

'Go ahead.'

'Ma ought to do it, I guess.'

Lafait grunted.

Major thought about it for several minutes. 'Maybe if we got both of them together, and then talked it over ... When you coming home, Lafait?'

Lafait was asleep.

Major listened to the wind breaking against the tough wall of boughs behind the hut. *Old mother hen ...* He smiled faintly and went to sleep.

CHAPTER SIXTEEN

On her seventeenth birthday Dorcas Whitlock looked at the world with considerable bitterness. Nobody but her even knew it was her birthday. That was all right for her brothers; more often than not they didn't know they were another year older until after their birthdays were two months past. But a lone girl on her seventeenth birthday ought to have some kind of attention, something beautiful to remind her that her life was slipping away. Then when she was an old hag of thirty-five, say, she could look back with bitter-sweet remembrance on the day when she was seventeen, alive, strong, loved by a man who was being denied her by her family.

She lay in the loft and listened to the wind fretting at the shakes. Ma was raking the ashes in the fireplace, breaking pitch splinters, blowing on the coals. Before the fire was pulling strong in the black throat of the chimney a little smoke would drift into the loft and Dorcas would watch it stream away through the holes where the shakes overlapped.

It was like something light and beautiful escaping from cruel captivity, from the clutches of a harsh family that denied its only daughter's right to love and happiness.

Who knew, or cared, that she was seventeen today?

The smoke came up and Dorcas watched it flee through the holes where daylight showed. Just her nose and eyes showed above the blankets, for it was bitter cold in the loft. Habit said she ought to get up and help Ma, and she always did without urging; but today was her birthday, forgotten by everyone, and so she wasn't going to stir until Ma climbed the ladder at least two times to call her.

She heard Major and Jude getting up. They went outside and she heard their voices later, thin in the wind, as they talked about some deadfall traps Jude had set for skunks. When they came inside, Ma had to run them away from the fireplace. It was much later when Jude got around to asking, 'Is Dorcas sick, or something, Ma?'

'No, she's fine. Don't talk so loud. Let her sleep.'

There, it took them half a day to realize she wasn't down there working her fingers to the bone as usual. Jude, you might have thought, would have noticed she was missing. Major, who acted like an old man most of the time, probably wouldn't have said anything if he had noticed she wasn't around as usual.

It was Major who was most set against Bill. Two weeks before when he went up to see Bill, he'd come back all stirred up, with arguments longer than a well rope against her having anything more to do with Bill. Even Ma had sided with him for a while, and then when she seen they weren't getting anywhere, she'd made Major shut up.

What did Dorcas care about the men who came to see Bill Gifford? She wasn't going to marry any of them, and nobody yet had proved to Dorcas that Bill was bad. Even if they did, she wouldn't believe it. Major was soured because he'd thrown Malinda away, so he didn't want anybody else to have any happiness. Well, they were in for a surprise, the whole bunch of them, even Lafait, who had been sort of on Dorcas' side. Lafait had given up living like an Indian and was now down at McAllister's trapping beaver.

Ma didn't climb the ladder and she didn't call, so Dorcas got up. She flipped her flannel nightgown off and scrambled into her clothes in a hurry. You didn't spend much time admiring yourself in this loft during winter.

Jude had edged as close to the fire as Ma would let him. 'Here comes the queen of Sheba, after sleeping all day.'

Major didn't say anything. He just looked at Dorcas like a solemn old owl-bird. The same cabin, the same smells, the same work—and nobody remembering it was her birthday. Right to the last, coming down the ladder, Dorcas had hoped there might be some little surprise. 'What spitey thing have *you* got to say now?' she snapped at Major, who blinked and looked surprised.

Dorcas went over to wash. She ought not to do a lick of work, seeing as this was her last day here, but from habit she began to help Ma. She wasn't quite as happy at the prospect of going to Bill as she thought she would be, and, to tell the truth, she was just a mite scared. There were a lot of things Ma would have told her, was she getting married; but running off the way she planned—Ma didn't know and so she hadn't told Dorcas.

Everything would be all right, though. She really loved Bill. At nights she dreamed he was holding her, and she could remember it all afterward too. He'd come down just once after Major had been to see him.

He was real polite when both Ma and Major told him not to come back again. He'd said if that's the way they were going to act, believing every wild rumor they heard, he guessed he wouldn't come back till they changed their minds. It like to broke Dorcas' heart, Bill acting so humble that way, but she knew it was because he loved her so and didn't want to start a lot of trouble with her family.

Out in the yard, when they had a chance to talk to each other alone before he left, Bill said, 'It just won't work, honey, me coming here. I'd wind up shooting Major.'

'But we love each other! You can't just stop—'

'Sure we do, honey.' Bill looked at her all

earnest and troubled. 'We won't be sneaky about seeing each other. You're too fine for that. There's only one thing to do.'

'What?'

'First chance you get, you come to my place. We'll light out to find a preacher, and once we're married, your family will just have to act different.'

The idea startled Dorcas. She'd always wanted a wedding like back home, with kin for miles around, the men whooping and getting drunk, the women laughing and giving advice, with the groom all happy but grinning sickly like because he knew the men were going to pull all kinds of tricks on him. Then afterward, everything would be wonderful and folks would leave you alone. That was her idea of a wedding, not just running off to a cabin she'd never even seen.

But she loved Bill so awful much, and so she said, 'I'll come as soon as I can get away.'

He gave her a smile and got on his horse.

Remembering back to that smile and the way he'd looked going away, straight and serious, Dorcas lost her fears about what she was going to do today. At noon the Whitlocks were all supposed to leave to go to the Sherman place for a dance that night. Only Dorcas wasn't going.

She and Ma were doing the dishes and tidying up, with Jude and Major outside somewhere, when Dorcas went to the table and

233

sat down suddenly.

'What's the matter?' Ma asked.

'Nothing much. It's just that time.'

Ma turned around slowly. 'You're some early.'

'I know it. I can't help that. I ain't going to that dance though, feeling the way I do.'

'Why, sure not, Dorcas. The boys can go and we'll stay home.'

'You ain't scarcely been out of here all winter, Ma. I won't have you staying home over nothing. If you won't go on account of me, then we'll both go on to the dance, no matter how I feel.'

Ma went to the window. She watched the wind blowing the light snow in crazy whirling patterns on the meadows. For a while she didn't say anything. 'You're real sure he's the man?'

Dorcas looked quickly at her mother. She might have known that Ma wouldn't be fooled. 'You're real sure Bill's the man?'

'He's the only one I'll ever want!' Dorcas said.

'Uh-huh.' Ma kept looking from the window. Tarnation, what was there to see out there? 'You aimed to go to him as soon as we left, didn't you?' Ma asked.

Dorcas jumped up. 'Yes, I did! You can stop me this time, but there'll be another time. You needn't think—'

'Hush. Nobody's aiming to stop you,

Dorcas. You've made up your mind, you're real sure about him, so there's no sense to fight over it. The boys and me will go on to the dance.'

'You're not fooling me, Ma? You really mean it?'

Ma nodded and smiled a little. Dorcas ran across the room to her. She'd never been a coddled youngun; Ma wasn't given to kissing and petting her children, but now it was wonderfully comforting to Dorcas to feel Ma's arms around her. Dorcas began to cry.

'Hush that.' Ma patted her back and stroked her hair. 'You're growed up now.' She was silent for a spell. 'I suppose you and Bill aim to light out up-country somewhere to find a preacher?'

'Yes.' Dorcas told her all about it. Ma kept nodding but she was looking out of the window again with a sort of sad expression.

'We'd best talk some,' Ma said.

'I know some things already. I overheard Lafait telling the boys about what he done with the Indians.'

Ma grunted. 'That's the man's side of things. Set down, Dorcas. We ain't got much time for what I've been putting off for years.'

*   *   *

Jude and Major were surprised when, just before dinner, Ma told them Dorcas wasn't

235

going to the dance. 'She don't feel well,' Ma said.

'She looks all right,' Jude said. 'What's the matter with her?'

'She don't feel well and she ain't going, but the rest of us will.'

Dorcas could see that Major was suspicious, but since Ma had done the talking, he took it for the truth. 'Well, then I guess we'd better have it now, huh?' Major said.

Ma nodded. Jude grinned and said, 'It's your birthday, Dorcas. I'll bet you forgot.'

It struck Dorcas real hard, after her thinking nobody knew how old she was or when she was born. 'I—I guess I did forget.'

Jude had built a little cedar box for her, with tiny hinges made from a scrap of brass. It was lined inside with dark blue velvet. 'You can put jewels in it,' he said, 'when you get some.' Major gave her ribbons, smooth, silky and beautiful. Most of them were some shade of green, which Dorcas didn't like, but she knew just what he had been thinking. Malinda had worn green ribbons in her hair and on her best dress. Dorcas couldn't look at Major for remembering the mean thoughts she'd had about him losing Malinda.

Lafait had not forgotten her either. From him there was a locket on a thin chain that was like a cool thread in her hand. With it was a printed note. *i maybe borro this backe forr a trapp chainne sumtime.*

236

From Grandma Ripley's chest Ma brought forth a gingham dress, the plaid material smooth and fresh and shining new. 'I had to measure from the old one. I think I left enough hem.' Ma was frowning, and she talked fast and stern, like the way she did when she was upset almost to crying. 'You scoot up in the loft and try it on. Help me get the dishes on the table, Jude.'

The dress was beautiful and it fitted. Dorcas kept running her hands down the front of it. She wanted to cry, remembering her bitterness when she woke up this morning. She didn't cry until she climbed down the ladder and stood at the bottom, shy and proud, and then Major said, 'By gosh, you *are* a pretty girl, Dorcas.'

Jude said, 'I don't see how you can stay home from the dance when you got a dress like that. Old Toby's eyes will fall out of his head when he sees you.'

Old Toby ... awkward and shy, but somehow as gentle and wistful inside as his sister Bessie. She was going to hurt Toby too, as well as her brothers, when she ran off to Bill; but they would understand in time. She loved Bill and she had to go to him. It was just that all this birthday stuff mixed her up and made it harder to deceive her brothers.

Dorcas held to Ma and cried again, while Major and Jude looked bewildered and embarrassed.

She couldn't stuff down one bite of dinner,

and she noticed that Ma didn't eat much either. In no time her brothers were up from the table and ready to get started. Dorcas wanted to kiss them goodbye and tell them it was on account of the presents; but she knew she'd start crying all over again, so she let them go with just a thanks.

Ma tied a shawl over her brown hair. She put on the blue greatcoat and an old pair of shoes. She had her best things in a little satchel Pa had brought home from the war. Ma was going to walk all the way to the Sherman place because she didn't have no faith in riding sidewise on a bareback Indian pony.

Ma was ready to go. The boys were calling from outside.

'Take Grandma Ripley's silver comb,' Ma said.

'Am I doing right, Ma?'

'I don't know. You have to find these things out for yourself. Come visiting as soon as you can, both of you.'

Visiting. That meant you didn't belong here any more.

'I will.' Dorcas was strong enough inside now. Like Ma, she realized that being married was a solid, lasting thing. You didn't go running back to your family because some little thing in the new life displeased you. You made your bed and slept in it.

It was a funny thing, Ma was old in years, but standing there in the greatcoat with the shawl over her hair, she didn't look old. She looked fine and strong, like she herself was young enough to get married again.

'Good-bye, Dorcas.' Ma went out.

For just an instant Dorcas wanted to run after her, but she steadied herself. She was all right; she was going to the man she loved.

She changed to her old linsey woolsey dress again. Quite calmly she went about cleaning up the table. Major had said Bill's cabin was a disorderly place. Well, that could be set right. It took a woman to spruce things up and make a cabin a comfortable, neat place to live. Dorcas knew she could do it as well as Ma, maybe even better because she could work without getting tired.

Oh, she could take care of the cabin well enough. It was the first night there that worried her. She just didn't know anything in spite of what Ma had told her. You didn't learn too much by listening; you had to get it by doing, like spelling out words in the sandboxes. She mustn't forget to take one of those boxes because she didn't want to have everything she'd learned about writing slip away from her.

It was time to go, but she was plagued by the thought of something undone, some little chore forgotten. She walked around the room slowly, knowing all the time that there was nothing left to do.

She changed again to her new dress, and over it put the heavy jacket that was too short in the sleeves. She tied a shawl over her head. The few things she was taking went easily into a tote sack. Walking outside was the hardest part of the trip. The wooden latch fell in place behind her and the latch string with the wagon bolt tied to the end of it swung and bumped a little against the door before it hung straight and silent.

Dorcas walked out to look around the corner of the cabin at the oxen shed. 'Good-bye, Fawn, good-bye, Steuben.' She struck out across the frozen meadows. The wind took her breath away as she climbed the south hill. She stopped to rest with her back to the cabin. Wind was blowing dry snow in long gusts on the mesa ahead. The bare ribs of the mountains were dark and harsh above the great snowfields lying in their hollows. Angry things, Ma called them.

Dorcas didn't look back. She walked on across the wind.

CHAPTER SEVENTEEN

It was something, the way folks busted loose and had themselves a time at the Sherman place. For a while Major couldn't quite get into the swing of things, and then Carl Burnine got him out in the barn with a jug; after that Major guessed he was about as lightfooted as anybody stomping around on the puncheon floor in the Sherman's big living room.

Everybody asked where Dorcas was and Ma told them she was home sick, and after that there wasn't much talk about it, unless it was out in the kitchen where the women congregated when they got weary of dancing.

There were men here that Major hadn't even known were around, mostly miners who had come down from the high country to spend the winter. Jude took up with them like they was old friends, and he asked a thousand questions about mining gold. Even Lafait had taken time away from his trapping. Major guessed that the McAllisters, or maybe Goodwin, had moved a mountain to make him come. He smelled some of beaver when he was close to the fireplace, but maybe not enough to run anybody out of the room.

At least Major didn't see anybody leave on account of him, especially Bessie, who was just about to give up on Jude.

Lafait was pretty disappointed because Dorcas was sick. It had been Lafait's idea, a long time before anyone else had even thought of her birthday, to have Goodwin bring some presents on one of his pack trips to Denver. He kept asking Major how she'd liked the locket, and was real pleased when Major told him he guessed it was her favorite of all the gifts.

'It was Jude's birthday too, Lafait.'

'That don't matter. He's a man.' Lafait

scowled. 'She ain't got a bad fever or something like that, has she?'

'Naw! You think Ma would have left her if she did?'

'She sure wouldn't.'

But you could see that Lafait was still a little puzzled about Dorcas. To tell the truth, Major was too, now that he'd had time to think on it; Dorcas wasn't one to miss a shindig because she felt a little bad. Major tried to find out something by watching Ma, but she didn't act like she was one mite worried about Dorcas.

Ma danced with Goodwin quite a bit. He wasn't wearing his dirty old buckskins now. In his black clothes, with his brown face all fresh shaved, Goodwin was a fine looking man. Major wondered why it bothered him to see him dancing with Ma, and both of them enjoying themselves. It was sort of unexpected, like finding out Shad McAllister was a fiddler. Who'd think that Shad, with his huge callused paws, could handle something delicate like a fiddle?

After a while Major stopped worrying about things that weren't easy to understand; they didn't matter too much, especially after he and Burnine made a few more trips to the barn.

Sometime during the evening he shouldered sort of accidental like into Jake McAllister when Jake was headed over toward Susan Burnine. Jake heated up right quick but Major just grinned and went on over to Susan. By

242

gosh, she was a prettier girl than he'd thought. One of these times after he had things in Deer Valley fixed up pretty good, with some cattle and hogs and other stuff, he'd get around to asking Susan to marry up with him. That's what he'd do, sure enough.

Susan eyed him close when they began to dance. She said, 'You better not try to drink with my pa, I'm warning you. Before long they'll be laying you away in the hayloft.'

'Not me. I'm a ring-tailed gator from down Natchez way. I can chomp a hundred pound catfish in one gulp and pick my teeth with his fins. I was borned on a mountain while the lightning was melting rocks. Nothing can get too hot for me. I'm a snorter from the canebrakes...' Major was a lot of things he'd heard from Uncle Lafe. He reeled them off and then he let out a whoop.

Susan smiled and shook her head. Lafait, dancing with Bessie, was startled to hear Major cut loose.

Major had himself a time. That's what he was here for. Let Jake McAllister stand against the wall and sulk.

From then on Major was a he-cougar on a downhill pull. He remembered, sometime later, having a little argument with Carl Burnine out in the barn when Burnine thought maybe Major had drunk about enough.

'Hell, I ain't started.'

'Every man's got to learn what he can hold, I
243

reckon. To tell the truth, I figured you for a kind of bluenose, Major, the way you acted at times, but you'll do.' Burnine leaned against a stall. He liked to do his talking around animals, leaning on a corral, or showing off a horse, or riding among cows. That's what he got started on now, cows.

Major said he guessed he'd wind up with a thousand of them, given a little time. Burnine started cussing when Major threw in a few hundred hogs just for old time's sake. Who the hell wanted to bother with a mess of rooting, grunting hogs? Major said they were real friendly things, once you got to understand them, but Burnine said he wasn't aiming to understand them. He stuck to cows. Major had another drink and allowed that he could reduce to a few sows if he had to.

Major didn't recall much about the fight he had with Jake McAllister. He remembered that the ground was awful hard and that once he got tangled up in a sawhorse and tried to hit Jake with it, until he realized the legs was froze into the ground. Everybody was having a whale of a breakfast about daylight when Major began to see straight once more. He was sitting beside Susan. Nobody seemed to think he had disgraced himself, and everybody was happy.

Jake was marked up some. Major couldn't tell how he himself looked but he knew he felt like he'd been dragged behind a wagon for about ten miles over rocky ground. It wasn't until he was on his way home with Jude and Ma that he felt free to ask what had happened.

'I guess you could say you licked him,' Jude said. 'Anyway, you was on top when Carl and Shad decided it'd gone far enough. Neither one of you could do anything but grunt by then. So you both went back and danced out the night and everything was fine.'

'You like to tore the Shermans' wood pile apart,' Ma said, 'flopping around like a couple of fighting badgers.'

Major wondered if they were making up stuff; he couldn't remember much from the time him and Burnine were talking about cows and hogs. Only twice more during his life was such a thing to happen to him. 'I feel awful,' he groaned. 'I think I ate too much breakfast.'

'I wouldn't be surprised,' Ma said.

Major was thankful that he lasted to get behind a hill out of sight of the Sherman place before his stomach revolted. He was feeling better when they came over the south hill above home. The first thing he noticed was the absence of smoke. 'Something's wrong!' he said, and started to kick the pony down the hill on the trot.

'No!' Ma said, so sharp it made Major stop and look back. 'Dorcas ain't there. She went to Bill. We'll talk about it after we get down there and have a fire going.'

She wouldn't say a word until the heat of the big fireplace drove the stale cold from the

245

cabin. Jude sat down at the table, dabbling in one of the writing boxes. He didn't like serious quarrels and he knew one was coming. Major walked around the room in a fury. Ma was standing in front of the fire, looking at them quietly.

'You knew she was running off to him!' Major said.

'I did.'

'And you let her go without saying anything.'

'I did.'

'Why?'

'I'm her mother.'

'That's just why you shouldn't've let her go!'

'The longer we didn't let her go, the worse it would've been for her,' Ma said.

'He's no good!' Major paced around the room. Jude dabbed away at the writing box with his head bent.

'Whiskey was no good for you last night,' Ma said, 'but you had to find it out yourself. Never was a Whitlock didn't learn the hard way. That ain't saying Dorcas and Bill won't get along all right. Maybe they will.'

'Sure they will!' Major shouted. 'He's a goddamn' robber and murderer, and Dorcas ain't got sense enough to know it!'

'Your yelling that at her didn't help none. She's got more sense than you think, Major.'

'How they going to get married? There ain't no preacher within—'

'Oh hush. I reckon they're searching out a preacher somewheres right now. There was no preacher around when your pa and me decided to marry, Major. You was three months inside me before we got to one.'

'Makes no difference. I'm going over there.'

'And what are you going to do when you get there?'

That was what was rubbing Major something fierce. If the whole business could have been prevented, like he wanted, there wouldn't be no problem about what he was going to do now; and if Lafait hadn't been so pig-headed about things, that would have been a mighty help too. 'Ain't much I can do now,' he growled, 'except make sure they get started to a preacher.'

'Won't that be fine—you standing with a rifle gun against them while the preacher marries them? That'll be something for Dorcas to remember all her life.'

Ma's words bit at Major's anger and made him feel foolish inside; but he had his head set and he wasn't going to quit now. 'Then I won't take no rifle, but I'm still going over there— right now.'

Ma nodded. 'I guess you mean well. You go along, Jude. Sometimes I think you got more sense than the whole family put together.'

They rode across the meadows and up the hill into the hard blast of the wind. Jude said, 'Looks to me like Dorcas has got a right to

247

marry him if she wants.'

'We'll make sure that's what *he* wants.'

'I like Bill.'

'You too, huh? I say he ain't no good, and you better believe it.'

Jude looked at Major calmly. 'You can't make me believe anything I don't want to believe. You ain't God or nothing like Him. So don't tell me who to like or what to think.'

'All this family does is fight!'

'That's all you been doing lately.' Jude grinned.

After a mile Major said, 'They just might have started toward South Park to find a preacher. Let's go to Pilchers first and see if they went by there. If they didn't, we'll go back to Bill's place.'

*   *   *

From the trees at the lower end of the meadows Dorcas looked for the first time at Bill's cabin. She didn't want to go there if a lot of men were around. To hear Major tell it, Cy Grove's bushwhackers were at Bill's almost all the time. There was more snow here than down in the valley proper; Dorcas' feet were cold and wet and her legs were freezing.

Smoke was coming from the cabin. Bill's horse was out on the meadow, but she couldn't be sure if there were others in the long shed behind the cabin. She stayed in the trees until

248

she was much closer to the shed, and then she could see that it was empty, so she struck out across the meadow and went straight toward the cabin. The horse threw its head up and trotted toward her eagerly. It knew her but it stayed out of reach of her hand.

The cabin was a sort of mean looking thing, with its low dirt roof and strips of rotting bark hanging from the logs. Dorcas was still some distance from it when the door opened and Bill stepped out with a rifle half raised.

'It's me, Bill!' Dorcas cried.

'Yeah, I didn't know till you came out of the trees.' Bill waited until she came up to him. He was smiling. 'I see you made it, finally.'

Dorcas was suddenly shy and scared. This was the moment for which she had waited so long. She pushed her shawl back. She stood there, young and straight and a little breathless, wondering why Bill was just smiling and watching her. 'My folks went to a dance at Shermans. I thought...'

'Sure you did.' Bill leaned the rifle against the doorway. He took Dorcas in his arms suddenly. 'You finally made it.'

Everything was warm and beautiful then and Dorcas knew she had made no mistake. After a time she said, 'Ow! Your whiskers scratch something awful.'

'You'll get used to that.' Bill picked up the rifle as they went into the cabin.

It was, as Major had said, the untidiest

boar's nest Dorcas had ever seen. The sourest odor of all came from cigar butts tromped all over the dirt floor. The mess didn't mean a thing; all bachelors probably lived like hogs. A day or two would make a big difference in the looks of things around here.

Bill sat down on a stool. He smiled at her. 'Take your coat off and make yourself to home.' He shook his head as if he couldn't believe she was here. 'So you finally made it! . . . Where'd your folks go, you say?'

'To the Shermans. They won't be back until tomorrow.' Dorcas hesitated. 'Ma knew I was coming here.'

'She did?'

'It was all right with her.'

'How about your brothers—Major?'

'He didn't know.'

Bill's eyes narrowed a little. He stared at the window for a moment, and then he smiled. 'Once we're married, what can he do, except bellyache a little? That's a right pretty dress, Dorcas. Come here.'

He swept her into his lap when she stepped toward him. He kissed her and his whiskers drove hard against the tender skin around her mouth. A scarey kind of warmth and excitement grew inside Dorcas and she found it hard to breathe. Bill's hands began to touch her where no man had ever touched her before.

Dorcas began to struggle suddenly and pulled away from him. It had been all right, all

250

right, she told herself—only he was sort of rough and hasty, and she was a little frightened. The walk hadn't tired her any but all the strain of leaving her folks had wearied her some.

'What's the matter?' Bill looked mad for a second, and then he grinned.

'It's daytime.'

'Hell, half the time it's daylight.' Bill started toward her.

Dorcas went to the stove quickly. 'I'll get something to eat. I'm terrible hungry.' She cast around wildly, looking for fixings. The fry pan was on the stove wood with hard grease in it, and the food seemed to be piled anywhere that was handy, some of it on the table, some of it on the wood pile, and some of it in a crookedy cupboard.

Bill went back to the stool. 'I guess there's no hurry. Go ahead and cook something. There's some deer meat hanging outside at the end of the cabin.'

Cooking brought back confidence to Dorcas, although she knew that when she got things straightened up a little, she could get a meal much better—and quicker, too. Sitting across the table from Bill, she felt more at ease, and it pleased her to see how well he liked her cooking.

'Take the first time you put a saddle on a horse—he's a little skittish, but once he's ridden hard, he forgets all about being scared.

251

You see what I mean, Dorcas?'

'I see what you mean, Bill—but I ain't no horse, you just remember that.'

He grinned. 'You'll be all right. I can tell that.'

Oh, so he thought he knew so all-fired much about women, did he? Dorcas' temper started to flare, but she held it down; this was no time to quarrel, him and her having their first meal together and all. She didn't know her ground well enough yet and she really didn't know Bill maybe as much as she'd thought. Give her a little time and she'd show him a thing or two.

'Where'd you get all the segars I seen in the cupboard?' she asked. Ten cents for each one, and there were three boxes of them!

'The boys left them. They had a-plenty.'

'What boys?'

Bill leaned back from his food. The narrow look came to his eyes. 'You know damn' well who I mean.'

'Cy Grove's bushwhackers?'

'They're not bushwhackers! That's all your ma and Major can think to call them. They're not bushwhackers.'

'Major called them robbers and murderers too.'

'We'll settle something right now!' Bill said angrily. 'I ain't going to listen the rest of my life to you bellyaching about my friends. Maybe they have killed a man or two when it couldn't be helped. Your brothers have come close to

252

that themselves, and they ain't been in this country a year yet.'

'Don't say nothing about my brothers.'

'As for robbing—Grove and the boys have done a little, yes. That don't mean anything. Half the stuff in this country is stolen. The Shermans got their start by stealing Indian supplies, until it got so bad the government switched to having Goodwin take care of the Utes. What does old pious Goodwin do? He hauls in the stuff for his store in government wagons, with a soldier escort, claiming it's Indian goods. Of course there's nothing so bad about robbing the government. Anybody that can does that.'

'Robbing anybody is still plain stealing,' Dorcas said.

'Sure! So how do you figure Goodwin is better than Cy Grove? Just because he's such a great friend of your ma's? Because he'd like to take up with her?'

'You keep your dirty tongue off my ma, Bill Gifford.'

'I didn't mean nothing. I'm just trying to tell you that everybody is a thief out here. You got to be to get along. Carl Burnine stole a whole herd in Texas and drove it up here when he had to leave the state.' Bill took a cigar from his pocket and lit it. 'Your brothers took up near five hundred acres of land, when they ain't entitled to near that much. What do you call that?'

'If that's true, they still ain't stealing anything from other folks and shooting them in the bargain.'

'They came damn' near shooting folks that tried to settle on that land. What's the difference? Don't try to be high and pious with me, Dorcas.' Bill punched the table with his finger. 'Cy Grove is my friend and he always will be. He does favors for me and I help him out a little now and then, so you may as well make up your mind you're going to see a lot of him and the boys while you're living with me.'

'I ain't living with you unless we get married.'

'We will.' Bill grinned. 'So that's what's bothering you? Tomorrow we'll light out for South Park to find a preacher.' He stood up, puffing a blue cloud of smoke from the cigar, looking down at Dorcas with his eyes smiling, with the you're-a-funny-little-girl expression that always made her feel shy and happy.

He'd talked so fast and hot about stealing that he'd sort of mixed the right and wrong of it up in Dorcas' mind. A man had to stick with his friends, she guessed, or else he wasn't much good; but she wished Bill's friends were some better than the ones he had. The thing of it was, he was the man she loved.

'I'll be gone for a while,' he said.

He was gone until almost dusk. Dorcas was grateful for the chance to get the cabin straightened up, and while she worked she was thinking ahead to the things that would have to be done to fix the room up a little. To start, the walls ought to be better chinked, and the stove ought to be set higher so a person wouldn't break his back leaning over it. Oh, there were a great many things that would have to be done, but she wouldn't tear into Bill to change it all overnight.

She scrubbed the table good and ran boiling water over it. She washed the grease scum from the cooking utensils and shined the outside of them. With a bunch of spruce boughs tied on a stick she swept the floor clean of its litter of twigs and food scraps and cigar butts and other trash. All the blankets on the bunks were dirty and twisty and they smelled of strong man odors, like Lafait when he came in from trapping.

The widest lower bunk had a tick mattress on it, filled with hay. When she took it off the poles to air it outside, she saw a mass of stuff piled under the bunk, rifles and pistols, expensive looking bridles, a silver trimmed saddle, and—why, there was a woman's hat under there, a velvety looking hat with fluffy feathers.

She moved some of the poles and picked up the hat. The feathers were all bedraggled and broken, but you could tell the hat was almost new and had been real fancy. She tried it on, wishing she had a looking glass. Then she took it off quickly and put it back under the bunk, and stood looking down at the strange assortment of things with a worried feeling that made her all uneasy. The crossbar on the end of a heavy gold chain was hanging from a leather tobacco pouch jammed in among the rifles.

Dorcas picked the pouch up slowly. It held three watches, two great silver ones as fat as onions and a gold one with beautiful marking on the outer case. Why, they must be worth hundreds of dollars! She put the watches back in the pouch and stuffed it away where it had been and went outside to get the mattress. Even when the bed was made it couldn't hide away from her mind the things she had seen beneath it.

She heard the clomp of hooves not long afterward. She ran to the door. Her breath came out in a long sigh when she saw it was Bill and not the men she had half expected to see. He had two horses now. She waited in the doorway for him.

His face was icy cold when he grabbed her and kissed her. 'I picked a gentle horse for you, Dorcas.'

'Where'd you get it?'

Bill smiled. 'Never mind. I don't keep everything I own right here in plain sight.'

'I—I'll fix something to eat.'

Right off, Bill noticed that the lower wide bunk had been straightened up. He walked over to Dorcas while she was putting wood in the tiny stove. 'What did you see under

256

that bed?'

'I didn't bother anything.'

Bill kept eyeing her sharp. He took off his coat and tossed it across the table. 'The boys now and then leave some stuff here for me to take care of for them. That reminds me, there's a real fancy saddle there that you can use tomorrow when we go to get married. The boys won't mind if we borrow it.'

He was so offhand about it that Dorcas tried hard to be relieved, but in the back of her mind she knew she couldn't swallow everything that came so easy and careless from Bill. If she couldn't believe, she had to overlook. What was that going to do to her in time, and just how much could she overlook?

Bill went to the shelf where she had put her things, the chest Jude had made, her folded clothing, the writing box. He smiled as he looked at the writing box. 'If that ain't the dangdest thing.'

'You'll have to get me some nice clean sand for it.'

'You won't be needing anything like this any more.' Bill tossed the box under one of the bunks.

Long afterward Dorcas had occasion to remember the incident with painful clarity, but that was in the happy darkness that veils the future.

That night in the warm gloom of the cabin she crossed the barrier of fear and uncertainty into womanhood. Bill was not as rough and hasty as she had feared he would be, but neither was he entirely gentle. Such things, Ma had said, were to be worked out over the long haul. Wildness and forgetting were enough at the moment, enough for the whole night perhaps, but there were still low moments between the high ones when Dorcas' mind worked steadily on practical lines.

A marriage couldn't be forever a mixture of wild, warm feelings that exploded in a heated embrace of bodies. Ma had tried to explain that there were years of looking at a man, watching him eat, seeing him in strength and weakness, learning about him until you knew what was inside him. Already Dorcas was understanding a little of what Ma had tried to make clear.

Love wasn't just wanting somebody as bad as she had wanted Bill. The mystery and fear were gone from that now, and no miracle had come from the mating to chase away the dark shadow of blemish on Bill. A fact that Dorcas had tried to walk around all afternoon still stood in her way: Bill Gifford was a no-good thief.

Lying awake beside him, Dorcas faced that fact.

Why, Cy Grove and the other bushwhackers at least ran risks in their devil's work, but all Bill did was hide stolen things for them. And him saying that Mr Goodwin and the

Shermans and Carl Burnine—and even the Whitlocks—were thieves; all he was trying to do was make decent folks as bad as himself.

This was the man she would have to live with if she went away with him tomorrow to find the preacher. Maybe she could have abided an honest robber as a husband, or any robber, if she loved him enough. Major—damn him anyway—had been right; Bill wasn't the man for her. At least she had been full honest in making her mistake, so she felt no sneaky shame about it, except that it had been a mistake. In one way she was mighty lucky, for if she and Bill had been married right off— well, you didn't up and walk off from marriage as easy as she was going to leave this place in the morning.

She slept a little before daylight came through the cracks and outlined the miserable room. In spite of what she had tried to do to clean up the place, it was still a pigpen. She slipped out of bed quietly and dressed in the bitter cold. She stuffed her things in the tote sack and began to put on her jacket.

All frowsy-headed, Bill watched her from the bed. He said, 'I think you'll have to split some kindling. The axe is—' He stopped when he saw that Dorcas was paying no attention. 'Hey, what are you doing with the sack?'

'I'm gitting.'

'Going where?' Bill jumped out of bed.

'Just going. You ain't no good, Bill Gifford.'

259

He turned dark at the insult. 'How would you know? I'm the first man you ever had. What—'

'It ain't that I'm saying. You're a low down thief, and if there's anything I can't abide it's a low down thief.'

'Why, you miserable little ridge runner!'

Dorcas slung the sack on her shoulder and walked out, leaving the door open. Bill stood in the doorway in his bare feet, shouting at her as she left. She kept on going. 'You'll be back!' he yelled.

Dorcas knew she never would.

She went down the snowy valley and turned over the cold hills toward the Pilcher place. She couldn't go home now. Ma had let her do what she wanted with the understanding that Dorcas would handle the whole thing, including mistakes. The whole thing had been a mistake, too, so Dorcas wasn't going crying back to Ma and her brothers. She'd do for herself. She guessed she could be just as tough as Lafait if she had to.

She *was* tough, too, of body and spirit. She wanted to go home, and because she couldn't she wept as she walked through the snow.

She was a mile short of the Pilcher place when Major and Jude came trotting on their ponies to meet her. Major jumped down and walked toward her and something he saw in her expression made him try to put his arms around her, but she backed away.

'You all right?' Major asked.

'Why wouldn't I be?'

Major and Jude looked at each other.

'Where you going, Dorcas?' Jude asked.

'None of your fat business!'

Major stood there like he was working up a terrible storm. He was pale and he was as angry as Dorcas had ever seen him, but he didn't blow up. He said, 'No use to visit the Pilchers. They're having one of their family fights and it might last for two days.'

'Who said I was going there? I suppose you asked all over the place if they'd seen me and Bill.'

'They don't know nothing about you and Bill,' Major said. 'We lied some and asked if they'd seen Lafait, and they said they hadn't seen anybody go by in the last few days, so we figured you were still at Bill's.'

'That's none of your business either.'

'Since you done left him, it is—a little.' Major wasn't near as mean and bossy as Dorcas had thought he was before she ran off to Bill. 'You did leave him, didn't you?'

'Yes. He's a no-good thief.'

Major didn't say I told you so. He looked at Jude and said, 'You take her home. I'll go see Bill.'

'He ain't worth wasting your breath on,' Dorcas said.

'I can spare some.' Major was awful quiet.

'I ain't going home.' Dorcas shook her head.

261

'Ma won't have me now. She give me my chance, so I won't ask her to—'

'What are you talking about? Ma never meant no such thing as you couldn't come home, no matter what you did.' Major shook his head. 'You thought that up yourself.'

'*No matter what I did!* I ain't ashamed, I'll tell you that.' Dorcas stood proud and angry before her oldest brother. He wasn't going to make her feel like she'd been a bad woman, because she hadn't been one. A trashy, filthy mind was what made you bad, not the mistakes you made in honesty. 'I ain't no Mary Magdalene.'

Major stood there quiet in the snow. 'All I tried to say was we love you and want you to come home.'

'Come on, Dorcas.' Jude took her hand. He was so gentle and appealing that Dorcas wanted to cry.

Jude helped her on Warty and led the pony away. Dorcas looked back and saw Major going swiftly up the trail she had made in the snow on her way from Bill's. He never told Dorcas what he said to Bill, but no word ever came back to her that Bill had given away her secret.

She went home to family love. Ma didn't try to pry and poke at her but let her tell her story when she was ready, and when Major came home from seeing Bill, he had nothing to say except that the wind seemed colder than usual.

Still, in a corner of her mind Dorcas always held a speck of resentment against Major because he, her brother, had been right when she had been wrong.

CHAPTER EIGHTEEN

Lafayette Whitlock—he liked the looks of his first name, and always wrote it correctly, though he couldn't abide the sound of it any other way than 'Lafait'—got into his first pistol fight on a warm day of false spring when he was about three months past eighteen. It was not his fault but it served to start him out on a long string of pistol fights that ran till he was past sixty.

He was alone at Goodwin's store one day when Goodwin had lit out for Denver with his pack horses. Lafait had trapped a heap of beaver on McAllister's place, working clean down the creek to Goodwin's before things slowed up. Maybe two hundred dollars worth, which was really stacking money up. Goodwin had taken the skins to Denver, where he was going to get Lafait a .45 pistol and five hundred rounds of ammunition. That was all Lafait figured he needed, and if there was any money left, Lafait guessed he'd just give it to Ma, even if she had thrown out the painter skin he'd put on the floor by his bunk at home. She said it stank.

Sitting in the doorway of the store, Lafait studied the cottonwoods along the creek. They were greening up just a bit; you could tell it all right, but it sure wasn't like any spring back in Kentucky. This sitting around was a hell of a thing. He had only about twenty rounds left for his Prescott, so he couldn't even do any practicing. He had a notion to shut the door and go visit the miners down the creek. If Goodwin wasn't trusting him to stay here and take care of things, that's just what he'd do.

He was having a little doze in the warm sun when he heard them coming. All five of them, a ragged bunch for sure, but good-natured and easy going, except Bohannon, the black-whiskered one with the eyes set so wide they looked like they was trying to bust out of the sides of his head.

They came tramping up and talked about the weather and one thing and another before Mike asked, 'What kind of eatables has Goodwin got—besides beans?'

'Ain't even got beans,' Lafait said. 'He went to Denver for stuff.'

'And'a left *you* in charge?' Bohannon looked at the others. 'He must be out of stock for sure, huh, boys?'

'There's some saltside.' Lafait stood up, glancing at the heavy belt knife and the Army revolver Bohannon was wearing.

'Saltside.' One of the miners made a face. 'I

264

was hoping somebody passed a law against making any more of it.'

'Aw hell,' Bohannon said, 'let's get a jug of whiskey and go shoot our own meat.'

'Out of whiskey,' Lafait said.

'The hell you are!' Bohannon made an insult of it. 'What kind of place is Goodwin trying to run anyway?'

Lafait tried to ignore him. He spoke to Mike. 'I got a saddle of venison I'll give you.'

'Fair enough.' Mike grinned. 'We've been missing deer right and left lately.'

Lafait went to get the saddle of deer meat hanging at the cold end of Goodwin's cabin. When he returned, the miners were in the store. Bohannon was sitting on the counter with the jug Lafait was saving for McAllister. 'I thought you said Goodwin was out of whiskey, Whitlock.'

'That belongs to somebody else.' Lafait handed the deer meat to Mike.

'Somebody else just lost a jug of whiskey then.' Bohannon hooked his thumb in the ear of the jug and tilted it for a long drink. 'Here, boys, drink deep.'

The other miners hesitated. Mike said, 'Maybe you'd better leave the man's whiskey alone, Bo. No use to—'

'I said have a drink.' Bohannon was as mean as a rattler in one quick instant. The man closest to him took the jug and had a drink and passed it on.

Lafait said, 'Put it back where you found it, Bohannon.' He moved two steps to the side of the doorway. The light came through directly on Bohannon then, and in later years men were to make much of Lafait's stepping out of the doorway, but it was only accidental. Lafait was scared and uncertain; he didn't know why he took those two steps.

The jug came back to Bohannon. 'Who says put it down?' He laughed. 'You tell that somebody else you claim this whiskey belongs to to come down and collect for it from me when he gets ready.'

'Put it back,' Lafait said.

'Take a snot-nosed brat and give him a little authority...' Bohannon shook his head. 'I knew a lieutenant in the Army like that. One night he got shot, sort of accidental, you might say, when he went out to inspect the pickets.' He took another drink. 'You be a good brat, Whitlock, and I may let you have a snifter out of this.'

'Last time, put it back where you got it.'

'You got a big mouth, boy. You sound just like that lieutenant I was telling you about.' Bohannon put the jug down and slid off the counter. 'You ain't running everything on this crick, you know.'

'I'm running this here store.'

Bohannon laughed, and then you could see him figuring to himself that he'd been insulted so bad he'd have to do something about it.

'Younker,' he said, 'I'm going to wipe this floor up with you to learn you a little respect.'

'Don't come no closer.'

Bohannon stopped. Half of him was in the wide streak of sunlight coming through the doorway. It made his face queer looking, with the eye that was in the sun all bulgy and starey. 'You asking for *that* kind of fight?'

'Don't come no farther.'

For just a little Lafait thought it might end up with no trouble. He didn't care if Bohannon cussed him some and got real mad, because then Bohannon might stomp out and that would be the end of it. But Bohannon got to thinking again, hurting because he figured Lafait was making a fool of him. You could read it easy on his face.

Bohannon dragged away at his Army revolver.

Lafait didn't know all he himself did. He knew the first rimfire in the Prescott didn't go off, so he pulled the trigger again. It seemed like he missed. Bohannon got his revolver out all right, but he didn't do anything with it. He ducked his shoulder and came at Lafait with a terrible look on his face. Lafait kept shooting. His back was hard against the logs when Bohannon fell, almost at Lafait's feet.

Half blind from powder smoke, Lafait could see Bohannon's legs stretched out into the path of sunlight. The feet were twisted funny-like. The way Pa's had been. Lafait knew Bohannon was dead, all of a sudden dead and laying there. Lafait couldn't move or do anything for a moment.

Mike said, 'Jesus Christ, boys, he killed him!'

Lafait moved then, over toward the corner of the room, with the pistol covering Mike and the others. He didn't know how many shots were left in it. But Bohannon's friends didn't seem to care about Lafait. They turned Bohannon over and unbuttoned his shirt. 'Look at that!' one of them said. 'You could cover them three holes with a dollar!'

'At that range—sure.' A miner looked hard at Lafait and then dropped his glance.

'He started it,' Lafait said.

Mike straightened up. 'That's right.' He too stared at Lafait and then looked away.

'What are you going to do about it?' Lafait asked.

The one named Kansas said, 'Well, I reckon we'll bury the poor sonofabitch, that's what we'll do. He never did do nothing but cause us trouble anyway.' He went to the counter and took the cork out of the jug and started to lift it before he thought, and then he put the whiskey down quick, like it was something red hot.

'Go ahead,' Lafait said. 'Drink it.' He wished now he'd let Bohannon have the jug.

All the miners had a drink. When they started to carry Bohannon out, Lafait said, 'Take the whiskey with you.'

Mike came back later for the saddle of deer meat. He was about half drunk, for he and the others had killed the jug while burying Bohannon, and then they'd left it as a marker with rocks piled around it at the head of the grave. Lafait was walking slowly back and forth in front of the counter.

'No use to blame yourself,' Mike said.

'I wish I'd let him have the jug.'

'Wouldn't have done no good.' Mike shook his head. 'When Bo was out to pick a fight, he always kept trying till he made the riffle.'

'It was a hell of a thing.'

'Yeah, it was. I keep thinking now that Bo wasn't so bad. He was ornery and quarrelsome and always knocking somebody around, but ... Well, he asked for what he got!' Mike took the meat and went out.

Ma was the one who was going to think it was awful. It would be hard to look at her and tell her about it. Even if it had been Cy Grove, who had killed Pa inside these very same walls, Ma still wouldn't like it.

Kansas brought Goodwin's tools back and left them by the cabin, and then the miners went back to their camp. Lafait could see the grave over against the hill. It had all been so quick. One second Bohannon was alive and loud; now he was over there and Lafait was the cause of it. Maybe Bohannon hadn't figured to use his pistol, except as a bluff. Who knew that at the time, even if it happened to be so?

Every shooting that he was in always brought Lafait back to this lonely, puzzled moment.

He wished Toby would come down, like he did sometimes in the evening. He wished somebody would show up. Bill would be a good one, for he talked easy and convincing, and maybe he could make Lafait feel better about what had happened.

But no one came to the store until Goodwin returned five days later. Above the trees Lafait could sometimes see the smoke of the miners' camp, but he didn't want to go see them and they didn't come to see him. The false spring weather died before a blizzard that made a white mound over there where Bohannon's grave was. Every time he went outside Lafait couldn't keep from glancing that way.

Goodwin came back during a wolf-fanged wind at the tail end of the blizzard. He was half frozen but in good spirits. Lafait helped him unload the packhorses.

'I stopped by for a few minutes to see your folks on the way in,' Goodwin said. 'Toby McAllister was visiting, right in the middle of the day, mind you. It seemed to me that Dorcas was a lot more taken with him than she used to be. All the time I thought it was Bill, but your ma said he hadn't been around for quite a spell.'

'I guess not.'

They carried the goods inside. Goodwin

270

squatted by the fire. 'How were things while I was gone?'

'Fine.'

Goodwin kept looking across his shoulder at Lafait. 'What went wrong?'

He was like Ma when it came to smelling out things. 'Nothing went wrong,' Lafait said.

Goodwin let it pass. 'We did fair with your hides. I didn't fool with regular buyers. I found some fellows that wanted beaver coats and hats.'

From his saddle bags Goodwin took a pistol, heavy, long, some worn in places but still a beautiful weapon. 'It's a Walker Colt .44,' he said. 'I think you'll find caps more reliable than your rimfires. A ball from this will stop a man quick.' Goodwin smiled. 'Of course I ain't saying you intend to—' The smile died as he studied Lafait's expression.

'I killed a man the other day.'

'My God! Who?'

Lafait told Goodwin all about the shooting. Goodwin was silent for a long time. 'He started to draw on you, and that put you in the right.' Goodwin looked at the pistol in his hand. 'But that ain't going to help me with your ma.'

'It don't make no difference that you gave me my first pistol,' Lafait said. 'I would've found me one somewhere. I like guns, just like Jude likes tools, that's all.' He reached out and took the Walker. He liked the heavy, solid feel of it the instant it was in his grip.

271

You couldn't blame a pistol for causing killings. Look at Pa, he hadn't even been wearing one when he got shot. Lafait didn't aim to go around looking for trouble; most likely he'd never have any more. Still, if you were going to have a pistol at all, you'd best have a good one.

Lafait aimed at a dark knot in the wall. He tested the balance of the Walker Colt. He could hardly wait to get to practicing with it.

CHAPTER NINETEEN

The arrival of spring was about the draggiest business Major had ever lived through. Sudden warm days fooled him. He thought it was spring, and two days later it was snowing. This went on till the end of May, and by then summer was just a spell away, and if spring had preceded it, you were so weary with false alarms you sure couldn't say just where spring had sneaked in.

Ma and Dorcas got some seeds from Kate McAllister and put in a garden. That was a sure sign of a settled place and Major was glad to see it. Dorcas wouldn't be around to help eat the stuff out of the garden because she was going to marry Toby McAllister in about a month. Major guessed there wasn't any real bad effects from her being with Bill that one night, or else they'd have been noticeable by now.

He went on with his stubborn work of fencing. Jude and Lafait had given him considerable help getting out poles, but now they weren't around home much. Jude was at Goodwin's more than he was home, learning about surveying. Lafait was working for Carl Burnine. Pretty soon Dorcas would be gone and then just Major and Ma would be left. He guessed they'd be in Deer Valley to the end of time.

Jude came fogging in one evening, just when the Whitlocks were getting ready to eat. You could see he was so excited he was ready to bust. He was shouting even before he got off Warty and came inside. 'I got me a start in the surveying business!'

He came busting in, grinning and happy and the story poured out of him. A United States deputy surveyor named Beach was at Goodwin's with his party. One man was sick and was going back down the river as soon as he could travel. With Goodwin's help Jude had got the fellow's job, and had already taken the oath. He was to be a chainman, for which he would get a dollar a day and food.

'Where will you be,' Ma asked. 'All over the valley?'

'Naw. Somewhere way up the river, finding out where Indian land starts and ends.'

Major had known it was coming, but it was

still a shock to think of Jude going far off by himself with strangers. 'When do you start?'

'Tomorrow. When they come by, I'll just join 'em.'

'Just like that.' Ma smiled sort of sad and turned away to look at the mountains.

'Don't you want me to go?' Jude asked.

Ma nodded. 'That's the thing for you to do.'

Jude left, just like that, early the next morning. The surveyors came by, four of them, and hardly stopped to say hello to the Whitlocks. Beach was a whiskery, nervous little man in a hurry. Ma said he looked more like a politician than anything else, which happened to be the mortal truth when the facts about him came out some months later.

Jude went away happy, riding bareback on Warty. He waved from the north hill and that was the last Deer Valley saw of him for more than a year.

Ma went over to her garden. It was just sprouting good in the rich light soil where cottonwoods had been the year before. She shied a piece of bark at a chipmunk. 'Them pesky squirrels will likely eat everything in sight.'

'I guess I'd best dig another post hole or so.' Major walked away quickly. He would miss Jude forever. Jude was the kind of person you'd love even if he wasn't your brother. Until noon Major sweated at his digging. He didn't want to go back for dinner and see all the things that Jude had done, and feel close at hand the heaviness that had come from Jude's going away. He forced himself to go.

The oxen followed him across the meadows. When Fawn was just an ugly little fellow Jude had named him. A spindly legged, graceless creature named in memory of the tiny deer Lafait had killed so long ago. So many of the gentle things Jude had done lay across Major's heart.

Silent during the meal, all the Whitlocks felt the loss of Jude. They were never to see much of him again.

Travel that summer was heavier than before. It got so that Major no longer went to the house when he saw travellers. Ma made a little money right along serving meals to miners and other wanderers without families.

The meadow crossing became all chopped up again and people began swinging their wagons wide to find firmer ground, and finally, to keep the whole valley from getting rutted, Major hauled logs and rocks to fill the worst places and made a sort of road across the meadows. He wondered what ideas Jude would have had about it if he had been there.

Dorcas and Toby McAllister were married on the Fourth of July. Dorcas didn't much favor the date, but the whole country thought it was a great idea to have a double celebration. The whole country came. The travelling preacher from Fairplay held things down with

275

a two-hour sermon before he got around to the marrying, but after that he was taken aback by what went on.

The Pilchers got in a fight with a bunch of miners who had happened to stop by. One of Burnine's dogs chewed up a wolfhound of Tad Sherman's, while everybody was making bets on the outcome, and then Sherman and Burnine like to have got in a shooting fight before Goodwin cooled them off.

Ma was plumb worn down when everybody left. That night some of the Pilchers and Lafait and others went over to Toby's new cabin and dragged Toby out of bed and threw him in a beaver pond. Right then Major made up his mind that when he got married, he'd do it real quiet and avoid all the shooting and hell raising that didn't have anything to do with the real event.

None of the Whitlocks of course expected Bill to show up at the wedding, and he didn't; but a lot of folks thought he should have been a good sport and joined in the festivities. On their way home after keeping Dorcas and Toby up all night, the Pilchers, still full of steam, went to Bill's place to josh him about the wedding. Bill wasn't in no mood for such fun; he stood the Pilchers off with a rifle and sent them on their way. They laid it to the fact that they'd had the trouble at the wagon train with him the year before, so the Whitlocks were content to let it stand that way.

Watching the preacher ride away the day after the wedding, Ma said, 'Did you notice how she kept looking to see if Bill was in the crowd?'

Major was ready to go out to his fencing again. 'No, I didn't notice.'

'Maybe I'm the only one that did. I reckon it was natural enough for her to wonder if he'd show up. It would've suited me better if he had.'

'Bill ain't going to trouble Dorcas any now.'

'I guess not, only in her mind, and she'll wear that out in time.' Ma looked at the mountains. 'You're the last one, Major. Lafait ain't going to be home more than now and then. This family is growed up and taking care of itself.'

Ma's quietness made Major uneasy. 'You're not thinking of going back to Kentucky?'

'No, I'm not thinking of going back, Major.' She looked at the mountains. 'I said I never would settle under those rocks, but it seems I did.' Ma went inside the cabin.

There was something she hadn't said, but Major couldn't figure what it was. It worried him as he worked. Now and then he paused to look at the smoke from the cabin. Somehow, that smoke didn't mean everything it had before Dorcas and Jude left the family. For a while it had been proof that about all the creature comforts the Whitlocks needed were provided for, but those things weren't enough now.

It struck Major that he, the old mother hen, was actually the last one of the family to grow up, and maybe that was because he'd over-fancied himself as the only one who could take care of the Whitlocks.

CHAPTER TWENTY

The cattle came up the river a week or two after Dorcas' wedding. They raised enough dust for an army, and long before they poured down into Deer Valley, Major could hear the strange sounds of the herd, the bumping of horns, isolated bellowing from the dust, and a tramping rumble. Major ran out into the meadows to get Fawn and Steuben and put them in the corral.

It looked like all the cattle in the world. They came out of the dust on the south hill and crashed down the gravelly slope, brindles, reds, patchy-colored brutes, long-horned and wild looking. They crowded through gaps in Major's unfinished fence, and then the gaps enlarged and the poles and posts were smashed down, and riders out in front turned the cattle into the rich grass of the valley.

A lean, dark-faced man in a hat that was cracked at the folds of the crown, rode up to the cabin and stopped before Ma and Major. His clothes were hard worn, a toughness showed in the cast of his face, his eyes looked out of his dusty features with startling cold blue directness.

'If you got no objections, I'm going to hold the drive on your land a few days.'

'You're busting down my fences, mister,' Major said.

'That can't be helped.' The man wasn't mean about it; he was just saying a fact.

The cattle already were spreading up and down the creek. Major didn't see that he had much choice about giving permission; at a glance he'd known this fellow wasn't like the Rusks or the others the Whitlocks had run off the land. 'Go ahead,' Major said.

The man touched his hat to Ma and spun his horse away. There were eight riders with the herd and they had a lot of horses with them that Major hadn't even noticed at first. It didn't take much to settle the cattle on the grass, and then some of the riders started making a camp at the spring down the valley.

Before long one of the camp-makers came trotting toward the cabin. Major thought he knew the horse, dusty as it was, even with a saddle on. He was right, the rider was Lafait. His clothes were sounder than any of the others, but he looked just as tough as the lean man who had stopped at the house.

'What are you doing with that bunch?' Major asked.

'Hired me. I'm going up to South Park to

help deliver this here herd of cows.'

'What do you do, Lafait?' Ma asked.

Lafait lost some of his big-man manner. 'Well, I help around camp some, and a few other things. They been short-handed ever since they left their wagon way down the river.'

'I ain't too happy about having those cows eat up all the grass in sight,' Major said.

'What are you saving it for?' Lafait asked. 'Besides, maybe you can talk Blake out of a few of them calves that are all worn down from the trip, in trade for the grass. They been leaving calves behind ever since they started from Texas.'

Ma said, 'It sounds like you done talked to this Blake yourself, Lafait.'

'Yeah, I did—some. He wants to rest the herd and sort of scout around up the river before he goes on. They could have gone an easier way from downriver, but Blake says—'

'What does he say?' Ma asked.

'Well, I guess he knows his business. He brought this here herd all the way from Texas. He sort of figures somebody is going to try to grab off the cows before he delivers 'em.'

'You mean steal about ten thousand cows?' Major asked.

'There's only a little over a thousand.' Lafait got back on Smoke. 'You talk to him about them calves, Major. He ain't no thief, even when it comes to using grass that's doing nobody any good.' He trotted away.

Ma shook her head. 'They're a hard bunch, them cowboys. I've heard about what goes on in Texas—and now Lafait is right in the midst of them, and him already killed a man.'

'It wasn't his fault.' Major was wondering how many calves he should try to get from Blake. It was a pretty tricky thing; Blake didn't have to give him any. Major got a fair idea of Blake's character when Colorow's bunch showed up the next day.

There were only men in the Ute party, ten of them, stripped down for war. Blake talked with them easily in sign language, and the Indians said they were on their way to fight Arapahoes. At once Lafait was torn between going with them and staying with the herd. He decided he'd better stick with Blake.

The Indians camped near the cabin as usual. Ma baked them some bread, but you could tell from the way they watched the cows that they had their minds on something better than bread. Major was visiting the cowboy camp when Colorow told Blake that the Utes needed a beef.

'Cut him out one of those steers we picked up in Short Grass, Billy,' Blake said to one of his riders.

'Give that damn' Indian a good steer?'

'That's what I said.'

'How about one of them old dry cows?'

Blake just kept looking at Billy, who said, 'You ain't afraid of no scraggly bunch of

281

Indians like these, are you?'

'Not one bit,' Blake snapped. 'Get him a steer.'

Billy argued no more. He cut a big brindle steer out of the herd and the Utes took it up on the south hill for a buffalo run. It was well their ponies were nimble or some of them would have been gored when they tried to keep the steer from turning back to the herd in the meadows. They drove arrows through its lungs and brought it down, and then they dragged it to the Whitlock yard for a feast.

'How come you gave 'em a good steer?' Major asked Blake.

'Because I wanted to. Maybe for good luck. I ain't quite got this herd where it's going yet.'

'I figure you owe me something for using my grass,' Major said.

'So does your brother.' Blake gave Major a cold look. 'What if I say I don't?'

Major's temper rose instantly. Anything that seemed a threat or an insult to the land of Deer Valley would always bring him to a fighting pitch. Still, he spoke quietly enough. 'I ain't going to try to take what you owe me, if that's what you mean.'

Blake looked at him a long time. 'I ain't so sure you wouldn't try. My orders is to deliver one thousand head, mixed herd. I got that many and then some. It's just possible I could leave you a few calves in trade for your grass.' He looked out toward the north hill.

'How many?'

'What do you know about Cy Grove?'

'Only what I've heard.'

'Yeah,' Blake said. 'Ever since I came against the mountains, that's what I've been hearing too. You know him?'

'I've seen him.'

'There's easier ways into South Park from the plains, I guess you know. I came the hard way on account of your friend Grove. I sent a man to see what was stacked up along one of those easy ways, and he didn't come back. I'm thinking Grove has got men scattered all through these hills, Whitlock.'

'That might be, but don't call him my friend.'

'I don't feel right about the last of this drive. You want to join up with your brother and come with me? For that—and the grass—I'll leave you ten calves.'

It was clear to Major that Blake didn't need him for his knowledge of cows. He said, 'I ain't altogether like Lafait when it comes to shooting.'

'About half like him will do.'

'I'll go,' Major said. 'Maybe you could get the Utes to ride along, since you—'

'Oh hell,' Blake said, and rode away. He went somewhere up the river that day. Lafait, who was staying in the cowboy camp, said Blake didn't return till well after dark.

The Indians left the next morning while

Blake's riders were getting the herd started. The cows didn't much want to leave the valley, but after a time the drive was lined out. Lafait and Major, who was on a borrowed horse, were at the rear. It wasn't Major's idea of the cattle business, this getting choked with dust at the drag end of things, but he liked the sight of the long-backed animals rolling along before him, and he thought about the ten bawling calves in the corral at home. He'd have cows all over the mountains before he wound up.

Lafait was carrying the long rifle and his heavy pistol. Major had the buffalo gun. When the herd crowded along the hill above the Pilcher place, all the Pilchers came out to goggle. Major and Lafait spit dust from their mouths and tried to look tough and important.

From the scouting trip Blake had taken the day before, he knew just where he was going day by day. He bedded the herd that night on a flat under the hills. There was a little stream but there wasn't much grass. The cows were restless about settling down. Blake divided the night into two shifts, telling everybody to have a saddled horse on short picket close to their blankets when they weren't standing guard.

Major and Lafait were on guard the first half of the night. The whole idea of riding along slow beside the cows and listening for danger in the night filled Major with a thumping excitement at first; but about the time his shift was half gone he got tired and sleepy, and he began to think that Blake was worrying over-much. The idea of anyone, even Cy Grove, stealing a whole herd of a thousand cows was pretty big.

When it was Major's turn to roll in, he was glad of it. He drove a pin in the ground and tied a fresh, saddled horse close to his bed, and hoped the horse would have sense enough not to tromp on him during the night. Lafait was already asleep by then. Just before he dropped off Major thought that driving a herd as far as Blake had brought this one must be a terrible job.

It seemed only minutes later when he woke up in a bedlam of noise. His horse was snorting and dragging at the picket pin. He heard gunshots and the bawl of terrified cows and men shouting curses and orders. The faint gray, smoky light of early dawn was on the land.

Lafait grabbed him by the shoulder and shouted, 'Get on your horse!'

Already the Longhorns, monstrous in the early light, wild with fright, were booming close to the camp, kicking dust, colliding, bawling. It seemed that guns were firing everywhere. Lafait disappeared in the murk while Major was getting on his horse. Suddenly it looked like the whole herd was coming at Major. He held tight to the buffalo gun with one hand and let the horse run, figuring it knew what to do better than he did.

It surged away in a wild run. Major didn't try to slow it until he saw that he was fairly in the clear. Small groups of cattle were streaking through the dust all around him but he was away from the solid front of them. The horse leaped suddenly and almost threw him, and then he realized it had jumped over a saddled horse struggling on the ground. Ahead he saw a man running clumsily and it looked like Marty, one of Blake's men.

Major caught up with him and brought the horse to a plunging stop. 'Get on!' he shouted, trying to keep his horse under control while the man was leaping up behind him. 'Where are they?' Major asked, and then he got his first close look at the man.

It wasn't Marty. It was a man Major had never seen before. Close crowded against Major's back, with a vicious look on his face, the man was raising a pistol to club Major over the head. Major swung his elbow into the fellow's throat. The blow from the pistol came down across Major's shoulder.

Again Major heaved back violently and this time his elbow caught the man in the mouth and knocked him off the horse. An instant later the animal leaped away as frantic cows pressed close to it. Against the hills, all over the flats, the shooting was still going on. Later, Major knew that most of it had been only to stampede the herd.

He could see now where he was; he had gone

a long way toward the river. He circled back toward the camp. In the confusion of dust he went clean beyond it and came against the first rocks of the hill. He saw another dismounted man, crouched behind a rock with a pistol. He swung the buffalo gun on him until he was sure he was not making a second mistake. It was Billy this time.

Billy signalled angrily at him, 'Get down!' Major leaped off his horse and went forward in a crouch, and as he did a bullet chugged the dust at his feet and he heard the crash of a rifle up in the rocks. He fell behind the rock where Billy was.

'Three of the bastards up there,' Billy said. 'They're the only ones I've seen to shoot at. You seen any of our bunch since it busted loose?'

Major shook his head. He peered over the rock. The light was getting stronger all the time, although dust was still hanging in the air.

'See 'em?' Billy asked.

'I see three horses about a hundred and fifty yards—'

'They're this side of that.'

After a moment Major said, 'Yeah, I think I see where you mean.' Somewhere off to his left he heard two shots close on each other. The sounds of the cows were far away now. Except for what little part he'd had in things, he had no idea of what had happened.

'They wasn't sure I didn't have a rifle,' Billy said. 'That's why they ain't run for their horses before this. They will, though, pretty soon.' He looked at the buffalo gun. 'Can you shoot that thing?'

'I reckon.'

'Stay here then. I'll work around the hill and try to chouse 'em out.'

'I can shoot their horses from here.'

'We don't want to do that!'

'Why not?'

'We just don't want to, that's why. Jesus Christ, shooting horses!'

'Stay here yourself,' Major said. 'I'll sneak around the hill.' He ducked away before Billy could speak. He made the shelter of the next rock and then he leaped on behind a second rock. He crouched there, knowing deep in his insides that they were going to shoot at him when he made his next jump. He looked across the flat toward the river. The cows were scattered from hell to breakfast, but he could see two or three riders out there in the dust and they appeared to be trying to bunch the cows.

On beyond the next rock was the beginning of a wash that would pretty well hide him—if he got that far. The longer he stayed where he was, the harder it became to move.

Major dug his feet in and ran, standing straight up. They shot at him, more than once, he was sure. He didn't stop behind the rock but went all the way to the wash and flung himself down. After a while he decided they hadn't hit him.

288

As long as he stayed on his hands and knees, the wash gave him complete protection. He scrambled up it until he was sure he was about as high on the hill as the three men. Billy yelled shrilly. Major peered over the bank. The men were running toward the horses. Billy began to shoot his pistol, but he was too far away to do any good with it.

Major levelled the buffalo gun on a rock. He sighted down the heavy barrel and pulled the trigger. One of the running men, almost at the horses, went down. He staggered up an instant later, hopping on one foot. One of his companions paused long enough to help him into the saddle.

Major had time to reload fast and get in another shot, but he kept staring at the three men. They put their horses in a hard scramble among the rocks and up the bleak hill, and Major lay against the bank and watched them go.

Reloaded after his first burst of firing, Billy cut loose again at an impossible range. The riders disappeared into the winding hills. Major reloaded the rifle slowly. He went down the wash. He had to find Lafait.

'Sonsofbitches! I guess we put 'em on the run!' Billy said.

'I guess.'

'You hit one of 'em. You saw that, didn't you?'

'Looked like it,' Major said.

289

They found their horses and rode out across the trampled flat. Major kept looking for the man he had knocked off his horse, thinking maybe the fellow had got tromped flat by the cattle, but apparently the man had got away. They came to one of Blake's men holding a small bunch of cattle. He said he hadn't seen Lafait.

'Jim and Ike Peeples are down on the river. They're the only ones I seen since the thing busted loose—our bunch, I mean.'

Major turned back toward the hills when he saw two riders coming out of the rocks about a half mile apart. One of them was Lafait, sure as the world! The two men had come together before Major crossed the flats. They were standing where the camp had been, beside the body of a man all shapeless and dusty.

'Grub Box didn't have no wagon to dive under this time,' Blake said. His face was hard and bitter. He looked at Major. 'How many men down toward the river?'

'Four, far's I know.'

'We'll look around,' Blake said.

When Major swung up to ride beside Lafait, he saw two pistols tied on his brother's saddle.

Two hundred yards below the rock where Billy and Major had been for a while, they found the bodies of two of Blake's riders, both shot. 'They come in from the hill,' Blake said. 'They tried to run the herd right over us.' He looked at the pistols hanging on Lafait's saddle.

'Grove's,' Lafait said.

Blake looked at Major.

'I didn't do much good.'

Billy galloped in to report that Clint Ferris was down on the river unharmed, and that the cottonwoods and the river itself had fairly well stopped the scatter, although a dozen or more cows had busted their legs plunging over a steep bank. Then he looked at Major and said, 'You tell Blake about knocking the legs from under the guy up there in the rocks?'

'It wasn't much,' Major said. He saw Blake watching him sharply.

'I was out of range with my pistol,' Billy said, 'so we worked it out that—'

'Go back to camp and get Grub Box's shovel,' Blake said curtly.

They buried their dead. Lafait took the shovel then and looked toward the hills. 'I reckon I'll … It would sort of worry me if I didn't.'

Blake looked bitterly at the graves of his own men. 'These are the ones that worry me.' He paused. 'But since you're so damned ambitious, Whitlock, you'll find two more up that gulch to the north.' He mounted and galloped off toward the river.

'Yeah,' Major said, 'I'll go with you.'

They buried Cy Grove. On their way to the gulch Blake had pointed out they found a stray horse with an empty long gun in the boot.

'Privateer booty,' Lafait said grimly, and took the horse in tow.

One of the men Blake had killed was Limber Jim. Major remembered how he'd talked to him in Bill's cabin not so very long ago. Lafait took the pistols from both men. Following the orders Blake had given them, they went back to the wrecked camp to salvage everything they could, and then they rode on down to the river to help round up the herd.

By nightfall Blake's drivers had gathered up about nine hundred head, bedding them across the river from the first camp. It took all the next day to bring in most of the stragglers and the rest of the horses.

The Pilchers got their start from a small group of cows that Blake's riders didn't find.

They went over the dry hills to the wide grasslands of South Park, and Blake delivered the herd to a man near Garo. The Whitlocks had done their job, and Major guessed they'd earned their pay too. Now it was time to go home.

Lafait said, 'I didn't figure on going back— not right away.'

'Where you going?'

'I reckon I'll just ride down to Texas with the boys. There's a lot of country I ain't seen, and it's high time I started looking around before I get too old.'

Lafait was going. No argument was going to turn him, Major knew, so he didn't give any.

'What'll I tell Ma?'

'Why, say I went visiting down Texas way, what else?'

'Yeah, visiting—ten thousand miles away.'

'Blake and the others come up. I reckon they know the way back. I ain't made for setting still, Major.'

'That's for sure.'

Lafait gave his brother the Smoke horse, saddle and all, and one of the Grove's pistols. Lafait had been doing some trading with his spoils of war and now, besides the horse he had picked up near the flats, he had a second pony. In the things that interested him Lafait was a trader from away back.

When Major parted with the trail drivers, Lafait was as offhand about it as Blake and his riders. The Texans had come a powerful way with the herd, they had left dead friends behind them in a strange country, but there was nothing of that in their manner when they rode away, and Lafait was just as careless as any of them.

Alone, Major rode back across the wide stretches of the park, over the dry piñon hills until the awesome peaks of the mountains that split the running waters of America to east and west crashed suddenly into the sky ahead of him. He went past the graves of Blake's men, graves that he wouldn't be able to find in a few years. Far away he saw a small wagon train making slow dust.

He guessed they would keep coming until there wouldn't be a place left to light where there was grass and water; and maybe even a town would grow somewhere in the big valley under the peaks as the years went on, and Major would be here to see it come about.

At the Pilcher place he stopped to visit a minute or two without getting down. He hooked one leg around the horn like he'd seen Billy do sometimes. Matt Pilcher did most of the talking. He was bigger than his pa now, and the way he acted, brushing aside about everything his old man said, showed that he was pretty well getting to be boss of the tribe.

Ross Pilcher asked, 'See any of the folks we come out with when you was in the park?'

'Who cares about them?' Matt said. He eyed Major's saddle and pistol. 'We heard you had some trouble up the river a piece.'

'Yeah.' Out in the field near the river Major saw six cows from the scattered herd. He guessed the Pilchers had as good a right to them as anyone; just so Matt didn't start making such rights reach too far south. 'Cy Grove got himself killed.'

'That's good!' Matt said. 'Who done it?'

'Hard to tell. One of the Texans, I guess.' Major watched the cows idly. 'Seen Bill around lately?'

Matt shook his head and his eyes tightened up. He never had had any use for Bill. Now, with a few cows, not considering how the

Pilchers happened to get them, it was sort of funny the way Matt's view of Bill would screw down even tighter. 'You think he was in it?' Matt asked.

'No, I don't hardly think he was.' It was likely though, Major thought, that Bill had known about the raid beforehand. Major started up the hill, noticing that not a single one of the whole Pilcher-Broome tribe seemed to be missing. They hadn't built big enough to start and now they were adding lean-tos to their two squatty cabins.

It wasn't often Major approached home from the north hill, and this time it seemed that he had been away a terrible long time, and awful far. Deer Valley looked better than ever, though even from the hill he could see how a thousand head of cattle had changed the look of the grass. But it would grow again in that deep soil fed by water that came underground from the snow streaked mountains.

He could see Ma over there hoeing in her garden. She'd turned the calves out and they were bunched in the upper end of the willows with Fawn and Steuben. Major reckoned he'd best go over and take a look at them before he went to the cabin. As he rode across the deep sod of the meadows he looked up and down the valley. Mainly it was chance that had stopped the Whitlocks here, but it had been darned good luck at that.

With just him and Ma left now, maybe they

did have more land than the law said they were entitled to. Bill had thrown that in Major's face the day Major had the violent talk with him about Dorcas; but Major had been interested in only one thing that day, solemnly promising Bill to kill him if he ever opened his mouth about Dorcas staying with him that one night.

I'll keep this land, no matter how, Major told himself. The law was a faraway thing; ownership was everything.

He looked at the calves. They seemed to be doing fine. You'd swear that the oxen were trying to mother them. About tomorrow Major would go see Carl Burnine and get some advice about this herd of cattle. He was grinning as he went on toward the cabin.

The first thing Ma said was, 'Where's Lafait?'

'He figures to visit a spell with them Texas boys.'

'Visit a spell?' Ma said.

'Well, he went to Texas with them.'

'That's a long way.' Ma leaned her hoe against the fence she'd built around the garden. 'But I ain't surprised. I expect you're pretty hungry, Major.'

'Some.'

You'd have thought that it didn't mean much to Ma, having Lafait up and leave for Texas without warning. She started fixing something to eat, talking about the neighbors who had been by while Major was gone. Susan

296

and Mrs Burnine had been there, and Goodwin had visited for a while one evening. Ma talked about how her garden was coming along and how the oxen had taken up with the calves, but she didn't say anything at all about Lafait.

She'd showed her feelings considerable more when Jude, first, and then Dorcas, had left home. Major guessed that Ma had been ready, deep inside her, to see Lafait go away ever since he was little. It gave him a faint stirring of jealousy to think that those who ran away to far places often were better loved than those who stayed at home; but there wasn't enough jealousy in his makeup to make him bitter.

Nobody could love different people, even brothers and sisters, just the same amount or in the same way. Jude had always been Major's favorite.

Where was Jude now? He didn't have any of Lafait's toughness, but in his own way Jude would be able to live among the hardest kind of folks and get along fine, without any of the danger that would always come to Lafait.

'I've got something to tell you in the morning,' Ma said softly.

She was sitting at the table with her Bible open before her when Major went to bed. She wasn't reading it; she was just sitting there looking slowly around the cabin.

CHAPTER TWENTY-ONE

When Ma told Major that she and Goodwin were going to be married, it just didn't seem possible that time had passed so quick to make such a thing possible. Major hadn't figured that Ma would marry again, but when he got to thinking he realized Pa had been dead more than a year, and that Ma and Goodwin had been friends most of that time.

'When's it going to be?' Major asked.

'Next week. The preacher will be down this way then for a meeting at McAllisters'.'

'It appears there's a lot that goes on that nobody tells me anything about.'

'You've got your own problems, Major, and one of these times I reckon you'll be getting married too.' Ma studied him sharp for a moment. 'The longer I stay here, the longer you're going to put off getting married, though that ain't the reason I told Mr Goodwin I'd have him.'

'But next week—and I didn't even know about it.' So that was why Ma had sat so late the night before, just looking at the cabin. Not that her mind wasn't already made up, but she had been having a long moment of peace and quiet while she said good-bye to her family, no matter if most of them was scattered high wide and handsome. The cabin had held them all together for a while at least.

'Goodwin is all right, I guess you could say, but I never thought of him as no stepfather.' For the first time in a long time Major remembered sharply a lot of things about Pa, good things and bad things. Mixed all together, the good things probably were greater than the bad.

'Stepfather?' Ma shook her head. 'I ain't got any younguns that need a stepfather, have I?'

Major felt the sting of shame. He shook his head.

On the morning of the day of the wedding Major left Ma at the McAllisters' and went over to see Dorcas. A pretty good crowd was already gathered at the McAllister place and Major figured the preacher might work up a two hour storm about sin any old time; besides, Major hadn't visited his sister since her marriage.

Dorcas was fixing to go to the wedding. Toby was already dressed in his best clothes, but he was outside looking at a half-finished corral and you could see he was itching to get back to work. Major visited with him a spell before Dorcas called to her brother to come inside.

She looked fine, Dorcas did, maybe just a mite fuller in the face than she used to be. There was a glow in her eyes and you could tell she was mighty proud of her own place. It was a sight neater inside than one would figure from looking at the outside, and none of the furniture was homemade. Major guessed the McAllisters had been downright generous.

Dorcas poured her brother a cup of coffee. They talked about Lafait and Jude for a while, and it dawned on Major that he and Dorcas were sort of strangers now.

'You look happy, Dorcas.'

'I am. Toby's got a fine start, and his family don't interfere at all with us. When are *you* going to get married, Major?'

'There's no rush.'

Dorcas smiled. 'Just wait till you have to do for yourself for a month or so—then you'll wonder if there's a rush. You never could cook a lick.'

'Cooking ain't everything. I'll get along.'

Dorcas was insistent. 'You talked any to Susan about getting married?'

'Not yet. Danged if I don't wish I'd gone with Lafait, if this is the way it's going to be from now on.' Major grinned. 'But I got to admit you and Toby sure look like you're hitting things off good.'

'We are.' After a moment Dorcas said, 'I'll worry some about you being up there alone in Deer Valley, but still I got to say I think it's a fine thing that Ma is marrying Goodwin.'

'It startled me at first—but you're right.'

Toby came in. 'You about ready, Dorcas? We can all go over together.'

Major rode with them back to the

McAllister place, but he knew he was an outsider.

The wedding ceremony, once the preacher got to it, was quick enough. Ma wasn't a Whitlock any more; her name was Goodwin now. It wasn't so much the event itself that made Major feel puzzled and alone, but the fact that it was the last one of a chain of events that had completely separated the family since Pa's death.

Major had a few drinks with Burnine, and talked to him about cows. 'I'll come up in a day or two and show you what to do about them calves,' Burnine said. 'Cows themselves ain't no great problem in this country where there ain't no ticks or fever. Grass is going to be the problem.'

Major watched Susan talking to Ma, the two of them all happy about something. They glanced over at Major and he turned his attention back to Burnine quickly.

'Land with good grass during the winter is the big problem,' Burnine said. 'This ain't Texas. You see that you hold your valley up there, Major, until the time you can own every bit of it legal.'

'I figure on holding it.'

'There's ways. And if it happens you ever need some help, just let me know.'

'Thanks. I will.'

'To tell the truth, I don't think you'll ever need help.'

Goodwin had supplied plenty of food and drink and the McAllisters had added more. Things were working on toward a big evening of dancing when Major told Ma he guessed he'd better get home and see about the calves.

Goodwin protested about Major's leaving so early, but Ma said, 'No, it's all right, Jim,' and then to Major, 'We'll see you in a few days when I come up to get Grandma Ripley's chest.'

As he rode away Major realized at last and in full that everyone but him had made a clean break with Deer Valley.

He didn't go home, but went instead to the original site of Goodwin's store. Grass and bushes were already growing along the edges of the flat place where the building had stood and across the river the ruts the wagon train had made coming down the bank were now washed into one narrow gully by the runoff of winter snows.

Spring floods had changed the course of the river, so that Pa's grave was now deeply covered with sand and gravel. Even the rock headstone was buried. Major stood there remembering the quarrel he and Pa had got into just before Pa was killed. Long ago all the heat had vanished from the memory. Cy Grove was dead too and so there was no use to look back on what he had done. To tell the truth, it had been useless to come here at all, but Major guessed he had been making one last effort to

302

hang onto the feeling of the Whitlock family as it once had been.

Ma had done the right thing by getting married again. Pa was gone, all his orneriness, his love, and everything else about him buried here. Major looked at the blue river, fast moving, shallow, slipping without great argument around the black rocks that had caused a pounding terror the day Pa went out to save Joe Marion.

Major rode away.

By early moonlight he went over the south hill and down past the dark house. Night gave Deer Valley a mystery of bigness as he went up the meadows toward the end of the grove, riding slowly until he saw the shadowy forms of Fawn and Steuben. Behind them in the deeper shadows of the trees the calves were rising in alarm.

'All right, all right, there's nothing to get spooky about.'

He went back toward the house, bracing himself to face the quietness of it. There was a power of things he had to do around the place. He'd keep so busy there wouldn't be time to think about being alone. As he started to carry the saddle inside he remembered what Ma had said the day the wagon broke down. *Fix one wheel at a time.* That was the way he'd work out all his problems.

His life here was just beginning.

Major took a long look at the shadows, at

the meadows reaching toward the friendly, guarding mountains. This was the place. This was home.

Steve Frazee was born in Salida, Colorado, and for the decade 1926–1936 he worked in heavy construction and mining in his native state. He also managed to pay his way through Western State College in Gunnison, Colorado, from which in 1937 he graduated with a Bachelor's degree in journalism. The same year he also married. He began making major contributions to the Western pulp magazines with stories set in the American West as well as a number of North-Western tales published in ADVENTURE. Few can match his Western novels which are notable for their evocative, lyrical descriptions of the open range and the awesome power of natural forces and their effects on human efforts. CRY COYOTE (1955) is memorable for its strong female protagonists who actually influence most of the major events and bring about the resolution of the central conflict in this story of wheat growers and expansionist cattlemen. HIGH CAGE (1957) concerns five miners and a woman snowbound at an isolated gold mine on top of Bulmer Peak in which the twin themes of the lust for gold and the struggle against the savagery of both the elements and human nature interplay with increasing, almost tormented intensity. BRAGG'S FANCY WOMAN (1966) concerns a free-spirited woman who is able to tame a family of thieves. RENDEZVOUS (1958) ranks as one of the finest mountain man books together with such excellent works as Guthrie's THE BIG SKY and Gulick's THE MOUNTAIN MEN. Not surprisingly, many of Frazee's novels have become major motion pictures. According to Bill Pronzini in the second edition of TWENTIETH CENTURY WESTERN WRITERS, a Frazee story is possessed of 'flawless characterization, particularly when it involves the clash of human passions; believable dialogue; and the ability to create and sustain damp-palmed suspense.'

We hope you have enjoyed this Large Print book. Other Chivers Press or G.K. Hall & Co. Large Print books are available at your library or directly from the publishers.

For more information about current and forthcoming titles, please call or write, without obligation, to:

Chivers Press Limited
Windsor Bridge Road
Bath BA2 3AX
England
Tel. (01225) 335336

OR

G.K. Hall & Co.
P.O. Box 159
Thorndike, Maine 04986
USA
Tel. (800) 223-2336

All our Large Print titles are designed for easy reading, and all our books are made to last.